La Vida

La Vida

Catalina McIsaac

STUDIO 221

La Vida is a work of fiction. Names, characters, geographic locations, places, and incidents either are a product of the author's imagination or are used fictitiously. The author's use of names of actual persons, places, and characters is incidental to the plot, and is not intended to change the entirely fictional character of the work.

Copyright © 2022 by Catalina McIsaac
Published April 2023

All Rights Reserved. No part of this book may be reproduced or transmitted in any form or by any means, electronic or mechanical, including photocopying, recording, or by any information and retrieval systems, without the written permission of the Publisher, except where permitted by law.

Studio 221
318 Lloyd Avenue #16
Santa Barbara, California 93101

ISBN: 979-8-9860949-0-8 (paperback)
ISBN: 979-8-9860949-1-5 (e-book)

Library of Congress Control Number: 2022907567

Song referenced is in public domain

Cover and book design by Ryan S. Bruemmer
Cover photo by Catalina McIsaac

Break open this La Vida piñata filled with word candy and taste sweet Latin soul.

— CATALINA

Viva La Vida (Long Live Life), Watermelons
by Frida Kahlo, 1954, her last painting

Contents

ONE	1
TWO	5
THREE	9
FOUR	15
FIVE	21
SIX	31
SEVEN	35
EIGHT	47
NINE	55
TEN	63
ELEVEN	75
TWELVE	87
THIRTEEN	99
FOURTEEN	109
FIFTEEN	115
SIXTEEN	127
SEVENTEEN	135
EIGHTEEN	143
NINETEEN	153
TWENTY	165
TWENTY- ONE	179
TWENTY-TWO	191
TWENTY-THREE	203
TWENTY-FOUR	215
TWENTY-FIVE	227
TWENTY-SIX	237
TWENTY-SEVEN	251
TWENTY-EIGHT	263
TWENTY-NINE	275
THIRTY	287
THIRTY-ONE	301
THIRTY-TWO	315
THIRTY-THREE	327
THIRTY-FOUR	339
THIRTY-FIVE	353

ONE

Prologue

Vanessa Taylor is eighteen years young today. Her blond-curly hair shines and frames her face. Her green eyes sparkle. She calls her best friend.

"Hello…?"

"Susie, guess what. . ."

"What. . . ?

"I have an appointment to sign on the dotted line with the armed services today!"

"Yeah right, and I have an appointment to join the circus. Get out."

"No, seriously, I'll sign up, leave this place, travel and get my education paid for after four years … if I still want to go to college."

"You're kidding, right?

"No. I'm an adult now. I'll do what I want. Go where I want."

"What are you doing? You're an honors student, a stand out athlete in soccer and tennis, and you want to go be a grunt in the military? You're crazy!

"I'm sick of school. I don't know what I want to do. It will help me find out who I am. There's no future in this town. Besides, it'll be an adventure and something totally new!"

"The recruiters certainly sold you the bag of candy."

"Stop it! Nobody sold me anything! I want to join the military. No mean, stupid thing you say is going to stop me."

"Yeah, and you're totally out of your mind."

"You're just jealous!"

"Uh, no, joining the military isn't anything I would do. They own you. You become government property."

"Oh come on, they don't own you. They train you and give orders, but they don't own you!"

"They certainly do own you, and they give you a folded flag and military burial when you die. Trust me they own you. Only times they stop owning you are when your time is up, if you're wounded and get an honorary discharge, you do something bad and earn a dishonorable discharge, you have a medical condition and get a general discharge under honorable conditions, or you go cuckoo and fall off the radar.

"Wow! Where'd that come from?"

"My uncle, he's a wounded veteran, a decorated alcoholic, homeless and cuckoo. Trust me. You don't want to sign on that dotted line."

"That's your uncle. That's not me."

"Just sayin' . . ."

"I don't care what anyone says. I'm signing!"

"God help you, Girlfriend."

TWO

Vanessa leans over to look for the cocktail napkin that came with the drink. Her head pounds, and the alcohol doesn't help. Nothing helps. Vanessa has been here every night for the last three weeks, and nothing blocks the agony of her migraine. She sleeps all day and drinks at Paradise Roadhouse every night. She feeds the retro-jukebox quarters and dances by herself or with anyone who asks. Sometimes she plays pool, but tonight the light from the ceiling lamp over the pool table feels like a knife plunged into her eye. She stops and lays her head on the cool resin of a nearby table-top for relief. Night after night, a table becomes a pillow for her enraged consciousness.

Tonight, Vanessa puts her head down on a fork, and the dull tine stabs her cheek. She jumps up then crouches to hide from the incoming blaze of bullets that come from the empty Afghanistan desert dotted with boulders that roll onto the dirt road. Vanessa wipes her mouth and pushes her margarita glass over to the edge of the table. She puts her head down again to feel the satin touch of the glossy resin on her forehead. The glass teeters, falls to the floor and shatters. The ice lands in the middle of the mess and starts to melt. Unconscious, Vanessa follows the glass in a slow slide to the floor and lays sprawled with her mouth a gaping hole in a silent howl.

"Hey, Dave, call a taxi for Vanessa. She's wasted…a waste. Get her out of here."

Dave's a new hire. He doesn't know Vanessa.

"What's wrong?"

John rolls his eyes.

"You've got to be kidding …what's wrong? She's had five shots of tequila, and God knows what she started with… pills, who knows, who cares . . . just get her out of here."

Dave calls a taxi and gathers Vanessa's purse and coat.

"Leave my purse alone . . . idiot."

Vanessa rolls over and struggles to get up then flops down in a heap under a table for four. Dave puts her purse and coat by the front door in anticipation of the taxi. He comes back to see if he can help Vanessa get up, but she's curled around the center stem of the table and tangled in a web of chair legs. Dave takes her arm and tries to pull her free.

"Leave her for the taxi! When it gets here, we'll carry her out."

Dave reluctantly pulls back. He's never worked in a bar before. He isn't comfortable leaving a woman on the floor. He sees John is disgusted and takes his cue from the man in charge.

Vanessa is a mess. Her hair is dirty like the peanut shells she's passed out on. Her hoodie is unzipped and leaves her t-shirt to mop the floor. She drools in her bliss. Her jeans are dirty, and her tennis shoes are shot.

"If she comes back tomorrow, bounce her. Don't let her in. She's a foul ball."

Dave looks at Vanessa for more signs of consciousness. John starts to wash dishes. It's late, and he wants to get out early. The taxi arrives, and the driver, Tom, and Dave pick up Vanessa and carry her to the car. They lay her out on the back seat.

"Tom, here's some cash with a tip and her key. Take her to this address and leave her on the couch. Dave, you lock her in, then come back here with the key, and we'll close up."

"Should we call someone? Does she have a friend who can check on her?"

"Trust me, Dave. She doesn't have friends. She torpedoes them. Twice shy. Take it from me. When she's on the wagon, she's sweet as sugar. Off the wagon, she's vicious. I mean cruel. Sarcasm is her specialty. A friend of mine fell into her barrel, rode in the wagon, suffered through multiple wagon crashes and finally ditched her. He still bears the scars. Be forewarned."

Dave sits in the front seat with Tom. No one says anything. They weave through late night traffic to apartments behind the strip mall "decorated" with twinkle-lights on palm trees. GPS guides them to the address, and Tom and Dave carry Vanessa to her apartment door. Dave unlocks the door and flips on the light. They carry Vanessa inside and lay her on the couch. It's a one room studio apartment. There's a fold out couch, a coffee table, a wall calendar with pictures of California-wildflower landscapes and a TV that sits on top of a breakfast table.

Dave opens the door next to the kitchenette to look for a blanket. The top shelf has blankets and towels stacked up with perfect edges. The entire closet is in military order, and the clothes are coordinated by color and purpose. Dave is mesmerized by the faint scent of perfume. He remembers that he bought a scarf once for a girlfriend in a store like this closet. He also remembers a friend in high school who had a closet like this and hung himself in it.

The driver stands back and waits to return Dave to the Roadhouse. Dave takes a blanket and gently lays it over Vanessa.

"Did you see the closet? Perfect."

"Yeah, the service really teaches how to fold clothes – this is a military town full of tidy drunks."

"You see a lot of this?"

"Enough to know I never want to join the military. These people are broken. I've heard war stories that give me nightmares, and I wasn't even there. Drunk or sober, these vets are busted."

"You think that's what's going on with her?"

"Could be . . ."

Vanessa is still passed out as Dave shuts the door and locks it. She is imprisoned in unconsciousness, and no one cares. Even Dave, who has a small measure of curiosity about Vanessa, drops his interest when he closes the door of the apartment and heads back to Paradise.

THREE

It's noon. The light, through the split in the curtain, hits the back of Vanessa's head. Her curly-blond mop is dull and matted. She rolls over and squints to block the sunlight. She pulls the blanket over her head and lies still while the fog in her brain is pierced by a slice of sunlight that penetrates the shroud that covers her from head to toe. She's disappointed that she's still alive – dressed in yesterday's clothes and tennis shoes. The tequila and prescription meds fail her again.

Vanessa sits up, and, not exactly sure where she is, combs her hair with her fingers, sees her purse on the coffee table and pulls it over to get her phone. The face of her smart phone is black with the exception of the white numbers of time and the tiny date beneath them. The numbers begin a count down. Vanessa throws the phone across the room. She ducks for cover, as a secondary explosion rocks the suicide-bomb site where she picks up pieces of body parts for analysis. She finds the back of the head and one foot of the exploded bomber, but the rest of the body is pulverized into confetti to celebrate the Cause. She stumbles and stretches her hand out to break her fall. She lies in a soup of bone bits, shreds of fabric and blood. Her right hand lands on something squishy, like a piece of liver. She grabs hold and pulls up the face of a child.

Vanessa remembers her appointment at Veterans Services. She flops back and pulls the blanket over her head to ward off the migraine behind her temple that threatens to strike her blind.

"Get out of here!"

Vanessa obeys her inner voice and opens the door of the apartment to another perfect day on California's Central Coast. She sees a military-transport plane fly like an airborne snail through the bright-blue sky. She boarded these bloated slugs, when she was whole, before she broke on the barren Afghanistan landscape – so rich in precious stones and minerals.

"Hallelujah!"

The liquor store in the strip mall is open. The short walk from her apartment to the watering hole clears her head. She's coherent as she buys a bottle of tequila from the market purveyor of foreign descent who looks and sounds a lot like her former enemies. She smiles and thanks the indifferent cashier.

Vanessa cradles her bottle of bagged tequila and heads for the bus bench facing the boulevard. When she sees a police car drive past, Vanessa changes her mind, walks back through the parking lot and sits on a bench in front of Anton Dance Studio – two doors down from the liquor store.

A mother, toddler and stroller, with a bag from Glenn's

neighborhood market perched behind the stroller handle, glide by. The toddler starts to cry at the sight of Vanessa. The mom shoves a pacifier into the child's mouth and scurries past. Vanessa laughs out loud.

"Pacifiers should be standard issue in the military! Think of all the money they would save. All the war babies would suck pacifiers and shut up until the pain and frustration subsides, and the universal PTSD from simply being born would dissolve . . . genius."

Vanessa takes a swig from her pacifier of choice and continues to laugh while she visualizes battalions sucking pacifiers.

"Screw it. I don't need the VA. I have the perfect pass-out pacifier."

A driver of a compact sedan waits for an oversize SUV to back out then slips into the parking space directly in front of Vanessa. A slim-medium-height man steps out of the non-descript vehicle and walks past Vanessa to the dance studio behind her. His soft-black-leather shoes take quiet steps to the studio. He finds the studio key on his key ring and unlocks the door.

"What a cool guy with such an uncool car. Oh, I know, you're a foreigner, barely able to pay the rent, right? An illegal alien, I guess that makes you from outer space."

Vanessa laughs at her own joke and takes another long draw from the bottle camouflaged in a brown paper bag. A sleek sports car drives past and finds a space in front of the liquor store. A woman in a black tank top and flowing black skirt gathers her dance bag with her purse inside. She steps out of her car and strides towards Vanessa and the dance studio. As the woman gets closer, Vanessa reads "Anton Dance

Studio" printed on the tank top.

"He must be Anton, and you're a wanna-be dancer, right?"

"Exactly!"

The woman smiles at Vanessa, stumbles on the uneven sidewalk and catches herself.

"Must be the dance lessons that saved you, right?"

"Exactly!"

The woman laughs and continues on to the studio door where Anton greets her, ushers her in and locks the door behind her. Vanessa lies down on the bench and looks up. Little white puffs of cotton-candy clouds float through the sky, and a seagull sails by just below the clouds. Another seagull follows, then another, another and another.

"Rain, it's going to rain! Seagulls on the fly! Those gulls are smart. They know when to get out of the rain."

Vanessa rolls back over and sits up. She hears the Latin music and feels the rhythm. She turns and watches Anton, and the woman dance flamenco in fitted-smooth-leather boots and high-thick-heeled shoes with a strap and buckle. The dancers crack the floor with a rain of rapid fire from their nail studded heels. Anton clicks a remote, and the music stops. He, once again, shows the woman the steps while Vanessa watches. The music starts up. Vanessa stands in front of the window and mimics the dancers until she falls down and passes out.

Anton has his back to the window while the woman dancer concentrates on his feet. No one notices Vanessa crumpled on the ground below the large studio window. The busy strip mall is full of purposeful people. Vanessa is invisible in this world absent of Good Samaritan purpose.

The little clouds grow into bigger-dark-cotton balls, and the sunlight is robbed of space to shine. Darkness overtakes the light, and the bloated-opaque-cotton balls smother the afternoon. The mall people hurry to get to their cars before the sky drips onto them and drenches the thirsty asphalt.

Anton closes his studio and runs on tiptoes to his car with his key ready to unlock the door. He jumps inside, bows his head and tastes the water dripping off his cheek. He shivers and starts the car. He squints to see where he can start the windshield wipers. Rain out of season throws him off. He leans over the steering wheel to get a glimpse of the sky and notices the homeless body folded up under his studio window. His Catholic schooling kicks him out of the car and chases him over to Vanessa who is peacefully unconscious of the rain that pours over her and soaks her black hoodie and jeans.

Without hesitation, Anton reaches under Vanessa, wraps his arms up and around her armpits and, with a dancer's core strength, easily pulls her over to the studio door. He lays her down on the sidewalk, runs on tiptoes like a deer to his car, grabs the keys from the ignition and dances back to Vanessa. He fumbles with the keys until he finds the one that unlocks the studio. He carries her to the back of the studio and sets her down on the soft-well-used-siesta couch. He takes the throw his students gave him for his afternoon naps and lays it over Vanessa.

As quickly as the thunder storm gathers, it dissolves, and the wind blows away the darkness. The sunlight paints a rainbow beginning and ending over the subdued town. People begin to trust the light and take up where they left off. Anton, the only Good Samaritan in the all-American mall today, stands, looks out of his studio window and wonders what's next for Vanessa. He looks down at the bench outside, sees the bag with the tequila and Vanessa's purse behind the bottle. He retrieves both and sits at his desk to examine the contents of the purse for clues about this stranger. The purse doesn't reveal any secrets. The only things inside are comb, compact mirror, lipstick and perfume.

Vanessa is restless in her semi-passed-out state. Anton gets up, goes to see what's causing her unease and bends over her trembling body. Vanessa punches him full force on the chest, jumps off the couch and runs to the door. Like a trapped animal, she cowers and waits for the approaching enemy. Her terror is palpable. Every cell in her body is on high alert. There's no back-up on this mission. Vanessa reaches up to the studio door behind her, turns the handle, slips out through the small opening and runs to her apartment.

The key to the door is in her pocket, along with her debit card. She unlocks the door and thinks about where to escape from the migraine that continues to expand from her temple into her whole head. She locks the door and hides in her closet from the pain and fear that now engulf her. Mercifully, she passes out in her ordered sanctuary.

FOUR

It's 5:30 a.m. A one bedroom casita lights up a motionless-dark street. Anton is pouring coffee into his favorite cup. His cat, Luisa, wanders into the kitchen and insists on breakfast. Anton obeys and puts his coffee down next to his laptop on the kitchen table. Luisa sits and waits for room service. Anton chuckles and scratches her head with affectionate fingers while his other hand takes a fistful of kibble from the bag on the bottom shelf of the pantry and puts it in Luisa's nearby bowl.

Anton, still in pajamas and slippers, sits down at the table. He opens his laptop and begins to read *Havana Times* webzine. Cubans are never far from Cuba, no matter how long it's been since they left, and they prefer the independent publications over government news. Anton clicks on Entertainment and reads the article on dance. The photo at the top of the story features an intense dancer with sweat dripping through his shirt, and a bandana tied around his head to keep his hair out of his eyes. Anton scrolls to the video below. He sees his good friend, Alvaro, hover over legs and feet that move like high-performance-engine pistons. Alvaro is lost in the sound of a flamenco guitar, clap rhythms that compete with each other and the soulful cry from a powerful female singer.

Anton shouts "Bravo!" Luisa jumps up and runs into the other room. Anton laughs, closes his laptop and gets up ready to embrace the day. He dresses in his usual black everything and slips on his lace-up-black-leather-ballroom-dance shoes that work double time on the street. He checks his appearance in the full length mirror attached to the back of his bedroom door. He applauds his signature fashion choices and heads out to pick up a pastry from the local Mexican bakery.

While he drives through the sleepy neighborhood, Anton thinks about the strange-young-homeless woman that slugged him and darted out of his studio like a wild animal. He says a little prayer for her and touches the Rosary that hangs from his ash tray where he keeps his spare change. He remembers other friends and acquaintances and continues to move his fingers across the Rosary. Anton isn't particularly religious, but he's fond of his version of the Rosary habit established in childhood.

The dawn invigorates and the pastry satisfies. The town continues to dream, before alarm clocks shock citizens and the undocumented awake and into action. Anton unlocks his dance studio and warms up with stretches. He shuffles through some favorite flamenco guitar composers. He prefers his cherished vinyl LPs and CDs over cloud sources for isolating what he needs for his choreography practice. He selects his favorite composer and listens to the musician's complete mastery of an instrument shaped like a woman's torso. Carved hardwood, finished and polished to perfection with strings stretched to exact tension, voice the orchestra inside the wooden body cradled in the arms of a flamenco guitar player. This is Anton's addiction. He used to play classical guitar, but gave it up when he discovered dance and the symphony inside himself.

The sound of the flamenco guitar transports Anton to his beloved Cuba. He puts on his dance boots, closes his eyes and, in blind obedience, begins to move in creative sync with the music he hears. His imagination moves him in striking patterns unhinged from the confinements of tradition. Anton, unbound, creates visionary expressions of the composer's moods with his body and adds punctuation with his heels.

A firm knock on his studio front door interrupts Anton's dance gymnastics. Sweat drips through his black shirt while he unlocks the door and welcomes the early-to-rise-alcoholic woman that he helped off the concrete yesterday.

"I think you have my purse."

"I do."

"Give it to me, before I report you to the police."

"Of course, let me get it for you. Please come inside."

"No. Just give me my purse."

"Certainly."

Anton walks across the dance floor with straight-stiff posture that betrays his shock at meeting this rude-American drunk demanding her purse from him – as if he stole it. He approaches the table desk, and his body softens. He recognizes it's the alcohol speaking. He returns the purse with grace.

"You shouldn't take what doesn't belong to you."

"No, of course not."

Vanessa stinks, and her hair fast approaches matted-beyond-saving. She grabs her purse and leaves but doesn't go far. She flops down on the bench in front of the studio and tells herself stories that make no sense. Anton returns to his choreography practice and allows the music to take over. He forgets Vanessa and dances with passion and abandon. Vanessa hears the music and dabs her hair with the perfume that she pulls from her purse. She jumps up, and mimics the dancer she sees through the window. She is uncanny in her ability to match Anton's choreography until she gets dizzy, slams against the window and falls down. Anton stops when he hears the window rattle and sees Vanessa disappear beneath the windowsill. He hurries outside to check on the woman that moments ago accused him of stealing her purse.

"I see you enjoy dancing. Come inside and join me. It will be safer for you."

Vanessa struggles to get up and follows Anton into the studio. She waits by the door with her purse tucked under her arm. Anton restarts the music, puts the remote in his pocket and resumes his practice. Vanessa watches intently. She puts her purse on the floor and begins to copy, a semi-second behind, Anton's expressive dance moves.

Anton is amazed but says nothing. He continues to dance and watches Vanessa follow with awkward precision. He has never witnessed this level of intuitive imitation of complex dance moves, let alone from a mean-alcoholic-street person.

Vanessa immerses her whole being into the Latin rhythms and the intense finger rolls that fan a flamenco guitar. She grunts and twists oblivious to Anton who observes in amazement the accuracy Vanessa is able to demonstrate in spite of her obvious alcoholic haze.

Anton and Vanessa continue to dance their awkward duet. Anton is graceful as a hummingbird while Vanessa lumbers around like a slim-drunken rhino, but her ability to match Anton's rapid moves is supernatural. Vanessa's stamina is remarkable considering the volume of tequila she drinks daily. This unusual combo brings a passerby to the window. He watches with amusement and admiration as the consumed dancers continue their shared passion for hot rhythms and soulful music. Vanessa finally reaches her limit and dives onto the floor.

Anton, surprised by Vanessa's crash landing, continues to flutter like an exotic bird. Vanessa watches but is too spent to follow. Anton gives a final blast of heels and a flip of a graceful bird-hand to end his practice. Terrified, Vanessa covers her head from the incoming gunfire and runs for cover under the desk. The abrupt silence makes her hypervigilant. She scurries to the door, struggles in panic to get out and runs back to her safe-house-studio apartment.

Instinctive by nature, Anton responds and, determined to know more, follows Vanessa at a distance. As he rounds the corner, he sees Vanessa and hides behind the trunk of a palm tree wrapped in little-white-unlit lights. He catches a glimpse of her as she tries to unlock her door while looking right and left to see if the enemy has followed her. She trusts the all clear feeling, calms down enough to stop shaking, opens the door and disappears inside the apartment.

Anton returns to his dance studio in a state of compassion and frustration. Obviously the woman is disturbed, but she interrupted his morning practice. This, in retrospect, is an inexcusable violation. Anton decides to exercise compassion over irritation and considers what he can do. He concludes "nothing."

While Anton continues to muse, he notices the woman's purse on the floor next to the wall. He thinks he should return it right away then catches himself. No, let her pick it up herself. That's how you handle a stubborn-angry-alcoholic creature. He leaves the purse where it is, goes to his desk, pulls out a fat-black-felt marker, a piece of copier paper and writes in all caps, "STUDENTS AND GUESTS LEAVE THIS PURSE WHERE IT IS. THANK YOU! ANTON." He reaches inside the desk drawer again and pulls out scotch tape. He takes the paper and tape and attaches the sign to the wall above the purse. He stands back and relaxes.

"That should do it."

Students and guests come and go, and no one touches the purse. Anton continues his day at the studio with consistency, determination and joy. His choreography feeds his spirit, and he relishes each workout while he anticipates the time he can resume his career as an innovative flamenco artist. In Cuba, he was a rising star. On the California Central Coast, he's nobody, and like the unpleasant drunk so aptly shouted, "BARELY ABLE TO PAY THE RENT!"

FIVE

Vanessa sits in her dark closet and waits for her heart to stop pounding. She lies down and anticipates the blinding headache that will follow her flashback. It's becoming harder to discern if the images are present circumstances or nightmares from Afghanistan. Vanessa recognizes her boundaries between reality and insanity are blurred. She's afraid her own shadow will start to do her harm.

Vanessa closes her eyes, watches the vice as it begins to squeeze her temple, enlarge its grip and squash her head. It crushes her vision and leaves her blind. She vomits and passes out. Three hours later Vanessa wakes up. The dim light in the closed-curtain studio apartment is tolerable, and she moves to the bathroom, but the light from the bathroom window assaults her. She starts to faint. She reaches out, grabs the sink and leans over the basin for support. Bent over, she manages to keep her balance.

Vanessa hasn't had a shower in a month. She can smell her own stench and braves the fear that overtakes her, as she steps into the tiled-glass-shower cage fully dressed. She backs out, undresses and leaves her clothes that reek of alcohol on the floor. Still afraid, she locks the bathroom door. She steps into the shower and adjusts the water to warm. She shampoos and conditions her hair, feels the water's caress and begins to feel safe in spite of being naked.

The fear that overtook her subsides as the bubbles slide down her skin to the drain. What a luxury to stand under a shower while she remembers being out in the field in the Afghan desert. Habit prevents her from wasting water. She shuts off the shower and steps out to dry off. She stands near the sink, turns and sees her reflection in the mirror.

"Well, hello there, you're back. Look at you girl! You're clean, and you smell like lavender! There's hope!"

Flashback and migraine fade, and Vanessa laughs out loud in a happy way. It's been a long time since she felt clean. Her hair is a thick mass but manageable with the conditioning treatment.

Vanessa takes a brush from the medicine cabinet, brushes her hair and works out the tangles. Her hair is past her shoulders. Vanessa is able to pull handfuls across her collar bone and brush out the ends to create a crown of wet curls. She sees the pile of dirty clothes and gathers them up. She puts them outside the bathroom door, wraps a towel around her torso, runs to the closet and flips on the light. Her eyes land on a dress.

"What the heck, it's spring!"

Vanessa puts on matching lace bra and panties, slides the dress over her head and feels it shape itself over her strong body. The scoop neck and mid-length sleeves make a fashion statement. She can't remember the last time she wore a dress. She sees her earrings lined out in her jewelry box. She selects a gift from her high school friend, Susie – a simple pair of green stones to compliment her eyes and match the green background of the floral-print dress she wears. She studies the row of shoes and picks out a pair of simple tan-colored flats. Her feet are delicate, and the flats emphasize the beauty of her sturdy yet refined feet. The mirror on the back of the closet door is full length, and Vanessa turns left and right to get a panoramic vision of this new-old self.

"Dang girl, aren't you the belle of the ball. Down. The Bomb. Cha, Cha, Cha!"

Vanessa does a few ballroom dance steps and laughs.

"You've been away too long! It's nice to see you again!!"

Vanessa bounces out of the closet, goes to the refrigerator, opens it and sees rotting vegetables and out of date milk.

"Time to go to the Glenn's, and oh yah, they have that great deli!"

Vanessa, in her euphoria, looks around for her purse and remembers the dance studio. She remembers bits and pieces from yesterday.

"I'll pick up my purse, if it's even there, then go to the market! Thank God I keep my debit card in my pocket!!"

Vanessa pinches her nose shut and digs into her dirty-pant pocket for her debit card. She goes to the breakfast table, sits down and checks her bank balance on her cell phone. She navigates the site and sees all the charges.

"Holy moly, who knew tequila would take all my cash! I've got to find another way to placate the demons!"

Vanessa laughs and is ready to take on the day. She's got enough money for some groceries and feels exhilarated. Her hair is dry and fluffy, and her skin is like a peach with little rosy patches on her cheeks. She has a big smile full of naturally-white-straight teeth. Vanessa has it all going for her on the outside.

Vanessa skips down the sidewalk, rounds the corner, and passes the liquor store on her way to Glenn's market. She feels a joyful dance inside her happy steps. She notices a woman dressed in a black tank top and skirt in Anton Dance Studio dancing with Anton. The woman stops often to have Anton show her the steps. Vanessa is mesmerized by the patterns the two dancers draw on the floor, and the percussive sounds of their heels. She can't help herself and stands at the front window staring at Anton and the woman. The woman's effort to sync her steps in time with Anton's moves, and the music that seeps out from under the front door inspire Vanessa.

Anton looks over and sees the pretty-young woman at the window. He excuses himself from the woman trying to learn the dance steps and goes to the front door to invite the young woman to take a seat in the back of the room and watch. Vanessa is relieved Anton doesn't recognize her. On the way to the back of the studio, Vanessa sees her purse and a handmade sign taped above it telling everyone in the studio, in letters that shout, LEAVE THE PURSE WHERE IT IS. Vanessa is embarrassed to the point that she temporally disowns the purse. She continues to walk to the back and sits down on a chair by the desk to watch.

The music transports Vanessa to Spain, where she lived abroad in her junior year in high school. Her feet tremble with energy at the sound of flamenco guitar. She sits on the chair, but her whole being is alive with the vibrations that fill the room. Her fingers drum imaginary castanets and her hands fan against the chair while the dance partners in front of her perform the elaborate choreography.

Anton looks at the studio clock and sees there are only a few minutes left in the lesson. He repeats the song and shows the woman, once again, the sequence of steps that would be a challenge to a professional dancer, let alone a student. The woman doubles down and finally puts it together. Anton claps his hands in rhythm with the music and cheers,

"Olé Margret! Bravo! That didn't take too long."

They both laugh which washes away any residual frustration. Anton gives Margret a hug. Vanessa notices Margret adores Anton and is grateful for his praise. Margret slowly lets go of Anton and laughs at herself. She waits for Anton to dismiss her, but hopes he'll want to continue the lesson. Anton breaks the spell.

"Okay! Tomorrow, same time, same place. You have your recording. Just go slow until you have it on automatic without thought."

"Exactly, I'll get it if it kills me. Thanks for allowing me to record the steps. See you Thursday!

Anton waits for Margret to exit before he walks back to speak with the potential student sitting on the chair by the desk.

"You're a wonderful teacher – kind and patient."

"Is that your purse?"

"Yes, and I apologize for my behavior, that I don't remember, but I do know I can get out of hand . . . I hope you can forget it and forgive me. I'm on my way to Glenn's Market. I vaguely remember that I might have left my purse, which I now see on the floor over there with the sign posted above it."

"You don't wear alcohol well. You were extremely rude. You also smelled like a Cuban trash heap, and worse you were mean. There's no excuse. There is an explanation, maybe, but no excuse. I grew up under a cruel government, and cruelty is something I will not tolerate. I forgive you, yes, but if you ever come to this studio drunk, I will throw you out and lock the door. Now, take your purse, go to Glenn's and buy some vegetables. If you want to learn to dance flamenco, come back to sign up."

Vanessa bows her head and studies the floor. She watches one tear splash on her shoe then another. She slowly walks to the wall, stoops down and picks up her purse. Her shoulders begin to shake, and the tears flow. She stumbles in a river of despair out the door and down the block to Glenn's market. There's no bench to sit on, no couch to curl up on and no place to sob.

A small mutt watches Vanessa and wags her tail but hides under a newsstand. Vanessa sees the little creature, goes to the stand and pretends to take a free publication. The dog sniffs Vanessa's wet flats and licks the salty tears. Vanessa bends down, scoops up the dog and squeezes her tight against her chest. The dog wiggles and tries to get away. Clutched in Vanessa's hold, the little savior yields to her destiny. She lies still in Vanessa's embrace and allows Vanessa to cry tears onto her matted fur with her face buried under Vanessa's chest.

There's a pet store, *All Creatures Great and Small,* on the other side of Glenn's market. Vanessa passes the market and walks to the pet store for a leash, collar and dog food. She has no intention of advertising the lost dog. The stray unburies itself from Vanessa's protective chest to look around the store. The sales clerk at the register is charmed.

"What a cute dog! What's its name?"

"Susie."

"If you want a name tag to go with the collar, I can make one for you. The tags are behind you on the top shelf."

Vanessa turns around, picks out a bright pink heart and gives it to the clerk to engrave.

"What do you want on the tag?"

"Susie, and her phone number 805-007-7007."

The clerk laughs.

"Is she a double agent?"

Vanessa answers with a grin,

"Yes!"

"Here's a biscuit for the little spy. We have a sink, shampoo, conditioner and blow dryer if you want to give her a bath."

"How much do you charge?"

"It's five dollars"

"Really, only five dollars?"

"Yes. Right there, in back."

Vanessa carries Susie to the back and bathes her with all the amenities. The blow dryer uncovers a foxlike face with fluffy-honey-colored fur. Susie loves the bath. She relishes the massage with shampoo and conditioner, hot air and attention. Vanessa laughs.

"We'll both be going to the spa for make overs!"

Vanessa hugs Susie, pays with her debit card that she now carries in her purse, and they sashay into the sunshine.

The market is next. Susie is on the leash with her bright-pink-dog tag. Her cherub face is framed in soft-thick fur and her foxlike ears twitch with interest. Vanessa loops the leash around the leg of the newsstand and leaves Susie tied at the place where they first met.

"Stay. I'll be right back. No barking."

Vanessa goes through the neighborhood store with a cart, finds the pet section and selects a toy and dog brush. She goes to the freezer and picks up organic frozen vegetables and berries. She stops to get bread, bananas, butter and milk, picks up a premade Italian sub and asks the cashier to add a sturdy bag. Vanessa figures the canvas bag is perfect to carry Susie if necessary. The cashier packs the groceries and sandwich in the canvas bag with Glenn's Market logo on the front and a farm scene on the back. Vanessa is aware that her budget is blown. She looks down at Susie prancing along beside her. There are no second thoughts.

The Anton Dance Studio is busy with a small class of adult women that follow a simple routine. Anton repeats the steps multiple times so each dancer can perform without looking down. Vanessa picks up her pace and looks straight ahead as she and Susie pass by the studio. The music follows her down the block. She swings as she walks, bounces her heels a couple of times and mimics the dance patterns she saw out of the corner of her eye when she passed by the bench and studio. She stops to concentrate on her dance steps then looks up and sees the liquor store with all the inviting-booze-filled bottles on display. She pushes ahead, rounds the corner and heads for home.

SIX

Anton stops at Glenn's Market and buys tortilla chips, a soda and homemade salsa from the deli. He drives three blocks. Before he turns right onto Sunset Avenue, Anton pulls over, parks and enjoys the fact that he lives on Sunset. He often stops here after work where he can see his street sign and eat a snack. He visualizes the sun dropping into the sea beyond the harbor at Havana Port. He remembers the large natural bay that he explored on his bicycle on Sundays, and the sunsets that soothed away a week's worth of frustration, as he drilled his dance company to create innovative dance routines. The sky's rainbow-sherbet colors drip over the bold colors that decorate the old buildings and wrap them in romantic hues that hide the crumbling history like soft light hides the age of a beautiful woman.

    The Caribbean island nation has a firm grip on Anton's imagination and is the birthplace of his award winning choreography. The harbor is the seed of the sound and motion in everything he now creates in his modest studio. That and baseball. Like most Cubans, Anton is crazy for baseball. He played in school and now often plays in the nearby park on Sundays. He watches the pros on TV, studies the posture of each player and incorporates their moves into his choreography. He imagines a big contemporary production with a "baseball" floating from dancer to dancer in a dream sequence of slow-motion-baseball-body language. He laughs out loud when ideas of titles for the event run from *"Homerun"* to *"You're Out."*

A neighbor honks his horn and interrupts Anton's daydream. Anton waves, starts his engine, continues to his driveway mid-way down the block and parks in front of his single-space-detached garage. He likes his historical casita surrounded by equally-aged-larger houses. The neighborhood is part of the Old Town District, and Anton feels at home here.

Luisa runs out from a bush along the side of the house and races inside when Anton opens the door. She hurries to the pantry and demands her dinner. Anton is obedient and fills her dish with premium cat kibble. He opens a can of salmon and tops the kibble with the juicy fish. Luisa is chubby and has fixed mealtimes – free feeding is not an option.

Anton checks his mail and prepares his dinner. Tonight, its rice and beans with vegetables and his preferred Cuban beer *Bucanero* to wash it down. The liquor store in the strip mall is well stocked with imported beers to accommodate the diverse neighborhood. He sits at the table and reads his mail while he eats dinner and drinks his beer. The alcohol takes the edge off seeing the bills, and a postcard from his mama assures him all is well in Cuba.

Anton sighs and puts his emotions on hold, as he thinks about his mama and his large extended family. Anton's father died when a drunk driver plowed over him while he smoked his favorite cigar at a sidewalk café. When he died, the family lost everything except basic social services. Anton, being ambitious, came to America to advance his prospects and sends home what small amounts of money he can to help. His dance credentials gained him entry to the United States – music, dance and baseball keep Anton grounded.

Anton finishes his dinner, clears the table and washes the dishes. He picks up Luisa, who lies grooming herself, and they go to the living room to watch TV. Anton subscribes to a satellite provider for *MLB Network – National Pastime All The Time,* so he can watch *Caribbean World Series* in February. He keeps up with his *Havana News* and *MLB Network* on his laptop and cell phone.

Anton is an animated viewer. He takes mental notes, always relating the game of baseball to flamenco. Luisa, curled up on his lap, leaps away when a homerun becomes a flurry of hands waving above his head. A line drive is a series of fast footwork on his heels, and a hit to left field is a graceful ballet move before a long slide on the floor. Anton laughs, picks himself up and goes to his bedroom ready for bed. He keeps his pajamas and his slippers at his bedside. Anton has another Rosary on his bedside table. He gives special attention to his mama, three brothers and one sister and Cuba. He says goodnight to Havana Port and the little cafe where his father smoked his last cigar. He can still smell cigar smoke and hear the ocean sloshing against the dock.

Almost asleep, Anton remembers the young woman, and how she walked past the studio window looking straight ahead. He wonders if he was too harsh about the purse and her drunken behavior. No, he did the right thing, but …

"Ay Caramba! That young woman is born to dance."

He takes the Rosary up once more, fingers the beads and prays. He closes his eyes, falls asleep and hopes she'll return to take dance lessons.

SEVEN

The studio apartment feels like a prison, and Susie needs to go out. Vanessa changes into a dress and old-but-clean-tennis shoes. She puts on a sweater, hooks the leash to Susie's collar and grabs her purse. The key and debit card are inside her purse only because there are no pockets on her dress. Vanessa makes a conscious effort to steer clear of temptation and decides to walk through downtown Old Town. It's just three blocks away in the opposite direction of the strip mall and the liquor store.

The street names call out the shades of day – Dawn, Morning, Sundown and Sunset. Vanessa lets Susie pick the trail, and they end up on Sunset. It's dark and lights are shutting off, as residents go to bed. Midway down the block, Vanessa turns and heads home unaware that Anton and his cat, Luisa, live here on Sunset Avenue in Old Town.

Vanessa is at peace, and Susie is a happy companion. Street lamps are sparse in this neighborhood, but an early full moon takes the night watch and illuminates the way.

Vanessa feels as if she's walking inside a black and white photograph. The beauty of the houses and landscaping bathed in silver light is comforting. Susie is as intrepid in the moonlight as she is in sunlight. And now that Susie has Vanessa, she is increasingly bold and edges out ahead as they walk home.

Inside the studio apartment, Vanessa pulls out the bed from the belly of the couch. Susie is terrified of the dark-cave mouth of the couch. Vanessa brings out sheets, blankets and a pillow from the closet and makes the bed into a nest. She closes the curtains and whispers, "Goodnight moon." She puts on a comfy *"Save the Whales"* t-shirt, silk-pajama pants from India and goes from the closet to the bathroom to brush her teeth. Susie follows her from place to place with playful curiosity and bites the floating pant legs. Ready for bed, Vanessa invites her hesitant nestling to join her. She falls asleep on her side with her arm curled around Susie.

Vanessa wakes early without an alarm, lies on her back in bed and thinks about yesterday. She wonders what dance lessons would cost. The sting of humiliation is erased by a desire to learn to dance flamenco. Susie is cuddled up to Vanessa's side and is sound asleep. Vanessa's fingers tickle Susie's fur. It's like having a teddy bear that breathes. Susie stretches out and snuggles into the blanket. Vanessa considers her budget, and where she could squeeze the numbers to find more cash for dance lessons. Bingo.

"Susie, get up. We're going to dance flamenco! No more tequila adjusts the balance – tequila out equals flamenco in!"

Susie wiggles, stretches and yawns. Susie is a late sleeper and pushes the snooze button. Vanessa, invigorated by her budget solution, gets up. When Susie hears kibble spill into the stainless-steel bowl, she runs to the kitchenette and, proper as a Victorian Duchess, nibbles her breakfast. Vanessa prepares a soft boiled egg with toast and eats while she watches Susie finish her meal.

"Susie girl, you can teach me manners. You're the Queen. Look at you dressed in fur while you nibble your crumpet."

Vanessa gets up, tidies the kitchen and heads to the closet to dress for dance. She's found her passion, and Anton, hopefully, means what he said about signing up for lessons. She trades out her sleep wear for leggings, a long-tailed shirt and chunky-heeled shoes. Her hair is still fresh and bouncy. Susie is already at the door. Her Imperial Highness isn't used to waiting and jumps up and down trying to hurry her courier. Vanessa laughs.

"You really are a Duchess!"

Vanessa puts Susie on the leash, and they power walk to the studio where, sure enough, Anton stretches. Vanessa knocks, and Anton stops to let her in. He sees Susie and is fatally charmed. The Duchess has another servant. Anton reaches down and picks up the Duchess.

"Her fur is so soft! And her eyes sparkle. What's her name?"

"Susie."

Anton gently puts Susie on the floor and stands back up to welcome Vanessa.

"How can I help you?"

"Did you really mean I could take lessons here?"

"Yes."

"I'm ready to start today. How much are lessons?"

"Group classes are $60 a month with one lesson a week. Months with an extra week are $75. Private lessons are $75 a lesson."

"Sign me up for a group class, please."

"Okay. Come back later today. The adult beginning class starts at 5:00. Arrive fifteen minutes early, pay your fee, sign the release and pick out shoes and skirt from the loan closet."

"See you at 4:45! Come Susie."

Susie isn't eager to leave the side of such a friendly man, but her affection for Vanessa is established. She tiptoes out the door and leads Vanessa to the next stop. They walk around the block to avoid the liquor store and return to the apartment. Vanessa doesn't drive because of the flashbacks. She's on disability with a military general discharge under honorable conditions.

Inside the apartment, Vanessa checks her bank balance. This month looks good in spite of falling off the wagon. She hopes the wagon stays on the road, and she stays on the wagon. She thinks her furry companion and flamenco dance should help.

"Susie, we're on a special mission to save me. This is a battle for my sanity."

Susie looks up and wags her fluffy tail. She circles twice then sits down and stares at Vanessa.

"If anyone can pull me out of this trench, it's you Susie."

Vanessa pulls her phone out of her purse and calls her Mom.

"Hello?"

"Hi, Mom."

"Oh, heavens, Vanessa how are you? It's been weeks. Are you doing okay? Are you taking your meds? I miss you! What's going on?"

"Mom, I got a dog!"

"O Lord, a dog. What kind of a dog?

"I have no idea. She's a stray. She's adorable. I named her 'Susie'."

"Are you sure a dog is a good idea? I mean, with all the troubles, do you think that's wise?"

"Oh yes, she's my savior, my angel. I should have found one straight out of the service. She's my guardian and best friend – my only friend."

"Oh Honey, you have friends, lots of friends."

"No, Mom, I don't have any friends. But now I have Susie! How's Dad? Any better?"

"No, no he's 'bout the same. He still can't talk, and he's in a lot of pain. His left side still isn't able to do anything. It's sad . . . awful. The church has been wonderful, but it's mostly unbearable. Do you miss Texas at all? Do you think you'll be able to visit soon?"

"I don't miss Texas one bit, but I'll visit as soon as I can. I miss you and Dad, but Texas not one-tiny bit."

"We should have never allowed you to spend that summer in Austin with Aunt Janet and Uncle Jim."

"Ah, Mom, don't blame them. I just wanted to get out and see the world."

"I do blame them. They should have kept a closer eye."

"Mom, I just have an independent streak. No one could have stopped me. I don't regret it. I just have to get through it."

"I know dear. I'm glad you have a dog. What's her name again?"

"Susie."

"After your friend, Susie from school?"

"No, she's Susie, because that's the name that came to me when the clerk asked what I wanted on the dog tag."

"Was your friend, Susie, in the service with you?"

"God no, Mom, it was a dog tag for my dog!"

"Okay. Well, send me a photo of her. I'll show it to Dad. He loves dogs."

"I know. Too bad Ralph didn't live longer. He would have kept Dad happy."

"Yes, he was a sweet dog. Cost an arm and a leg to feed, but he was pure goodness."

"Yes he was . . . he was special . . . I have to go, Mom. I love you guys. Give Dad a big hug for me. Bye now."

"Bye dear. . . Send a photo of Susie and call me. . ."

The phone goes black. Vanessa taps, and the phone lights up again. She scrolls to camera, hits the camera icon and takes a quick picture of Susie curled up at her feet. She messages it to Texas. Vanessa is hyper aware of the time. Susie is at the door whining.

"Okay, we'll go out, but we need to be at the studio fifteen minutes early."

Susie bounces up and down while Vanessa gets the leash. Snapped in and ready for the open door, Susie backs up and waits. Vanessa opens the door and out they go. Vanessa walks towards the strip mall. Susie tugs her in the opposite direction. Susie wins. The neighborhood has landscaping which Vanessa and Susie both enjoy. Vanessa recognizes Susie guided her away from the temptation to visit the liquor store to buy a lottery ticket. Vanessa smiles and gives Susie a thumb's up.

"You are my guardian angel, you little puffball."

Susie looks up and wags her tail. The landscape at each home is unique. Susie appreciates the smells, and Vanessa loves the colors. Vanessa sighs and feels peace replace the excitement of possibly winning the lottery.

"You know, Susie that ticket could fix everything. That liquor store is exactly like the ones that sell the numbers that win. It's an anonymous-little-bottle shop in a small town. Even the cashier looks the part. I tell you, Susie, we missed our shot."

A snoozing cat wakes, as Susie and Vanessa approach. Susie grows bold on the leash and barks. The cat panics and runs away.

"Susie! Stop it! I'm that cat. Leave it alone!"

Susie settles down, and Vanessa sees herself for the first time in a cat. She sees her own panic, and how she runs away in blind over reaction. Susie, on the other hand, forgets it all and moves on to the next bush eager to explore new smells.

"Oh, to be a dog,"

Back at the apartment, Vanessa checks herself in the mirror, picks up her purse and calls Susie away from the toy she bought her at the market. Susie sees Vanessa at the door and jumps up ready for adventure. They skip to the dance studio and ignore the store hawking bottles of alcohol and prizes. Vanessa remembers,

"One day at a time."

The dance studio is empty, but the door is open. Vanessa is twenty minutes early. She sits on the chair by the desk and waits. Susie sits beside her, curious but restrained. A chubby woman walks in and sits on the couch. She's dressed in the same black skirt and Anton Dance Studio tank top as the woman Vanessa has seen dance with Anton.

"Hello, I'm Vanessa. Can you tell me where the loan closet is? I signed up for lessons."

"It's down the hall, first door on the left. You can change in the closet, in the hall or in the restroom across from the closet. We hang out here and wait for Anton to start the class. I'm Maria."

"Thanks, Maria."

"Let me know if you need help with anything."

Vanessa tries to hide her excitement. She goes to the closet and is stunned when she opens the door. It's organized like a store! Skirts are hung up by size. Tank tops are folded and sit in piles according to size. Shoes are laid out in pairs along the floor next to the wall. A sign above each group of shoes tells their size. A check out sheet hangs on a clipboard with a pencil hanging from the clamp.

"I wonder if Anton ever did military service. He has all the marks."

Susie stares at Vanessa.

"Oh, Susie you wouldn't understand. What do you know about rank and file?"

Vanessa changes into a tank top and skirt and slips her feet into size seven flamenco dance shoes. Her toes wiggle inside the black-suede footwear with the nail studded heels.

"I should have signed up here a long time ago. Who knew I had Spain inside me?"

Susie looks up at Vanessa and wags her tail.

"How different my life would have been if Mom had enrolled me in flamenco dance lessons! Not! Mom would never even hire Mexicans, and she was always afraid I would pierce my ears. How can anyone be so out of step?"

Susie bounces up and down.

"Settle down, Susie. We're here to dance not bouncy house."

Vanessa signs in on the clipboard for dance clothes, and Maria registers Vanessa for lessons and runs her debit card. It's official. Vanessa is a flamenco dancer. She walks to the wall of mirrors and studies her reflection. Susie, tied to the couch leg, watches Vanessa look in the mirror, settles down and sighs with her nose propped up on her paw. Vanessa swings her skirt and twirls. She stamps her feet and laughs.

Anton arrives with a soda in hand and tells everyone to line up facing the wall of mirrors. The sound of the clumping shoes causes a foggy veil to spread over Vanessa. She feels the panic rise and races to Susie. She frees Susie from the couch and squeezes her to her chest. The yelling and confusion increase as the marketplace fills with smoke and body parts fly through the air. Susie and Vanessa race out of the studio and dive under the bench outside. The whole class is looking at them from inside the studio, as Vanessa and Susie hide under the bench.

Anton tells the class to return to the mirrors and practice last week's footwork. Maria takes the remote from Anton and starts the music. Anton goes out to the bench and reaches under to take Susie and help Vanessa unfold and sit up. Vanessa trembles and cries.

"I wish I had never been born."

Anton sits next to Vanessa in silence. Vanessa reaches for Susie and buries her face into Susie's fur. Anton is patient and waits for the tears to subside.

"Let's get up and return to the class."

"What if it happens again? I can't stand it."

"If it happens again, you can run under the desk."

Vanessa looks at Anton and sees his smile.

"I'm really messed up aren't I?"

"No. Just sensitive and hyper aware, which makes you a natural dancer. If a trigger sends you running, go ahead and run. Just run to the desk. Then I don't have to watch you get hit by a car!"

Vanessa half laughs. Anton stands up and offers a hand to Vanessa. She takes it, stands up and carries Susie back to the couch to tie her up again. Vanessa rejoins the class and mimics the dancers as they review last week's lesson. By the end of the hour, Vanessa has the entire routine memorized and performs it with a measure of elegance. Her laser focus shuts out all distraction, and she's swallowed up in the rhythm. Her hands and feet accent the sound of the flamenco guitar. The gypsy inside Vanessa takes over her body and unleashes her passion.

The class ends, and Vanessa changes into her own clothes. She unties Susie, and students compliment her first day in dance class. Maria is particularly attentive, and everyone pretends nothing out of the ordinary happened. Vanessa feels safe, and there's no migraine. Anton is busy answering questions from students, and there's a feeling of celebration unlike anything Vanessa has ever felt before. Anton keeps the music playing while the next class for children begins. Vanessa watches the children line up, and Anton turns off the music to count, clap and start a new routine for the class of young butterflies.

On the walk home, with Susie eager to get home for dinner, Vanessa wonders at the irony of a liquor store directly in her to path to her new passion. It's as if it's a test of her resolve with the bait two doors down from the dance studio.

EIGHT

Anton sits at the studio desk going over the same bills again. He shoves them aside, puts on his favorite LP of flamenco guitar and claps along. He walks to the drum near the wall, brings over a chair and sits down to beat the drum. Restless, he starts to do patterns with his heels and toes and begins a solo dance that takes him to a bullring in Andalusia. He stands fearless in front of the bull then kneels and opens his arms. The bleeding bull stands exhausted, falls forward onto his knees and topples over dead. Anton cuts off one ear and holds it up to the crowd. The crowd roars. This is the last time he enters a bullring even in his imagination. Anton became a vegetarian after he watched his first bullfight on TV, when he was seven years old.

    Anton understands Vanessa's horror. He isn't sure what triggers her flashbacks, but he knows what it's like to be in a world of viciousness that destroys innocence. Most problems arise when one tries to make everything black and white and doesn't see all the shades of gray. Anton is a master of painting shades of gray inside a black and white structure. Each student is seen in detail and taught with these shades in mind, but a black and white structure demands that they ultimately compromise, put aside the ego and become part of the whole. Vanessa is a puzzle. She's an extraordinarily gifted dancer but has a severe mental handicap. Her black and white is shattered into a thousand shades of gray.

The clock on the wall reminds Anton that Luisa is at home waiting for dinner. He puts the drum back near the wall, tucks the bills back inside the desk, turns out the light and locks the studio door. He stops at the liquor store and buys soda, chips and salsa. He passes the Sunset road sign on his way home to feed Luisa.

After dinner, the two of them sit on the couch. Luisa purrs while she shoves her head under Anton's hand. With his other hand Anton eats his potato chips and drinks his soda for dessert. Vanessa continues to circulate through Anton's thought. He considers how he can help her banish the demons. Luisa, annoyed with Anton's indifference, jumps down and curls up on the floor.

Anton forgoes TV and gets ready for bed. He slides under the covers and tries to think of what he can do for Vanessa. He leans over and reaches for his Rosary. As he fingers the beads, he falls asleep. Two hours later, the light still on, Anton wakes and decides he will offer Vanessa private flamenco dance lessons for free. He sighs, turns off the table lamp by his bed and falls into a dreamless sleep.

Anton follows his morning routine and stops at Lupe's Panaderia to buy a pasteles and cappuccino. Lupe and Anton chat for a moment then out the door he flies. Anton's metabolism is super-efficient. He could eat all the baked sweets on the tray and never gain an ounce. At the studio, Anton repeats his stretching routine and invents new choreography. He uses flamenco guitar music for inspiration. A knock on the studio door gets his attention. Anton sees his neighbor miming "Turn down the music!" Anton mimes "Forgive me" and lowers the volume. His neighbor is the salon owner next door and lives in the back of his shop. It's not uncommon for Anton to forget he has neighbors when he does his early-morning dance practice.

Anton remembers his studio in Old Town Havana with its wooden floors and large windows that faced the harbor. His dance company flourished in the romantic ballroom. He won many awards and grew a large following, but he gave it all up to come to America. Now he doubts his decision to start over in a foreign country. He shakes off his uncertainty and resumes his practice.

A loud slam rattles his window. Anton rushes over and sees that an oversized pickup truck has backed into his car. In shock, he races out to assess the damage. The driver is apologetic, and they exchange insurance information. The truck driver is able to drive his truck away without a scratch, but Anton is left with a crushed trunk and broken rear window. The lifted pickup cleared the back of Anton's little sedan and smashed the rear window leaving the truck's big tires to mangle the trunk. He returns to the studio and sits on the siesta couch with his head in his hands.

The entire day is a series of setbacks with the truck mash-up to take first prize. Now, at the end of the day, Anton watches baseball on TV with Luisa. A player whacks a homerun with bases loaded in the ninth inning. Anton leaps, whoops, shouts, yells and claps his hands to flamenco rhythms. Anton's favorite team wins the game. Today is a good day after all.

Dawn, in this town, is pink. It's a pale pink that fades to a light blue when it's not foggy. Anton, still celebrating his team's win last night, buys two pasteles from Lupe and drives fifteen minutes to the ocean. There's no harbor here, but there's a large wetland and rough sea. Miles of sand dunes, dotted with ocean-friendly plants, provides a home for snowy plover. Regular passenger and freight trains race through this wilderness. The horn blast, as the train crosses the trellis, reminds Anton of Havana Port. This place isn't anything like Cuba, but it has the same salt air and seagulls.

Anton sits down on a large driftwood log and eats his pasteles. Two seagulls join him and war over the crumbs Anton tosses. The two sleek-bodied-avian beggars rob each other. There's no sharing on this beach. It's harsh, cold and the wind is often strong, but it gives Anton the same peaceful feeling as when he would sit on a warm beach across the channel from Havana Port and watch the ships unload their containers.

Anton throws the last bit of pasteles to his new-best friends and heads back to his crumpled sedan. He puts his shoes back on and re-enters the bustle of a town waking up to its purpose. Anton carries peace inside and opens his studio to offer the public the opportunity to dance flamenco. It's a modest offering, but Anton is renewed from his sojourn to the beach. He's ready to share what he has to give.

The woman with the polished sports car, dressed in her Anton Dance Studio tank top and black-full skirt, arrives a little early for her lesson. She has worked hard to memorize her footwork. She is eager to show Anton her progress.

"Well, hello Margret! Early bird, aren't you?! Please, give me a minute to set up."

"Am I too early? I'm so excited to show you what I learned!"

"Wonderful. We'll begin in a few minutes."

Margret stands in front of the mirrors and practices the routine she's been working on all week. She watches her reflection and allows her steps to unfold without looking down. It's a breakthrough for Margret. She is free, relaxed and graceful. Her hair is long, dark and shiny, which she ties up in a ponytail. Her nails wear candy-apple-red polish. When she smiles her hyper-white teeth shock and distract. She is beautiful by commercial standards, but the beauty seems painted on rather than an upwelling from within – she tries too hard.

Anton turns on the music for their dance and mentally prepares for repeated interruptions to help Margret remember the step combinations. He slips the remote into his pocket.

"Yes, Margret, let's see where we are with this dance."

Anton begins with his back to Margret and walks to the music like a lion stalks its prey. He turns and sees Margret and begins his patterns of dominance while Margret stands in the center. Her head is down in submission. The music shifts, and Anton flips his hands in the air, turns and claps in rhythm with unpredictable clap accents. Margret raises her chin and begins a dance of graceful rebellion. Her steps are confident, perfectly timed and without hesitation. She has mastered her routine. There is no need for the remote. The dancers end together in a flurry of heel toe exchange and a graceful embrace.

"Bravo! Margret, you did it! You mastered the steps and remembered the routine. Brilliant! Let's do it again. This time add something more from your soul."

Margret isn't sure what "soul" means, but she thinks Anton wants more energy. They take their places, and the music starts. Anton repeats his beginning, and Margret takes her rebellion to a whole new level. She drives her body, and the dance is frantic. The steps and the routine are perfect, but all the grace has disappeared. The driving quality is over the top, and Anton is unable to find a connection. They finish the dance in an embrace, but the air between them is still.

"Margret, you must settle down. Go inside yourself and let the dance come up from within."

Margret has no idea what Anton means, but she is determined to learn.

"You mean relax? I thought you meant more energy."

"I did, but a different kind of energy."

"What kind?"

"The kind you see in ocean waves."

"I rarely go to the beach. I'm not sure what you mean."

"Go to the ocean and watch the waves."

"What should I look for?

"Just go to the ocean."

"Okay."

Margret doesn't go to the beach, because she doesn't like the sand. She has to take off her shoes, and the car fills up with of sand. The sand goes everywhere. The beach is not her thing, but she adores Anton, so she does what she thinks he wants her to do. Margret is still unsure of what Anton means about soul.

"Good. Let's start a new routine."

Anton shows Margret another difficult pattern. She struggles to match the steps, but her determination overrides her lack of natural aptitude. She soldiers on. Anton is patient and slowly repeats the steps. Margret watches and tries to remember the sequences.

"Anton, would you mind if I recorded you doing my part of the dance? I can practice the steps at home.

"That's a good idea."

Margret goes to her designer purse and pulls her android phone from the custom made pocket. She films Anton dancing her routine, puts the phone away and comes back to continue the lesson. Anton shows Margret the difference between what it is to dance the steps and feel the spirit of the dance. Margret sees the difference, but has no idea how to make the change.

"No worries, Margret. Keep practicing. Go to the ocean and watch the waves. You'll get it."

Margret is obviously discouraged, but Anton gives her hope.

NINE

Vanessa is encouraged. Anton is kind. He lowballed her mental handicap, pulled her through, and the women in the class followed his lead. Vanessa has found her tribe.

"Susie, come! It's a beautiful evening. Let's walk around Old Town while it's still light. What do you say?"

Susie barks once and wiggles. Vanessa gets the leash, and Susie dances in circles. The leash confirms the promise. Together they power walk to the Old Town neighborhood. Susie guides them to Sunset Avenue with side trips through alleys. The smells and neighborhood dogs are Susie's interest. Vanessa loves the charm of the old houses and the manicured landscapes. Susie and Vanessa try to be patient with each other. Each one gives the other time to investigate their interests in the surrounding environment.

"What's with Sunset Avenue, Susie? We came here the last time."

Susie keeps going, sniffing the ground, and prancing

ahead. Midway down the block Susie stops. She stares at a casita standing in between two large-historical homes. Vanessa, curious why Susie is staring at the casita, moves closer. Vanessa sees the crumpled sedan in the driveway, and Anton in the window cheering his favorite baseball team to another win.

"Susie! You knew didn't you! This is where that kind man who picked you up and held you lives! You little flirt!"

Vanessa picks Susie up, so she can see Anton jump up and down and do his wild dance in front of his TV. Vanessa laughs.

"Susie, you have a crush on Anton! Well, move over, because there are a lot of women and girls ahead of you from what I see in the studio."

Susie wants down. She wants to visit Anton. Vanessa laughs and puts Susie on the ground.

"Oh no, not tonight, Girlfriend, some other time, but I'll let him know you're smitten."

Susie hangs back, but Vanessa insists, and they continue their walk through the neighborhood. Susie sniffs plants and forgets Anton. Vanessa marvels at Susie's discovery of Anton's house. She is also concerned about the condition of Anton's car.

"Susie, I hope Anton's okay."

Susie is absorbed in a special smell in the gutter. Vanessa tugs the leash. Susie yields and comes to Vanessa's side.

"Susie, I see you've moved on, but Anton could use a cheer up. We'll buy him a bouquet tomorrow for his injured car, and I'll let him know how much you like him."

They continue their walk down Sunset Avenue in silence. They circle back towards the apartment. Vanessa is still amazed that Susie led the way to Anton's casita. Animal GPS is uncanny. Vanessa and Susie snuggle on the couch. Vanessa moves Susie over, so she can get up and go to the closet. Susie watches her from the couch. Inside the closet, Vanessa turns on the light and looks for the chess set her dad gave her when she was twelve. It's a beautiful hand carved chess set of the palace hierarchy with kings and queens, bishops, knights and the foot soldiers. Vanessa hasn't played chess in years, but tonight it seems like a good thing to do. She takes out the book illustrated with strategies to win tucked inside the case. Vanessa thumbs through the pages.

"Perfect!"

Vanessa sets up the chessboard on the kitchen table. She reviews the positions of the various pieces and remembers how much fun she had when she played chess with her dad. Susie curls up at Vanessa's feet and falls asleep. It's 11:30 p.m. when Vanessa finishes her first solitary game of chess. Tired, yet satisfied, Vanessa pulls the bed out of the couch. She gets bedding from the closet and makes the bed while Susie watches from a safe distance. Susie's still not convinced the couch won't eat her.

Morning comes with sunshine, and Vanessa is up early. She feeds Susie, makes herself breakfast and plans her day. First thing is Glenn's market for a bouquet for Anton. She puts on another spring dress, flip-flops and puts her hair up in a ponytail. Curls break out of the elastic band and frame her face. She gives herself a high five in the mirror.

Susie and Vanessa race each other to the market. It's not easy to run in flip-flops, but Vanessa is agile and wins the race to Glenn's. Vanessa buys the bouquet for Anton, a mini chew for Susie and a sandwich for later. With Susie close to her side, Vanessa heads to the studio. She knows Anton doesn't like to be interrupted, so she leaves the bouquet at the doorstep. Anton sees Vanessa and stops his practice. He hurries to open the door. He sees the bouquet and calls out to Vanessa.

"Hey, come back!"

Vanessa turns around, and Susie strains the leash to get to Anton first. Anton is holding the bouquet.

"I didn't want to disturb you."

"Are these flowers for me?"

"Yes! It's a long story. Susie and I like to walk in the Old Town neighborhood in the evening. Susie leads the way, and, twice now, she has taken me to Sunset Avenue and, specifically, to your casita! I know it's yours, because last night I saw you dance and jump in front of your TV. I also saw your car and thought a bouquet would cheer you up. Actually . . . the flowers are from Susie. She has a crush on you!"

Anton puts the bouquet under his arm, scoops up Susie and gives her a kiss. Susie is beside herself and starts to lick his face. Anton laughs and firmly holds her until she relaxes. Anton invites them inside and continues to hold Susie close to his chest. Vanessa takes the bouquet and sets it on the chair by the mirrors.

"I've never received a bouquet from a dog before."

"I hope you aren't allergic to flowers. Susie picked it out."

"They're beautiful, Susie. Thank you!"

Anton scratches Susie under her chin.

Vanessa is pleased someone likes Susie as much as she does. .

"I guess the feeling for Susie is mutual. You two are quite the pair!"

"She's adorable."

Vanessa holds out her arms to take Susie.

"I didn't mean to interrupt your practice."

"No, no today it's okay. I want to talk to you about something. Now is a good a time."

Anton carries Susie over to the desk, and Vanessa follows.

"Sit down, and let's see if you like my idea."

Anton sits behind his desk with Susie in his lap. Vanessa sits in front of the desk.

"I want to offer you a scholarship. You have a natural talent for dancing. I would like to develop this gift, your talent, with private lessons. Would you be interested?"

"Yes, but I'm stretched as it is. I can barely pay my rent."

Anton laughs.

"That sounds familiar. No, this would be a full scholarship. There would be no cost. We would set a time, and you would come five days a week for forty-five minute lessons. You learn the dance patterns quickly, and we could focus on the details. The art is in the details."

Susie sits up and stares at Vanessa. She jumps down,

trots over, and jumps into Vanessa's lap. Anton and Vanessa laugh.

"I think Susie says 'Yes!' But are you sure you want to do this? I mean with my mental issues, you know, my flashbacks."

"I think we can get through that."

"Really? You think I can get past it?"

"Yes, I think flamenco can chase all the swine over the cliff and send all the demons packing!"

"I hope you're right."

"We can start and see how it goes. It's not like I own you. You're free to stop any time."

"Can I still keep the group class?"

"Yes. I think that's an excellent idea. You could stay after, and help with the children's class too."

"I could be a working student."

"Yes."

"When can I start?"

"Let's start tomorrow at ten. Come early to get dressed. We'll start at ten o'clock sharp."

"I can't believe it. I'm going to be a flamenco dancer."

"You are a flamenco dancer!"

"Thank you, Anton."

"You're welcome."

Susie jumps down as Vanessa rises. Vanessa sees the bouquet on the chair by the mirrors. She laughs.

"And Susie thought she gave you something to cheer you up! Now she gets to see you almost every day. I wonder if she planned this."

Vanessa walks over to the chair by the mirrors, picks up the bouquet and takes it to Anton.

"These need water. You know how to water things."

Anton, smiles. Susie is reluctant to leave. Vanessa picks her up and out they go.

TEN

A sleek-high-shine-sports car pulls into the isolated parking lot on the edge of the expansive wetlands. Margret's car is the only one in the lot. Bundled up in a warm-designer coat with matching tennis shoes, Margret opens the car door, steps into the wind, clamps her hands over her hair and jumps back into the car. She wants to drive away, but Anton's recommendation to go to the beach pushes her to put her hair in a ponytail and face down the wind. Her resolve carries her all the way to the ocean. The waves roll over each other. They flash aqua and light blue as they break, and the wind whips spray over their backs.

A flock of seagulls stands on the sand packed from the earlier high tide. The birds take flight at the sight of Margret. They fan out overhead, and Margret covers her head. She doesn't see the sunlight that shines off their wings and makes them look like glitter bursts against a background of the dark-gray-fog bank on the horizon.

Margret braces herself, walks to a driftwood log and sits

down. The wind annoys Margret, but she is determined to follow Anton's instruction. She watches the ocean churn with rows of waves that roar and slap against each other.

"What can he possibly mean? This is a nightmare! Get me out of here!"

A troop of pelicans fly in formation above the waves. Their prehistoric bodies, designed for power gliding on the wind, speed by without a glance at Margret who sits alone on the smooth-gray log. A congregation of Snowy Plovers race back and forth with the tide. They grab bites of seafood as they race in random directions. A sand dollar lies flat on the packed sand. Rocks, pocked with numerous holes embedded with tiny sea shells, roll around while the tide surges.

"This is crazy! I'm freezing. My tennis shoes are full of sand. I can't hear myself think because the ocean makes so much noise. And Anton tells me to watch the ocean. Maybe I'm at the wrong beach."

Margret pulls her coat up around her neck and walks against the wind back to her car. She empties her tennis shoes while she sits sideways on the driver's seat and unties her hair. She hears a train whistle and gets out of the car to watch the train race across the bridge that spans the wetland. From an open box car, two young vagabonds wave to Margret.

"How'd they do it? How'd they get on that train? They're in big trouble!"

Margret forgets the wind and watches the train disappear beyond the dunes. Margret revisits a childhood memory with her mother.

"Margret what are you doing??? I asked you to get me

coffee and here you are standing between two cars watching the couplings, the tracks and whatever else!! It's dangerous!! And where's my coffee?? You're in trouble, big trouble!!"

Margret hurries back to her car, slides inside, turns on the engine and dials up the heat. The image of the boys on the train remains along with the childhood memory.

"Margret! Remove your face from the window. Go back to your homework. Stop dreaming!! The train stops when we reach the terminal. You have two hours to get your work done!! This isn't a vacation. You're behind in school, and your teacher says you're a dreamer!! Stop it!"

The memory stings, and Margret cries.

"Go to the beach and watch the ocean. He wants me to watch the ocean? I go to the ocean and watch the train! I wish I was one of those kids in the box car! I don't understand how the ocean can teach me anything. I stopped going to the beach the day I got caught in that riptide and was carried out beyond the waves. It was the lifeguard who saw me and brought me in that saved my life. The ocean is a big-powerful-pot-of-danger. And Anton wants me to watch the ocean . . . hell, no! The boys in the box car are what I should watch! Talk about living the life. Can you imagine what I'd be like if I followed my passion? I'd be a gypsy! Ha! So there, Mother! Take your homework drumbeat and dream-killer self to the mall and leave me to my imagination, such as it is. I should have moved out years ago. Dad was smart. He upped and died to get out. Me, I'm stuck in neutral. Why else would anyone own a convertible-sports car? Rebel with the top down and born to be wild. I would kill for a life beyond Mother's undecorated walls!"

Margret is invigorated by her tirade.

"I guess Anton was right! Watching the ocean fired me up, but it wasn't the ocean. It was the boys that sat on the edge of that boxcar coupled onto that fast-moving freight train!"

Margret hurries to her car with her head down to escape the wind. She could care less about the wetland and the bright-white egret that watches her from the rippled marsh, or the ducks that swim in the slough that keep their eye on the only human they see in the parking lot. Margret is too much inside her head to notice much of anything on the wetland that might stir her soul.

All Margret wants is to get inside her car and turn on the heat. She wants to go home, pull the rug off her Masonite practice board and watch the video of Anton demonstrating her part in the new dance. Margret wants to be a gypsy and is determined to show Anton she can dance "soul" flamenco.

Margret returns to her mother's contemporary mansion that stands on the edge of a plateau with a view of the valley. She slips inside through the back door and tiptoes past the glass door of the entertainment room. Her mother lies asleep in a custom-designed-recliner-leather couch fitted with drink holders on both sides of each of the connected three seats. The TV is a monster flat screen equipped with all the bells and whistles while it continuously spouts news of the latest disaster. There's a full bar on one side, and a library of books and videos on the other side.

Margret runs upstairs and closes the door to her bedroom suite behind her. It's a separate apartment outside the elaborate arrangement of seven bedrooms each with its own bathroom. Margret plugs a speaker into her phone, puts on her flamenco dance shoes and methodically imitates Anton's moves. She doesn't notice her mother staring at her through the bedroom glass door. The house is concrete, steel and glass without a stick of wood. Margret looks away from the phone, sees her mother at the door and opens it. Her mother is drunk.

"Margret, turn that music down! Better yet, turn it off! Stop pretending to be a dancer. You have no rhythm. You have no feel for music. Unlike you, your sister could do anything. How a drunk driver crossed the line and took her is beyond me, but he did, she's gone and it breaks my heart. So stop pretending to be what you're not and will never be."

Margret locks the door on her mother and returns to Anton and flamenco dancing. Her mother remains standing at the door with her mouth spewing things no mother with a heart would say, and Margret, fortunately, can't hear.

Margret repeats the routine until every step is memorized. She sees the moves, but doesn't feel the music, so her effort lacks the element that Anton hoped she would discover in the wild.

Bored with berating Margret, her mother returns to the bar and TV in search of alcohol and more sleep-inducing entertainment. It isn't a surprise that Margret is dead inside. The house that shelters her from the weather is a cage that stifles her self-expression. To Margret, Anton and all things flamenco is her path to freedom.

Margret ends her practice session with a soulless flip of her hand above her head. She unfolds the rug again to cover up her dance board and gets ready for bed. Everything has a place including Margret. In the morning nothing is rumpled or thrashed. With one sweep of her hand, Margret makes her bed.

At her next flamenco lesson, Margret can perform her

part of the routine by memory. She finds satisfaction that she can now do complicated footwork without looking down or stopping to review the video. Anton is her lighthouse, and his approval is like blood to a vampire.

Margret stops at Glenn's market on her way to dance. She buys an apple and banana, gets back in her car and eats the banana. She parks her car to face the dance studio, so she can watch Anton practice his choreography. She's an hour early for her lesson but already dressed to dance. Margret sees a small dog prance into the studio accompanied by the now-clean-pretty-homeless woman who was sitting on the bench and made that comment, something about being saved, when Margret stumbled.

"She's going into the dance studio with a dog???"

Margret sees Anton pick up the dog, and the young woman disappear down the hall. She sees Anton dance around the room with the little dog in his arms. She sees the young woman return dressed to dance.

"What???"

Margret watches Anton and Vanessa warm up. She sees Vanessa mimic Anton and flawlessly perform the same routine Margret's been working on for a week.

"This can't be real."

Vanessa sails around the room in perfect sync with Anton and the music. Anton choreographs on the fly, and Vanessa stays in the dance milliseconds behind him. They dance Anton's flamenco with passion and grace while Susie and Margret watch.

"How does this happen? I work for weeks to master a dance, and this stranger comes in and learns the routine on the spot! Is this some kind of bad joke??"

Margret is on the outside looking in, and all she wants is to be in – in with Anton, in with the music, in with everything she thinks has left her out. She feels her frustration and pain converge. Her anger grows into rage. She can't bear the unfairness of it all. She puts her forehead on her leather-wrapped-steering wheel and sobs.

""Margret, you're never going to be a flamenco dancer. Give it up! Whatever made you think you could dance flamenco? Now your sister – that's another story! She could do anything! What makes you think you're in her league? God, I wish it was you in that car that day instead of her!!!"

A passerby knocks on the driver's side window.

"I noticed your engine is still running. Are you okay?"

Margret, her face red and wet with tears, looks up and stares straight ahead. She slowly rolls the window down three inches.

"Yes, I'm fine"

The passerby persists.

"Are you sure you're okay?"

"Do I look like I'm okay?

The passerby hesitates.

"No."

"Then I guess I'm not ok."

Margret rolls the window back up. The passerby waits a moment then turns and walks to her car parked on the other side of Margret. The passerby gets in her car, looks over at Margret, backs out and drives away.

"Okay? Okay?? I'll never be okay!!! As long as my mother is alive, I'll never be okay. As long as I live, I'll never be okay. What's okay anyway???"

Margret finishes her banana.

"Monkeys are okay. I'll eat bananas, and I'll be okay. That's what's they say. Be in the moment and be okay. That's a lot of moments. How does anyone stay in that many moments? Billions, trillions of moments, I'm not sure I'm up to it. Oh yeah, one moment at a time. I get it, but I'm still not sure I'm up to it."

The homeless woman leaves the studio. She skips, and the little dog trots in front of Margret's car. To see them pass in front of her breaks the spell. Margret picks up her bag, pulls out a makeup kit and touches up the paint job on her face. Under the layers of makeup, Margret is a classic beauty.

"'Margret, sweetheart you're beautiful. Never let your mother get to you. It's not her. It's the alcohol. We love you more than you'll ever know.' That's for sure! Not! Daddy left in a box of ashes, and look what the moment leaves me with – Mother! Not sure Mother and I can survive the moment by moment."

Margret enters the dance studio. She hides her inner turmoil under a big smile and calm demeanor.

"Welcome, Margret!"

Anton goes back to the water cooler in the corner behind the desk for a drink and returns refreshed. He's ready for a lesson with Margret.

"I went to the beach as you suggested."

"Excellent! How did it make you feel?"

"I wanted to run back to the car. It was so windy and cold. I hated it."

"Hate? That's a strong word! Did you like anything about it? Did you see the ocean and the birds? Did you see anything to like? Did anything inspire you like the sand on your bare feet, the smell of the salted air or the roar of the waves?"

"I didn't take off my shoes, and I couldn't hear myself think."

"That's the idea, to get you out of your head and into the moment."

Margret laughs.

"I was just thinking about being in the moment while I waited for my lesson."

"Good for you! Did you see anything that inspired you at the beach, anything in nature that spoke to you?"

"No, nothing about the beach or nature, but a freight train crossed the bridge with two young vagabonds, and I was mesmerized."

"Yes! Trains can hypnotize."

"I wanted to be on that train! I wanted to jump on that train like a vagabond!"

Margret is animated and tells her experience with her hands and body. It's the first time Anton has seen a spark of spontaneity in Margret. He listens while she tells how she felt when she saw the train with the young adventure seekers on board. And how they would be in big trouble down the line!

"Big trouble? Maybe not, maybe they get away with it and live to tell their grandchildren. Good for them!"

"I didn't see it that way. I like that! They didn't get in trouble!"

Anton laughs.

"At least you found something that inspired you! Let's dance!"

Anton clicks the remote and the music plays. Anton snaps his fingers and walks to the music like a cat stalks a bird. Margret stands to the side and watches, clapping her hands in a spontaneous rhythm that catches Anton's attention. He continues his walkabout then ushers Margret to the center of the room, and they begin to dance the steps Margret has rehearsed all week.

Margret hears a train whistle. She forgets where she is and jumps the train. She's in Spain in a cantina and dances on a table top. People in the bar clap and shout "Bravo!" A Spaniard jumps onto the table and parades around her while he claps his hands and stamps his feet. Margret adds her skirt to the routine and waves it like a flag around her feet. Her steps are accurate and inspired. Now her feet are on the track as she runs away. The music carries her faster and faster down the track. She watches another train and jumps aboard. She rides away, waves to Anton and disappears. The dance ends, and Margret is exhausted. Anton is astounded.

"I had no idea how much the ocean suggestion would transform you! You are a flamenco dancer!"

"I did it, didn't I? And I didn't get in trouble!"

"No. You're not in trouble! You must go to the ocean often. Get the train schedule and ride that train every day!"

They both laugh again.

"Thank you, Anton! Thank you a thousand-million times! I love the train! You sent me to the ocean, and I fell in love with the train!"

"I think that's enough for today. You mastered the steps, and, most important, you mastered the art! We will go to another level next week! Remember Margret, there are wild places that can speak to you. Take yourself to the wetlands or the mountains this week and experience the wild places."

"Oh, Anton, I will. I will. You have no idea what you have done for me."

"Not me, Margret – flamenco!"

Anton bows and walks Margret to the door. Margret is euphoric. Like a person falsely accused and in prison for years – she is now free, and it's out-of-this-world fantastic!

"Hasta la vista, Anton, I will take all the steps I've ever learned, carry them to the wild and dance. Flamenco has set me free! See you next week!"

Anton watches Margret get into her car and drive away. He turns around and goes to his desk to do some paper work before the next lesson. He sits still a moment to think about what just happened. Margret became a dancer today. She became a dancer, because he suggested that she go to the ocean to watch the waves! Maybe the studio should take a field trip to the ocean. It's not every day you get to witness a student's transformation. He remembers his own transformation when he put down his classical guitar and started to dance flamenco.

He was invited to join a prestigious camp in Cuba. He showed promise as a classical guitar artist, and it was quite an honor to be asked to attend the camp. It was a performing arts camp and included flamenco dancing. When Anton watched the dancers he knew this was what he wanted to do. His father had recently died, and Anton felt a constant sadness inside. When he watched the dancers, he felt the pain recede. When he watched the flamenco dancers, he felt reborn. He put away his guitar and started to study flamenco. He never looked back.

ELEVEN

While he sits under his Sunset road sign, drinks a soda and eats potato chips, Anton is amazed at today's events. Vanessa is the most gifted dancer he's ever seen (he's seen a lot) and Margret is transformed. She's a dancer after all. Perhaps, just maybe, his dream of a small Central Coast dance company isn't a pipedream. A knock on his window breaks his musing. Anton rolls down the window and looks up to see a head covered in a helmet and eyes shaded with mirror sunglasses.

"Driver's license?"

Anton starts to reach for the glove compartment, and the officer tells him to get out of the car. Anton is confused but complies. He gets out of the car and stands in the street.

"My license is in the glove compartment."

The officer doesn't answer and walks behind and around to the other side of the car, reaches in and takes the folder from the glove compartment that holds the registration and Anton's driver's license – which he left inside the glove compartment when the truck smashed his car.

Another policeman arrives in a patrol car and parks behind the police motorcycle parked behind Anton's crushed trunk. The officers start rifling through Anton's car looking for drugs. Anton continues to wait for orders. He grew up in a police state and knows how to handle the stress.

The helmet-and-shades officer comes back around and hands Anton back his license.

"Get your car fixed Cuba-linga."

Anton waits until the officers are out of sight, before he gets into his car. He finishes his soda and chips while he reflects on the unpleasant encounter.

"This is America, but today it feels like Cuba, except I didn't have to bribe the officer to get my license back. Tomorrow I go to the body shop!"

Anton shakes his head and starts his car. He shakes his head again and puts his car in gear. He shakes his head once more and drives home to his casita and Luisa.

"Hello, little Luisa, you better stay in your own yard. You could end up in jail!"

Luisa isn't concerned. Her focus is dinner.

Anton is still disturbed by the police calling him "Cuba-linga" and tries to distract himself from the racial slur. He remembers there's a baseball game on tonight and opens his laptop to read the Havana News while he reheats last night's Picadillo. His friend Alvaro is pictured in the Entertainment section again. Anton watches the video of Alvaro and Company at the *Gran Teatro de La Habana*. The choreography is visceral. At the end of the program the audience is on their feet to stamp and clap. Anton isn't jealous. He's happy for his friend. Anton just wants to share the spotlight. He closes his laptop and thinks about his family in Cuba, his mama, hermanos y hermana, and Havana Port.

"Tomorrow, I will get up and go to the ocean!"

Anton goes to the living room and turns on the TV. His team just hit another homerun and is ahead in the second inning.

"At least some Cubans are winning."

Anton continues to sit on the couch, and Luisa seizes the opportunity to crawl onto Anton's lap. He strokes Luisa while he watches baseball and drinks his one *Bucanero*. He's relieved to watch his team stay in the lead to the end, but cheerless as he watches the team and fans leave the stadium. He picks up Luisa and goes to his bedroom. He puts on his pajamas and crawls under the covers. He remembers his Rosary and brings it close to his heart. He whispers prayers for the police, for his family, especially his mama, Margret, Vanessa, and Luisa and Susie. He closes his eyes and visualizes the *Gran Teatro de La Habana*. He watches himself perform choreography as he blasts the floor with a rain of a thousand-rapid-hammer strikes of heels to an even beat of finger snaps. The spotlight fades and Anton falls asleep.

It's sunrise. Anton jumps out of bed and dresses for a visit to the ocean. He wears his usual dance clothes, but covers up in sweat pants and a hoodie to stay warm. He wears his street shoes and puts a knit cap on his head for extra warmth. He flashes on yesterday's police encounter but refuses to hold resentment. He carries Luisa to the pantry, fills her dish with kibble and layers the usual canned salmon on top.

The fifteen minute drive to the beach is filled with flamenco guitar music, and Anton's loud singing. He takes breaks for sips of black coffee and bites of Campechana with apple filling. He pulls into the parking lot and finishes his coffee and pastry while he watches the birds swim in the mist. The rose light of morning is backlit with the dark marine layer, and the wetland is alive with glossy-metallic-ripples of color. Anton zips up his hoodie, and adds the jacket he carries in his car for an extra layer against the cold. He is pleased there's no wind today and dances his way to the ocean beyond the bridge.

The entire wetland has changed its shape after the last rain. The river that flows into the wetland has pushed through to the ocean, and he cannot cross the channel carved by the river. The ocean roars with lines of waves rolling in and burying each other. The low tide leaves a vast dance floor for Anton to practice spontaneous choreography. He races along the packed sand, leaps with both legs together and bent at the knees. He lands and smacks the sand with his hands. The sand, though packed, is too soft for heels. Anton has trained in ballet to enhance his flamenco choreography, and it resurfaces as he joins the birds with cabrioles, tour jetes, grand jetes, pas de chats, ballons, and assembles. The tide swirls in and out while Anton dances in a trance. The salt taste, the smell, the damp, the cold, the roar of the waves, the mist and the rocks that he dances around, lift Anton into another realm – he transcends earth.

Back at the studio, after a morning of exquisite freedom, Anton preps for his dance studio enthusiasts. His students are the beneficiaries of years of dedication to his art. Each one derives a measure of freedom of movement, because Anton is able to translate his mastery of flamenco into his teaching. Anton is one of those rare individuals who share their skills with evangelical zeal, infect their students with enthusiasm and yield an adoring tribe.

The pile of bills on Anton's desk rob him of his peace of mind. He looks up and sees Vanessa approach the studio door. She cups the sides of her eyes and presses her face to the glass to see if Anton is in the studio. Susie bounces up and down sensing that Anton is there. Anton shoves the bills to the side and hurries to open the door.

"Good morning! Come in. Come in!"

"I wasn't sure you were here. I didn't see you doing your usual morning practice."

"I chose to go to the ocean and use nature's dance floor. The low tide is perfect for spontaneous choreography."

"You went to the beach to dance?"

Susie scrambles her front paws on Anton's leg to get attention. Anton picks her up and hugs her.

"Yes! I often go to the ocean for inspiration."

"That sounds fantastic!"

"It is! We'll have to schedule a lesson on the sand one morning. The ocean is the best teacher and packed sand is the best dance floor! And Lupe's bakery makes the best coffee and Campechanas for breakfast."

Susie is bored and struggles to get down. Once on the floor, she trots to the couch, jumps up and settles on the throw bunched up in the corner between the arm and the seat of the siesta couch.

"Oh yes! Please! I would love to dance on the sand!

Anton is thrilled to have a student that understands the essence of dance, let alone have the extraordinary ability to express it. He forgets his impending financial disaster and celebrates his good fortune. Vanessa goes to the back to change while Anton searches for the exact music he has in mind for Vanessa's lesson.

"The steps must be accurate, so I will show you the patterns. Then we will add the music."

Vanessa locks in and memorizes the complex footwork. Anton, uninhibited by the need to teach methodically, presents the whole dance in one continuous flow. Vanessa mirrors the sequence and is ready to add the music.

"Vanessa, you capture the whole dance like someone who plays piano by ear. Now I demand more. The details of how you move, and the butterfly hands that speak another language are as important as the accuracy of your footwork."

Vanessa watches Anton curl and uncurl his fingers. His arms sweep up from his sides, and his graceful hands flutter over his head.

"Think of your hands as butterflies that blink their wings in rapid succession and give the impression that they float rather than fly. Here, let me show you on my phone."

Anton goes to his desk, picks up his phone and pulls up a YouTube video of butterflies in a field of wildflowers. The camera zooms in, displays a slow-motion close-up of wings that wave and suspend the butterfly in the air. Anton freezes the frame. Susie wants to get down, but Anton encourages her to stay on the couch.

"Here's what I mean."

Vanessa watches. Her fingers curl and uncurl as she raises

her hands above her head, spins them around overhead and back down to her side.

"That's it, but your hands must float like butterfly wings. The hands in flamenco have to sing like the guitar player's fingers. The art is in the details, and the hands must dance like the feet."

Anton pockets his phone and shows Vanessa the effortless flow of butterfly wings on the tips of his arms that float up, around, and down as he turns in circles and walks like a proud peacock to address the imaginary audience.

Vanessa repeats his routine and struggles to achieve the butterfly effect. She discovers there's more to dancing flamenco than meets the eye.

"The patterns are easy for me. This is a new level that is much more difficult. I'll have to practice this!"

"Yes! Practice this until it is second nature. Without expressive hands that float, the dance is not flamenco."

Anton drills Vanessa in this singular movement, and Vanessa becomes discouraged. The movement is as impossible to her as a human floating over a landscape. Anton recognizes her discouragement and stops Vanessa before she gives up.

"The details are a challenge, and it demands dedicated practice to master them. You have extraordinary dance instincts. We'll build on your natural gifts."

Vanessa continues to curl and uncurl her fingers.

"Do you think I'll be able to get this? I wish I started flamenco when I was five like some of the kids in the children's class!!! This is not easy!"

"No. But if you practice, you will master it. You'll become the butterfly! This is enough for today."

Vanessa goes to the couch to pick up her dog. Susie jumps down and runs to Anton. Vanessa laughs and Anton picks Susie up and gives her a hug. Susie curls a front leg around Anton's arm and doesn't want to let go. Anton releases his arm and hands Susie to Vanessa. Susie lives with Vanessa, but Anton is her soul mate.

"Okay Duchess, you need to be subtle. You must kiss the hand that feeds you!"

"Practice your butterflies. I'll see you same time tomorrow. Susie, you make sure she practices!"

Vanessa remembers she's still dressed in her dance clothes and goes to change with Susie in tow. Anton returns to his desk. Vanessa changes, waves a classic flamenco goodbye, and she and Susie head home. They pass the liquor store, and Vanessa imagines she wins the lottery. She spends the mega millions on an estate in Spain.

At home, Vanessa fixes lunch and settles down for a game of solitary chess. It's difficult to lose when you play against yourself, and no one watches you. The book *Teach Yourself Chess* is full of strategies, and Vanessa is victorious. She sees her phone on the table and opens the link Anton sent to practice the butterfly hands. She sits in the chair, raises her hands above her head and lowers them back to her sides. The whole time she struggles to make butterflies out of clay. She holds her hands overhead while she turns and then folds her hands under and over each other with fingers that curl and uncurl at the same time. She stops and looks at her hands. Her nails are chewed short and her fingers are stiff.

"Susie! What do you say we go to the salon and get our

nails done?"

Susie, always up for adventure, jumps up from her nap under Vanessa's chair and runs to the door. Vanessa picks up the leash, hooks Susie in, and off they go to glamorize. Vanessa does the math in her head.

"Free private-dance lessons five days a week more than pays for a once-a-month manicure, right Susie?"

Susie trots with her head high, and her mouth smiling. She is out ahead and leads the way to the salon. Vanessa knows it's the prospect of a visit to Anton's studio that animates Susie.

"We aren't going there, Girlfriend. We're going to the salon next door. Your painted nails will have to be enough! This is business Susie. You didn't answer me about the budget!"

Susie doesn't look up or slow down. She continues to trot while she looks straight ahead.

"I take that as a 'yes' the math is good, and the budget fine."

They round the corner, pass by the liquor store, and Susie makes a beeline to the dance studio. Vanessa pulls on the leash and a tug of war ensues. Susie is a tough competitor, and Vanessa finally picks her up and forges ahead. Anton is asleep on the siesta couch. He doesn't see the Duchess try to tell Vanessa that Anton is why she agreed to come along.

"Susie, this has got to stop. When I say salon, I mean salon!"

Susie licks her face and settles into being carried into the salon.

The salon owner, who frequently asks Anton to turn down the music, welcomes Vanessa and Susie,

"Hello, what can I do for you?"

"Do you take walk-ins for nails?"

"Yes."

He nods several times, points to the tables and chairs set up for nails and disappears through a curtain on the back wall. A young woman emerges through the curtain and sits down in front of Vanessa ready to work.

"I'm Vanessa. What's your name?"

"Chi."

Chi points to the dog.

"This is Susie. She wants bright-red-nail polish, please. And I would like acrylic nails with the same bright-red polish."

Chi looks at the owner now at the front desk. The owner nods 'Yes.' Chi and the owner have a short conversation in a foreign language, and Chi paints Susie's nails bright red. She dries each nail with a hair dryer, so Susie can't mess things up. Vanessa puts Susie down while still on the leash. Susie quietly lies at Vanessa's feet with her nose inches from her bright red toenails.

Vanessa watches while Chi creates long-semi-pointed acrylics on top of her short-ragged nails and paints them with the same bright-red-nail polish she used on Susie. Vanessa, amazed at the change, stretches out her fingers.

"Can you paint a little butterfly on the first nail on each hand?"

Chi and the owner have another brief conversation before Chi responds,

"Yes."

The young girl paints a tiny-colorful butterfly on each first nail of each hand. Vanessa is mesmerized by the transformation. High school was the last manicure she had, and this is a first time for acrylics. Vanessa is fascinated with the process and admires the beautiful smooth hands of the artist in front of her.

"Your hands are beautiful."

Chi nods.

"How do they stay so soft and smooth?"

Chi smiles, but doesn't understand. Vanessa points to her hands and tries to tell her again how beautiful her hands are. The young girl finally understands and points to a plastic bottle with lotion. Vanessa is determined to transform her hands into butterflies.

"Can I buy a bottle of that lotion?"

Chi looks to the man who owns the salon. He nods "Yes," and Chi goes behind the curtain while Vanessa's nail polish continues to dry. She returns with a bottle of lotion for Vanessa.

"Oh thank you! Now I can have beautiful hands like yours!"

Vanessa pays for the acrylic nails, lotion and Susie's polished nails. She includes a generous tip. They leave and walk past the liquor store. Vanessa has second thoughts and goes in to buy the lottery ticket on the chance she can buy an estate in Spain.

"Oh, come on Susie. It's only five dollars and it could be the big winner!"

Susie sits at Vanessa's feet, looks up and cocks her head.

"I suppose I just want to show off my new nails! Oh well, no harm done with one beer to celebrate our future!"

TWELVE

It is early morning. The sunlight on the oak forest, inside the park, filters onto the ground and dapples the path. Margret marches under the canopy without a glance at the beauty under her feet. She's preoccupied with her last dance lesson. She knows she went to a new level because of the train, but she still wants to give nature another chance. Anton suggested the forest, so here she is for a walk in the park. A mountain bike whizzes by, and Margret watches the rider lean into the wind as the bike picks up speed. The rider furiously rides his bike. His legs pedal the way a flamenco dancer's legs jackhammer the floor. Margret is hypnotized by the bike and rider like a herd dog latches onto movement. She stumbles and lands spread eagle on the ground. She lies on the path and spits out the dirt she swallowed on landing. Her workout clothes are covered in dust, her squeaky-clean-white-tennis shoes are smeared with soil and her chin bleeds.

"Great! Just great!!"

Margret sits up, takes off her sweatshirt and holds it

against her chin. The blood begins to seep through the sweatshirt, and Margret decides she should go to the local ER.

"You idiot, get up!"

Margret stands up and hurries to her car with her hand cupped around the sweatshirt. Blood seeps through her fingers and drips onto her shoes. She opens the trunk of her car and grabs the towel she uses to wipe off her shoes. She forgets the dirt from her shoes is on the towel and pushes it against her chin. She throws the blood-soaked sweatshirt into the trunk, picks up her purse that has been locked in her trunk, finds her keys and manages to get the car started while she holds the towel in place. With one hand Margret Googles "closest ER" on her phone and gets navigation directions. Because blood has soaked through the towel, she gets immediate attention when she arrives.

Two hours later Margret leaves the ER with fourteen stitches on the bottom of her chin and a prescription for pain pills.

"Never nature, Anton, but that mountain bike hypnotized me!"

Margret arrives home and sneaks in through the back door. It's still early, and Mother is asleep in the master bedroom. Margret goes to her bedroom, undresses, puts on a silk nightgown and crawls into bed,

"This nature thing isn't for me, but if I hadn't gone to the park, I never would have seen that mountain bike! Wow! Anton is right. I'm waking up to me. The train and mountain bike aren't natural, but I discovered them in nature, and they stir my soul. I didn't even know I had a soul!"

Margret laughs in spite of her sore chin.

"What am I doing in bed? This is ridiculous."

Margret gets out bed, gets dressed in a designer sports ensemble and sneaks out the she way came in. Her car shines in the sunlight, and Margret feels a tinge of excitement when she asks her phone for "best bicycle shop." The answer is quick and gives a Top Ten list to choose from.

"These mighty-bite little computers really have everything on us! I don't even have to say where I am. It already knows where! I bet it knows more about me than I do."

Margret chuckles and asks Google "Where can I find my best soul self." The phone displays "Essential Tips to Discover Your Inner Soul and Live Better!"

"According to google, I'm having an "awareness crisis!" This list sounds like a prescription for what Anton is trying get me to understand!"

Margret scrolls through a vast array of answers for curing lost soul syndrome. She has completely forgotten her chin. One suggestion resonates, "Cultivate a passion."

"Okay! Flamenco, trains and mountain bikes! I can take the train up the coast to go mountain biking! Done!"

Margret puts the phone down on the passenger seat, starts her car and drives to the number one bike shop.

"Welcome. My name's Bob. Can I help you?"

"You sure can! I'm looking to find my way out of "Lost Soul Syndrome."

The young-sporty Bob laughs.

"You're in the right place. We specialize in helping people find their lost soul. Looks like you had a rough landing on your search for your lost soul."

"It isn't really funny."

Bob catches himself,

"No, of course not, what are you looking for?"

"I want a bike I can take on the train and travel up the coast to go mountain biking."

"Sure. I can get you started with a beginner bike and recommend some easy trails in a park on the Central Coast. You get a perfect mix of easy climb in nature and a safe descent on your way back to the parking lot. The train station is near the trail head. The scenery will blow you away."

"I don't care much about the nature and scenery part. I just want to ride one of these amazing bikes."

"Okay. No nature, no scenery, just mechanical magic for you. Lost soul for sure, I have just the bike for you!"

"What did you say?"

"I said, 'I have just the right bike for you!' "

Margret leaves the shop with a new mountain bike, helmet, backpack, rack to attach to her car to ferry the bike and an outfit that gives the impression she rides for sponsors. Margret shells out a small fortune for a bike ride. She sees that her car can't accommodate the bike and returns to the bike shop. Because she's beautiful in an icy way a few heads turn. Bob looks up and sees the lost soul heading in his direction. He finishes with his current customer and turns to help Margret.

"What's up?"

"The bike won't fit in my car. I need someone to attach the rack."

"No problem. I'll find someone in back that can help you. Where are you parked?"

"Right in front, it's a sport car."

"Yes, that would be a challenge to stuff a bike in a sports car. We can put the rack over the trunk and show you how to take the front wheel on and off. You know, if you fall in love with mountain biking, your found soul might tell you to buy a four wheel drive vehicle.

Bob smiles. And Margret actually laughs.

"You're right! I'll be back in a couple hours. Can I leave the bike until I get back, maybe, three or four hours?"

"Sure. We're open 'til eight. I'll help you bring the bike in."

Bob sees the polished sports car.

"Whoa! You could buy two four wheel drive vehicles for the price of this beauty!!"

"Yes, the lost soul needed a shiny exterior. The found soul needs a dirt master. I have no idea what I'm getting into, but I know I'm going in full throttle!"

"Good on you!"

Margret zips out of the parking lot and heads south to *King of the Rough and Rugged Sport Vehicles*. She walks in, points to the show room supreme-four-wheel-drive-dirt master and negotiates a cash purchase. They offer to drive her sports car home. They install the bike rack on the back of her luxury-four-wheel-drive Gorilla, and Margret is ready for any terrain. They drive the showroom model out to the front of the dealership and usher Margret to the driver's side.

"Thank you!"

A beaming salesman gives Margret double thumbs up!

"Enjoy your off road adventures!"

Margret waves off with a flamenco turn of her hand. She isn't fully aware that she has turned a corner and can't go back, but she loves the feel of it all. She arrives at the bike shop. Bob sees her pull up in an all-terrain vehicle that is the envy of every employee at the shop. He greets her at the door with her new bike. He helps her mount the bike on the rack and congratulates her on her new partner for off road adventures.

"You didn't hold back. I'd say your soul has a voracious appetite. Now, that it's out of prison!"

Margret laughs.

"Thanks Bob. You helped me get there!"

"Can I give you a hug? It's not every day I watch a metamorphosis. I have to say I'm impressed!"

"You certainly can give me a hug! I celebrate everything. It's a fiesta every day!"

Bob gives Margret a sweet hug, and they high five each other.

"Let me know how the maiden voyage goes. If you ever want company in the wild, give me a call at the shop"

"Thanks! I'll keep it in mind."

Margret is in shock. She drives her new Gorilla, with her mountain bike secured on the backend, home to her ice castle on the plateau that overlooks the valley well known for Pinot Noir. She parks outside the garage and enters by the back entrance near the pool. Her mother drinks a Manhattan while she trims the roses. She wears a straw hat and sunglasses.

"Where have you been Margret? I've been looking all over for you! And what in God's name are you wearing?"

"Hello Mother. I'm just home for a minute. I have an appointment with a mountain bike and a park. My sports car will be delivered late afternoon, so don't be surprised. I bought an off road sports vehicle, and I'm off to explore some new trails."

"What?"

"New trails, Mother, new trails!"

"You bought an off road vehicle? How?"

"Same way anyone else does. I paid for it, and drove it home. I'm discovering another side. You might try it. Feels amazing!"

"How did you pay for it? Who gave you permission?"

"Mother, I'm well beyond permission, and you know I have my own trust, which is none of your business. Now, I'm off to explore. You can stay here and cherish your favorite-dead daughter while I choose to live and cherish me."

"What are you saying? You're crazy!"

"Am I? If saying "no" to more nights watching you fall

into a drunken stupor, only to awake and berate me for being alive is crazy then I guess I am."

"What happened to your chin?"

"I'm surprised you noticed. Nothing, I like wearing bandages. I have to go."

Margret runs upstairs, grabs a jacket and stuffs an oversize designer purse with pajamas, toothbrush and toothpaste and races out the front door. The sports car delivery is timely. Margret clicks the remote, now clipped to the Gorilla visor, and opens the gate. The driver pulls in, followed by another vehicle. He hands Margret the keys to her sports car, congratulates her, comments on the spectacular view and departs with the second driver in the car lot's curtesy car. Margret steps up into her Gorilla and heads north for her first mountain bike adventure.

"I might be crazy but thank you God!"

The park is still open, and the late-afternoon-mountain-bike stragglers pack up. Margret guesses most mountain bike enthusiasts are morning people. She steps down from the Gorilla and stares at her bike on the rack. One straggler notices her confusion and offers to help. Margret is grateful. The straggler recognizes Margret is a newbie and points out an easy trail.

"Don't stay too long. You're alone and mountain lions like dusk and solo travelers."

Margret is undeterred.

"Thanks for the warning. I'm brand new to this."

"Take it easy and time yourself, maybe fifteen minutes in and fifteen minutes out."

"Good plan!"

"Have a great ride."

"Thanks, again!"

Margret hasn't ridden a bike since she was a kid. She and her dad would ride together often while her mother and sister played tennis at the club. She puts her phone in the pocket on her thigh and practices circles in the parking lot. Her cycling prowess comes back. Her confidence established, she rides to the trailhead, checks the time and starts the gentle climb up the hill. She thought fifteen minutes was nothing, but as she stands on her pedals to gain more leverage, she understands why the biker said, "Maybe fifteen minutes." The incline pushes her limits, and, when she gets to the top of the hill, she feels the burn.

"This sport is not for the limp-wristed!"

Margret checks her phone.

"How did that straggler know? Fifteen minutes is a perfect estimate!"

Margret needs some time to regroup and straddles her bike. She looks out over the landscape and sees the sun turning the hills pink.

"I can't believe I'm here in nature no less. Who knew?"

Margret sighs as the sun disappears into the ocean. She tests her brakes. She sits back on the seat, puts one foot on the pedal and walks the bike down the incline. After a few steps, she puts the other foot on the pedal and the bike starts rolling down the hill. Margret panics, squeezes the brakes and puts both feet down on the packed-firebreak trail.

"I'm not ready for this."

Margret walks the bike down to the bottom of the hill. She turns around and walks the bike back up about twenty feet. She gets on and allows the bike to pick up speed, before she stops at the bottom. She's ecstatic.

"I might become an extreme sports addict. What a rush."

Margret sees it's later than she thought and foregoes another downhill test. She rides her bike to the Gorilla, attaches the bike to the rack like a pro and heads home with purpose. She arrives at the gates and stops. She stares at the massive house and shakes her head.

"This is ridiculous. Two people living in this place who despise each other, and one who rarely leaves the entertainment room except to prune her roses!"

Margret clicks her remote, and the gates open. She parks in front of the house, gets out and drives her sports car into the four car garage. She comes back to the Gorilla, picks up her bag and backpack, climbs the three expansive front steps and rings the bell to the front door.

Mother is soused. She hears the chimes but can't imagine who could be at the front door with the gates closed at dark.

"Maybe it's Margret. I bet she lost her key!"

Mother gets up from the entertainment-room couch, shuffles down the hall and opens the door.

"What's going on? Why didn't you come in the back way?"

"Because, Mother, I came in the front."

Margret hurries past her mother and heads to her room.

On the way, she gets a large suitcase from the hall closet and pulls it upstairs. She takes clothes from her walk-in closet and starts to pack. She gathers skin care lotions, shampoo and conditioner and packs them. She scans the room, sees the framed photo of her dad fly fishing and places it under a layer of clothes inside the suitcase. She closes the suitcase, pulls out the handle and rolls the suitcase down the stairs and out the front door. She guides her suitcase to the Gorilla and lifts it onto the back-bench seat. Mother reappears at the front door, looks confused and calls out,

"Margret, what are you doing? It's nine o'clock at night! What's gotten into you?"

"I'm moving. I'll let you know my new address. Maybe you want to think about a senior residence with other people and activities. I'm done."

Margret climbs into the Gorilla and drives away. She remembers an exclusive hotel off Highway 101. She leaves the Gorilla with the valet and rolls her suitcase to the reception desk.

"I want a room with a view and a king-size bed.

"Certainly, let's see what we have."

"Also, can I get anything to eat?"

"I'll check with the kitchen. We stopped serving dinner at nine, but we may be able to give you dessert."

"Dessert is perfect. Any kind of warm pie or cake with vanilla ice cream! I'm celebrating!"

"We have a beautiful room on the second floor with a view of our garden and the park across the street. The staff can take your suitcase to your room, and you are welcome to have dessert in the dining room."

Margret registers for the room and goes to the dining room for peach pie a la mode. She watches the fire dance in the stone fireplace and thinks about the homeless woman who said "flamenco saved you, right?"

"How could she know? I didn't even know. Who knew? Anton won't believe it when I tell him I went mountain biking!"

Margret finishes her dessert, drinks her water, signs the bill, leaves a generous tip and goes upstairs to her room. Inside the room, she sits on the bed. She feels the bandage on her chin.

"Why bother?"

THIRTEEN

Cuba-linga gets under Anton's skin every time he thinks about the police, and how it is okay for them to make ugly remarks. The insult makes him address the unpleasant task of contacting his insurance company and repairing his car. He calls to set up an appointment for an estimate. He dreads the possibility it's totaled. The appraiser evaluates the damage, and Anton is out a car. The other driver's insurance company will issue a check.

"I can't drive a check."

"Do you need a ride?"

"Yes."

Anton gathers his few items from the wrecked vehicle and puts his Rosary in his pocket. He arrives at the studio in time for Vanessa's lesson. Anton lays his head on the desk. Susie pops onto his lap and wiggles to get Anton's attention.

"Ah, my angel, Susie, let me bury my face in your fur

and forget I left Cuba for this dream that is a nightmare!"

Vanessa is disheveled and stinks of alcohol. She puts a hand on Anton's shoulder.

"Welcome to my world."

Anton sees the day just got worse and escorts Vanessa to the door.

"I warned you. You're drunk. Get out."

Anton picks up Susie and pushes her into Vanessa.

"Go."

Vanessa holds Susie with one arm and flashes a perfect-floating-butterfly hand while she turns and walks away. True to his word Anton locks the door. Vanessa walks to the liquor store with Susie tucked under her arm.

"Screw it. Susie, he isn't what you think. Who needs him? Who needs flamenco? Let's party! Viva la vida!"

Inside the liquor store, Vanessa puts Susie on the floor and leans on the counter arrayed with lottery tickets. The cashier recoils in disgust. Vanessa points to the tequila.

"I'll have one bottle of that and one five dollar lottery ticket! Viva la fiesta! And what's a party without chips?"

The cashier obeys Vanessa's order and fills a bag with tequila, a lottery ticket and a bag of kettle-cooked-potato chips. On her way out, Vanessa stumbles against a wine display, and bottles crash and roll onto the floor. The noise triggers a panic.

"Go!"

Vanessa runs outside, crouches and runs for cover behind a truck. Looking both directions, she runs to the Humvee that is driving through ground fire and jumps in. One soldier is wounded and the driver is blindly racing through the square. He rolls over a child holding a doll. The smoke is thick and screaming people are running in all directions. Vanessa jumps out of the Humvee and rolls under a fruit stand. She clutches her bag of tequila, chips and lottery ticket and hurries to her apartment. She digs in her purse for her key and opens the door. She races around the room. She closes curtains, runs into her closet and shuts the door.

"Susie!!"

Vanessa is horrified. Suddenly grounded, she hurries back to the liquor store desperate to find Susie. The cashier puts the last few bottles back on the shelf. He sees Vanessa and shouts,

"Get out!"

"Have you seen my dog???"

"Get out of here!!"

Vanessa runs to the studio and looks through the window. She sees Susie lying on the couch, while Anton dances with the woman in the black Anton Dance Studio tank top and black skirt. She pounds on the window, but Anton ignores her, and Margret, consumed with dance steps, doesn't hear her. Susie stays on the couch.

Vanessa is defeated. She turns away and walks to her apartment. Her whole world has collapsed. She is too numb to cry. She takes the tequila out of the bag and sets it on the counter with the chips and lottery ticket. She pulls out her bed from the couch, gets blankets from the closet and covers herself from head to toe in swaddling clothes. The tequila stands unopened on the counter beside the lottery ticket and the sealed kettle chips. The party is over.

***

Anton congratulates Margret on her extraordinary progress.

"You have awakened your soul. You have found your muse."

"Who knew trains and bikes would resurrect a dead person into a living soul? Throw in flamenco, and I'm fully alive. Viva la vida!"

"It's time we perform for the public. I will set a date, and we will invite the community to a flamenco show. We have three solid dances that we can perform, and the children can share one of their routines."

"I can help. I'm good at organizing parties. When my father was alive, I was always busy helping at corporate events all over the country, even abroad."

"This is excellent. You can be in charge of promotion and ticket sales."

"What about the homeless woman that takes lessons. She's incredible. Could she perform too? Isn't that her little dog?"

"No. She doesn't dance here anymore. I adopted Susie."

Susie hears her name and runs to Anton. He scoops her up and squeezes her. Susie wiggles and snuggles under Anton's chin.

"Oh. That's too bad. She's an amazing dancer."

"Yes, she is."

***

Vanessa untangles herself from the blankets and takes a shower. She puts on clean jeans and a white-long-tail shirt. She decides on flats and bracelets on both arms. She curls and uncurls her fingers and floats her hands above her head while she twirls and taps her feet. She folds the blankets and returns the bed to the hungry couch. She thinks of Susie and how afraid she is of the couch.

"It's better this way. She and Anton are soulmates. She's safe with him."

Vanessa sits on the couch and tries to meditate. She learned a meditation practice in a mindfulness class recommended by her case worker at the VA. The separation from Susie is too traumatic to concentrate. Vanessa decides to give AA another try. She unplugs her phone on the table with the chess set and googles nearest Episcopal Church and a local AA meeting.

Vanessa tosses the bottle of tequila in the trash, puts the lottery ticket in her purse along with the other ticket she bought earlier and the bag of chips in the cupboard above the kitchen counter. She walks to the Episcopal Church on the other side of the Old Town neighborhood. She enters the office and asks if the sanctuary is open to the public.

"Yes, the sanctuary is open. The organist is practicing, but you are welcome to sit and listen."

"Thank you."

Vanessa sits in the front pew and listens to the organist practice Widor's *Tocatta in F*. He follows with Gigout's *Grand Choer Dialogue* and Handel's *Messiah*. She feels the hole left by Susie's absence fill in with the sound of music that echoes throughout the sanctuary. She remembers the joy of Easter Sunday when she would dress up, sit between her mom and dad and listen to the organ prelude music and the hymns. The organ pipes would breathe life into the church. The lighted candles on the altar would flicker from the draft created by the open doors and light would stream through the stained glass windows and create a kaleidoscope of color on the strip of carpet down the aisle.

***

Margret gasps for air. The practice of three consecutive routines demands more than Margret can physically deliver. Anton, on the other hand, is energized by the challenge and doesn't slow down. He internalizes years of frustration and disappointment, and breaks the bonds of limitation in every move. Margret stops the dance, sits in a chair by the wall of mirrors and puts her head between her knees. She sweats profusely, heaves, shakes and struggles to stay conscious. Anton stops the music and runs to get a cold-wet towel to put on Margret's neck.

"Forgive me Margret! I completely lost myself in the dance. I didn't think about how new this is for you."

Margret isn't able to talk. She forces herself to breathe deeply. The cold towel helps cool her pounding head, and the dizziness recedes.

"You remembered all the steps and exposed your soul, but you haven't ever been asked to give so much extreme physical exertion demanded by the choreography of these routines! It's like asking a casual hiker to climb Mount Everest!"

Tears drop to the floor, as Margret remembers her little

sister Annie, curly-blond-blue-eyed Annie, who followed her everywhere. She remembers the first feelings of jealousy when Annie would do everything she did only better. She remembers her mother scold her, because she left Annie to fend for herself when the neighborhood kids came over to play. She remembers the first time her mother told her, "I wish it had been you who died instead of Anne."

Margret's despair is no longer veiled under a cold exterior. She breaks open and sobs, because she misses Annie, her father and the mother she knew, before her mother turned to Manhattans when a drunk driver killed Annie.

Anton stands beside Margret and rests his hand on her shoulder. Susie tiptoes over, sits by Anton's feet then lays down with her head on her crossed paws to face Margret. The dance studio is quiet. Margret slowly regains her composure, but she will never be the same. Like the train and the mountain bike, flamenco has cracked the wall and pushed it until it tumbled down and crushed every hard place in her broken heart. Margret thanks Anton for his kindness, tickles the top of Susie's head and leaves to look for a new home.

***

Vanessa continues to listen to the organist practice. Tears well up and spill as she remembers that day the Humvee struck the child in the marketplace, and the bump she felt as the second set of wheels rolled over the child's lifeless body. She remembers jumping out of the Humvee and running to escape the bullets, but she couldn't escape the horror of killing a bewildered child. Her despair is wrapped up in the tones of the organ, and she cries silently in tune with the music that exposes her broken heart.

The organist notices his tortured audience-of-one and

begins to play the Pachelbel-Canon in D that has guided so many bridesmaids to the altar in anticipation of the bride's entrance. The sanctuary is filled with a kaleidoscope of colors that stream through the stained glass windows. Vanessa puts her hands over her face and tries to stem the flood of tears that finally start to wash away the stain of guilt. The infected wound that poisoned her with shame is cleansed by the healing balm of music and tears.

Vanessa stands and waves to the organist. She blows him a kiss, turns and walks out of the sanctuary into the prospect of a new day.

***

Anton finishes his time in the studio with a sideways glance at the stack of bills on his desk as he prepares to walk home. He stops and puts the bills in the drawer.

"I lost my best dancer today. Margret makes progress, but her stamina on a scale of one to ten is a two. Who is going to help with the children now? The adult class should have a part in the show, but without Vanessa to lead them it would be an embarrassment. Add to that, I have no car and no money."

Anton reaches into his pocket for the studio key and bumps into his Rosary. He pulls it out and the string of beads hangs from his finger-tips. In frustration, he throws the Rosary across the room. Susie thinks it's a game, chases the Rosary and brings it back to Anton. He is mortified. Susie senses something is terribly wrong and sits quietly at Anton's feet. Anton, in complete humility, closes his eyes.

"Forgive me, Father."

Anton is too ashamed to even say prayers. He puts his

Rosary back in his pocket and picks up Susie. He looks into her eyes and sees the fear that chased away the sparkle.

"Oh Susie, it will be okay. Everything will be okay."

Susie and Anton sit together in silence. Susie doesn't move, and Anton closes his eyes. Anton lifts Susie to his cheek and kisses the top of her head. Susie holds still. Anton hugs Susie, and they stay silent together. Susie peeks out from Anton's hug and starts to wiggle. Anton chuckles and puts Susie on the floor.

"Susie, you're an angel. I think Vanessa misses you! You're her little angel too. Let's go find her."

FOURTEEN

Vanessa sits at her kitchen table and concentrates on the queen's next move. The king is in danger, and the bishop is across the board with his head under water.

There's a knock on Vanessa's door. A panic rises, but she is able to quell the unease. She hears a little bark and runs to see if it's Susie. Sure enough, Susie bounces up and down and right behind her is Anton. He smiles while Vanessa bends down and opens her arms. Susie runs, jumps, and Vanessa catches her.

"Susie, Susie, oh Susie, I thought I'd lost you forever!"

"She missed you! So here we are. I apologize for being too harsh."

"No, no, it's exactly what I needed. I see things differently now. You were right to lock me out."

"My father was killed by a drunk driver."

"I'm so sorry!"

There's a long silence.

"Well, Susie insisted we find you."

"I'm so glad you found me! Come in!"

Susie leads the way, and Vanessa and Anton follow.

"Would you like some tea? I have potato chips and cheese."

"Yes, I love potato chips!"

Vanessa takes the chips from the cupboard and shakes them into a bowl. She places the cheese on her small cutting board and sets an indoor picnic on the table. She breaks off a small piece of cheese and gives it to Susie.

"A reward for coming home, although I have to admit, I thought it was better for Susie if she stayed with you. Here, sit down. Would you like a soda, water or tea?"

"A soda, please."

Anton can't believe he's offered his two favorite snacks. Vanessa pours a tall glass of water, and gets a soda from the refrigerator for Anton.

"You play chess?"

"I used to play with my dad all the time. I decided to pull it out and review the players. I put the board, players and this book on the table where I can see them. I thought I could use some strategy in my life."

"In Cuba people play chess in the square. I grew up playing baseball and chess."

"After I review my players and the rules of the game, would you like to play sometime?"

"Yes, I could use some strategy practice too."

"It must be a challenge to run a flamenco studio. Do you ever do shows or recitals?"

"Oh yes. There are recitals, shows and competitions. I'm ready to do our first show. Would you like to come back and help us make it a success?"

"You would allow me back? Are you sure? I plan to rejoin AA and go for help at the VA. I even sat in the Episcopal Church, on the other side of Old Town, and listened to the organist practice! When you locked me out and Susie chose you, I hit bottom."

"You are welcome back."

"You have no idea what this means to me. It gives me hope! You know without hope, we're dead in the water."

"That's an understatement."

"Hey! Do you want to review my chess rules and strategy with me? I bet you could give me some pointers. If you play chess like you dance, I'm in for an education!"

Anton drinks his soda, eats cheese and chips and studies the chess board. The hand carved pieces are in place. Vanessa opens the *Teach Yourself Chess* strategies book by William R. Hartston.

"Okay. First chapter, '*Rules of the game.*'"

Vanessa holds the book so they can both study the chapter on rules. Vanessa is captivated by the diagrams. Anton reads a little and looks at the board. He alternates between what he reads and what he visualizes on the board. There are copious details described in the first chapter. One sentence captures Vanessa's attention. It describes the unique attributes of each piece and sums up *"that the charm, beauty and indeed difficulty of the game lies in the cooperation and conflict between pieces with distinct patterns of movement."*

"This sounds like flamenco – just add music!!"

Anton studies the chapter, looks at the board and visualizes a game. Vanessa drinks her water and gets up to cut more cheese. Anton eats chips while he concentrates on the game he has going on in his head.

Vanessa returns to the table, picks up the book and sees a description of the queen: *"The queen is the most powerful piece on the board. She can move in straight lines along ranks, files or diagonals, so from any square she combines the possible moves of the rook with those of the bishop."* Vanessa is hypnotized by this description of the queen.

"So, this is what it means to be a woman! I'm not a victim. Embrace the power! Oh yes, this is the book and the game for me!"

Anton looks at Vanessa, smiles and returns to the end game of his mental exercise with chess. Vanessa exclaims,

"Chess should be part of a worldwide curriculum in all elementary schools, and a required course in every grade. I should never have stopped playing chess!"

Vanessa settles down, and she and Anton spend the next hour in concentration on chess. Vanessa reviews the game with the help of the open book. Anton starts moving pieces in sync with what he sees in his head. He plays a few solitary games and of course he wins every time.

"I'm not sure I'm ready to play chess with you, Anton. I'm just beginning to regain confidence. I'm not sure you would let me win."

Anton laughs.

"You're right there."

"We're out of chips and soda. Do you want to walk to Glenn's market and buy some more food for a picnic? There's that beautiful park on the other side of the boulevard, and Susie needs to go out. Anton answers,

"Yes."

Anton recognizes chess is exactly what he needs to play to get him back on track – chess and baseball. Vanessa calls Susie, hooks her onto the leash and opens the door to go. Anton clears the table of dishes, places them in the sink and follows.

Glenn's market sells submarine sandwiches, sodas and potato chips, and the park has a game of baseball just starting. One of the players recognizes Anton, waves him over, tosses him a mitt and points to first base. Vanessa walks Susie around the park then sits in the bleachers to watch the game. Anton hits a homerun with bases loaded, and his team wins. How can the day get any better? A food truck arrives and sells hot dogs! Anton celebrates a day of winning chess and baseball with a vegan hot dog loaded with mustard, ketchup, relish, onions, jalapeño peppers and Sauerkraut.

Anton, Vanessa and Susie walk back across the boulevard to the studio.

"Thanks for allowing me back."

"And thank you for chess and baseball. I now know how

to prepare for a flamenco competition! Study chess strategy!

Anton and Vanessa laugh. Susie pulls Vanessa in the direction of Old Town.

"No, Susie. You're coming with me."

Anton bends down and lifts Susie up, gives her a kiss on top of her head and hands her over to Vanessa.

"Take good care of my angel."

"See you tomorrow for my lesson."

Vanessa flashes a perfect flip of a floating-butterfly hand above her head as she turns for home. Anton mimics Vanessa and signs off with the same classic sign of dismissal and calls out,

"Hasta la vista, señorita Vanessa"

FIFTEEN

It's near the end of the day. Margret catches the last agent, at the premier real estate office, on the Central Coast.

"Hello, I know it's late, but would you have a moment to show me some properties? I have an urgent need."

"Certainly, what exactly are you looking for?"

"I haven't really thought about it. What do you have available?"

"Well, let's start with your budget. Do you have a ballpark figure of what you want to spend?"

"I have no budget. Money is no object, and I do know what I want. I want a three bedroom house with a view, a swimming pool and land. No mansion."

"Oh."

"I'm ready to buy something today. Do you have anything close to what I described?

"Actually, I do. It isn't listed yet, but the owner approached me this morning and asked if I would represent the property. It's empty, and he wants to divest immediately."

"Can I see it?"

The agent hesitates.

"I can call and see if I can get the key."

"Please call. If it's what I want, I'm ready to buy."

"Oh."

The agent finds the number and calls the owner.

"Hello, Tom. I have someone in the office, and your property is exactly what she says she wants. Would it be okay if I came by and picked up a key?"
The agent nods a "Yes" to Margret.

"Great. I'll be there in fifteen minutes. Leave the key in the mailbox."

The agent picks up her keys and purse.

"Leave your keys. I'll drive,"

"Oh. Okay."

"Thank you for doing this. I didn't get your name."

"Sandra Wells. Sandy."

"Thank you, Sandy"

"My pleasure."

Margret and Sandy climb into the Gorilla.

"I've never seen anything like this. It's like a cross between a luxury SUV and a Baja 1000 converted VW Bug."

Margret laughs.

"Exactly, it's a Gorilla. I just discovered mountain bikes, and I'm all in! Flamenco and mountain bikes – that's my thing."

"Oh."

Margret GPS's Tom's address, and they arrive in fifteen minutes. Sandy picks up the key from the mailbox and tells Margret the address of the property. They drive through classic California Central Coast wine country and pull up to an original farm house, surrounded by oak trees, a view of the valley and forty acres of gently sloping land.

"There's a new swimming pool in back and a large barn. The house is completely restored on the inside."

"I'll take it."

"Don't you want to see inside??"

"I don't have time. I want you to draw up the paperwork, so I can move in as soon as possible."

Sandy is shocked but doesn't argue. They arrive back at the office before the banks close. Margret contacts her private client banker and starts the sale. Sandi draws up preliminary paper work and calls Tom.

"We have a cash offer for the full price. I know it's unorthodox, but she would like to stay on the property tonight and start moving in as soon as possible. And yes, she more than qualifies."

"Tell him it's exactly what I want."

"It's fine with the owner to stay the night on the property. We can finish the rest of the paperwork tomorrow when you both are ready to sign and the funds transfer. But there's the title business which might take a few days to a couple of weeks, and I'm sure you'll want an inspection."

"I don't care a hoot about inspections. I can fix whatever needs fixing and bring things to code if there's a problem. You get the escrow and title business taken care of, and I'll spend the night at the house until I have the deed. Then I move in. Sound good?"

"Ah yes, sure . . . I'll confirm with the owner."

Sandy and Margret shake hands. Margret gives Sandy a little hug.

"You have no idea what you have done for me."

Margret climbs into her Gorilla and drives back to the property with the key to the house. She has the combination to the gate. She stops on the way at Dan's Sports Chalet and buys a down sleeping bag, memory foam pad, flash light, battery run lantern and matches. She also buys the deluxe picnic basket featured in the front window.

Antonio's Italian Restaurant is next door. Margret orders mushroom ravioli, Mediterranean salad and a local bottle of Pinot Noir to go. She borrows a cork screw and wine glass.

It's daylight-savings dusk when Margret pulls up to the property. She unlocks the gate and parks in front of her new home. She is beyond happy. It's like unwrapping a Christmas present when you have no idea what to expect, but you know it's a special gift.

Margret opens the front door and gasps. The restoration is perfect in every detail. The kitchen is updated, but fits the farmhouse theme. The master bedroom with a view of the valley, and a smaller bedroom with the same view are upstairs, and one bedroom downstairs is off the kitchen. Margret peeks into the bathroom and sees claw foot tub, toilet with overhead water tank and classic chain for flushing. She goes back downstairs and outside to bring in her suitcase, new camping gear and dinner. She scouts the yard for sticks, short branches and small logs to make a fire. She lays out her memory foam pad in front of the fireplace, unrolls her sleeping bag and changes into silk pajamas. She makes a pillow with clothes from the suitcase and puts the lantern by her new bed. She lights the fire like the Girl Scout she was until Mother said, "No more tomboy."

Margret sits on her camp bed and eats her dinner. The Italian food, the crackling fire, the dim room and manic day leave her feeling sleepy. She gets up and digs around for the photograph of her Papa fly fishing. She tucks it under her arm and wiggles into her sleeping bag. She watches the fire and smiles. Her soul is pure joy.

"Tomorrow, I start the day with a run around the property, and, if it's not too cold, a swim in the pool. Who knew what was inside me?"

She traces a heart with her finger over the photo of her father. She kisses the photo and whispers,

"Papa, you knew all along, didn't you?"

The morning sun burns through the curtains, and Margret wakes with a start. She remembers she bought a house yesterday. She rolls over on her back, blinks a few times and stares at the crown molding, patterned tin ceiling and overhead antique light fixture.

"This guy, Tom, spared no expense!"

Suddenly, Margret jumps out of bed and hurries to dress for flamenco. She will just make it if she drives straight to the studio. She looks at the clock on her phone and realizes she's an hour ahead of herself. She has time for a walk around the property.

***

Anton arrives at the studio by taxi after a morning of soul-searching. The beach isn't even on the radar. Nothing breaks his preoccupation with the precarious state of his finances. The Rosary he kept in his car is now in his pocket, and Anton touches the beads hoping for a sign. He puts the Rosary from his pocket next to the one he keeps in his in desk. Anton laughs.

"Is this faith or superstition? Two Rosaries are better than one."

Vanessa and Susie appear in the front window. Anton jumps up and walks to the door and unlocks it.

"Anton, this is rare. No music, no dancing, no blazing heels?"

"No car, no money, no hope."

Vanessa is stunned by his confession, and Anton is surprised at his naked honesty. Susie has already settled herself on the couch with the hope that Anton will sit next to her and scratch her head.

Anton sits at his desk and stares at the calendar he uses to plan the dates for the show and the timeline to get ready for his first community event to celebrate flamenco.

"I think you need another bouquet!"

Anton laughs. He pulls open the desk drawer and pulls out the stack of bills.

"How do you say it? Out of sight out of mind? These haven't been out of mind for the last week. The totaled car is the final blow."

"Good thing you don't drink!"

"I may start."

"We can go to AA together."

Anton half laughs and Susie gets her wish. Anton moves to the couch, picks up Susie and scratches her head. Vanessa checks her purse and finds the lottery tickets.

"Anton, I bought these tickets because it's stores like the one we have on the corner that sell the winning tickets you hear about. Maybe one of these or both can pull you from the abyss. You go, and I'll wait here. Take Susie for good luck."

"I can't take your lottery tickets."

"Yes you can! I don't want anything that comes from that store. Go!"

Vanessa hands Anton the lottery tickets, goes to the door and opens it for Anton and Susie.

"I'll stay here and practice my butterflies."

Vanessa waves them off with a flurry of butterfly hands circling her head and ending with another dismissive flip from both hands. Anton and Susie obey and walk to the liquor store. Vanessa continues to practice her singular way of floating her hands above her head. She seems to follow her hands like a curious child follows the flight of a butterfly through a garden full of spring blossoms. Vanessa is lost in a dream of a meadow in full bloom and the scent of lavender and sage.

Anton and Susie return empty handed. Vanessa lands on earth.

"No pot of gold. And you're right it is exactly the kind of liquor store you could see on the news as the source of the mega-millions-winning tickets – just not today."

"Dang, I was sure one would be a winner – back to chess and strategy."

"I'm afraid strategy is in the hands of a fickle queen."

"Anton, where did you learn to speak English like this? I'm astonished by your vocabulary! Fickle is no common word!"

"My father insisted that I learn to speak fluent English. I had a tutor, and her favorite word was 'fickle.' The 'fickle fingers of fate' was something she believed in. I'm not sure if she was bitter or resigned, but she used this word often."

"Lucky for you – just not today!"

The Gorilla almost parks itself in front of the studio, and Margret jumps down from the state-of-the-art-dirt master. She sees Vanessa, Anton and the dog are still engaged and starts to get back in the Gorilla, but Anton sees her and waves her inside.

"Margret, I want to introduce you to Vanessa. You two are my best dancers and the whole of my dance company! Vanessa, Margret. Margret, Vanessa. The three of us are the Anton Dance Company. And Margret, what are you driving???"

All three laugh, but Margret turns serious.

"Vanessa, I'm so pleased to meet you! I remember the first time I saw you, and you called out when I stumbled 'and flamenco saved you.' You were so right!"

"Margret, I don't remember saying it, but I hear you. It's a lifeline for me too!"

An invisible bond of survivorship takes hold between Vanessa and Margret. Vanessa recognizes it's time for Margret's lesson and starts to leave with Susie.

"Wait. Margret, what if we all three dance together now. It's a good opportunity to explore working together as a company. Vanessa has been working on her hands."

"And I've been working on my soul awareness. Yes!"

Vanessa puts Susie back on the couch, Anton picks up his remote and flamenco guitar music fills the studio. The three dancers begin to clap their hands in sync to the guitar. Anton adds steps and prances in the center. He abruptly turns back and forth between the two women and accents each turn with a loud stamp. He returns to the patterns of the three dances familiar to Margret and Vanessa. He signals to Vanessa to move to his right, Margret to stay at his left and they begin to dance the opening of the first dance. Vanessa adds butterfly hands, Margret expresses passion and arches her back while slowly turning and tapping her feet. Her arms are bent at the elbow, and she continues to clap her hands in front of her chest. Anton works his steps in the middle and continues to turn back and forth to face each woman. Vanessa continues to float her soft-graceful-butterfly hands on the ends of arms that arch over her head as she tilts up and back in complete abandon. The tips of her fingers are buttery and melt into a swirl of spinning butterflies above her head. Margret twirls, lifts the front of her skirt and swings it left and right with both hands. This reveals a pair of strong-elegant legs tipped with footwork that increases in speed and intensity in her percussive attack on the floor. Both women dance the same patterns but with entirely different interpretations. The eye of the hurricane and the tornado gradually resolve into calm rhythmic clapping.

Anton clicks the remote and all three dancers catch their collective breath. Anton is astounded at what just happened.

"What can I say? Señoritas, you are brilliant! We have a flamenco dance company!"

"I'm driving a Gorilla, and I'm ready to dance like I drive."

"So it's from train to Gorilla??"

"Yes, Anton. Vanessa, you don't know this, but Anton sent me to the ocean to find my soul, and I fell in love, as I watched two young vagabonds and the train that travels over the wetlands. Anton also encouraged me to spend time in nature, so I went to a park with an oak grove and fell in love with mountain bikes! I went to a sport outlet to get set up for mountain biking, and the salesperson told me to consider a four wheel drive vehicle because the bike rack didn't exactly work on my sports car! I went directly to *King of the Rough and Rugged Sports Vehicles* dealership and bought the showroom Gorilla. Here I am, with the awakened soul of a vagabond, except that I bought a house mostly sight unseen. And you know what's incredible? I've never felt freer. I'm busting through all the norms, because I can, all thanks to Anton!"

"Wow! I started to review chess to understand and practice strategy, but that seems tame compared to your Gorilla adventure."

"Vanessa, you have the soul part in spades. Maybe strategy is what you need?"

"Yes! Definitely!"

"And I started playing baseball on Sunday – after Vanessa and I reviewed chess and reignited my passion for strategy."

"Anton is a killer chess master."

"And I've abandoned my sports car for soul food – now I eat dirt."

"Anton's car is totaled."

"Oh my God, Anton, take my car. I'm shedding. Must be divine strategy working in your favor. I have a Gorilla, and now you have a sports car."

"I can't take your sports car."

"Sure you can. What better gift for all you've done for me. Besides it suits you."

"No, no, no."

"Yes, yes, yes! Don't mess with divine strategy

"Take it, Anton. You can't afford not to, and it's rude to turn down Margret's offer."

"Thank you, Margret. I'll borrow it until I can get another car."

"It's all yours, Anton. I don't need it, and I don't want it. I'm bonkers, and I like being bonkers. My father was super generous. And, he was incredibly strategic. He created an international bio-chemical company. He died and left behind his alcoholic wife, my mother, who has driven me to break out of prison. Thank my father."

Anton is silent, and Vanessa hugs Margret. "Congratulations Margret. Flamenco did save you!"

Margret starts to cry. She goes to the siesta couch and sits next to Susie. She takes the throw from the back of the couch and buries her sobs in its softness. Susie sits quietly by her side. Anton sits at his desk, and Vanessa sits on the chair in front of the desk. The crying subsides, and Margret talks into the blanket to hide her face.

"I've cried, but I haven't cried like this since Papa died. He was wonderful, and he loved me. I miss him so much. He left me a fortune of my own to protect me from my mother. She changed when my sister died. Anton, please take the car. My father would want you to have it. He would adore you, because you have been so kind to me."

Anton nods to accept the car, and Vanessa goes to sit on the couch with Margret. Susie jumps into Vanessa's lap. Anton clicks his remote, and flamenco guitar music spreads comfort beyond the couch and into the room.

SIXTEEN

Anton sits in Margret's sports car in the beach parking lot as the sun comes up over the far end of the Valley and casts a metallic-pink shine on the wetlands. One of his Rosaries hangs from the blinker-control arm on the steering wheel. Anton absently fingers the beads as he visualizes new choreography for the Anton Dance Company comprised of three dancers.

"I'm going broke, and I sit here in a valuable sports car that really isn't mine. I could sell this a car, because I have the pink slip, but Margret would have none of it. I could ask Margret to help, but I would have to show her my finances. What do I do?"

Anton shakes off his troubles and walks against the wind to his favorite dance floor. The low tide exposes a broad expanse of firm sand dotted with pebbles and clumps of seaweed. Here and there a moss-covered rock emerges where sea anemones cling to their home, and tiny shell-encased-sea-crabs crawl in the small pool at the crease of a sand and granite seam. Anton has traded visualization for action and races across the sand. He leaps and turns as he hears the ocean roar and the seagulls squawk. A curious seal pops up above the continuous zigzag lines of rough waves and watches Anton.

Anton, lost in his dance, tumbles over a half buried driftwood branch. He rolls with his fall and makes it part of his choreography. He does cartwheels and back flips, touches down, before he springs up and jumps over two sea-moss-covered rocks. His arms spread out as he runs. He wishes he could fly.

Spent and restored, Anton unlocks the sports car, towels off the sand on his feet, puts on his street shoes, drives to Lupe's for his usual breakfast of Mexican pastries, drinks his coffee and hugs Lupe.

"You're a happy man!"

"You're the best baker in this town, in the world, maybe the universe!"

Lupe laughs.

"Go on. Get out of here. Go to work! Someone has to pay for that car. The dance studio hums, yes?"

Anton dances out the door.

"It couldn't be better!"

Anton parks in front of his studio and closes his eyes. His hand reaches out for the Rosary, and he stops himself. He pulls his hand to his lap, bows his head and sits for ten minutes and waits for an answer when he hasn't even posed a question. A knock on his window breaks the quiet.

"Hey there, your lights are on. Are you all right?"

"Oh, yes. Thanks for telling me."

"No problem, get some sleep."

Anton puts a hand up and half waves.

"The lies we tell. 'Are you okay? The studio hums, yes?' Why didn't I tell Lupe the truth? Why didn't I tell this man the truth? Why do I pretend that everything is okay? The house of cards is about to collapse!"

Anton shakes his head.

"I guess that's why I dance flamenco."

Anton gets out of his metal cocoon and sees something taped to his studio door. It's an envelope with his name on it. He unlocks the studio, goes to his desk, sits down and opens the letter. No mystery here. Pay the rent or vacate in three days.

Anton touches the bottom and springs into action. He finds flamenco music that cries. Choreography leaps out, and he dances a desperate story. Today he is a refugee who flees government collapse and starvation. He spins through streets filled with smoke and danger. The castanets he turned to since teenhood, sound like rattlesnakes. His dance is both a plea for mercy, and a demand for something better. Sweat and fear pour from his body as he whirls around oblivious to Vanessa, Susie and Margret that stand at the door and watch.

The salon owner next door pounds on the wall, and Anton turns up the music. He is one with the singer that wails and guitars that race. An explosion rocks the square and the buildings collapse. A thick fog of dust buries the rubble and the town is suddenly quiet. Anton finishes his story with slow steps back to his desk and flips his hand above his head as he shuts off the music. He lays his castanets on the desk next to the eviction notice and slumps onto his chair.

Margret gently knocks, and Susie pushes her nose against the window. Vanessa unhooks the leash in anticipation of a reunion. Anton looks up and sees his dance company. Both women are dressed to dance. He opens the door and opens his arms for Susie. She jumps into Anton full force. She wiggles and licks the sweat that drips from his forehead.

"Wow! You make mountain bikes, and the Gorilla off-road look like a walk in the park!"

"Good thing I was on the outside and only watched your explosion. The scene would have sent me under the desk for shelter, and the VA for emergency therapy!"

"Yes, it's good you didn't interrupt. I was out of my mind. I might have run out into the boulevard and caused a traffic disaster! I must apologize to my neighbor."

Anton carries Susie, and they all go next door to the salon. Anton puts his hands together and bows "Namaste." The salon owner bows "Namaste" in return, and the dance company goes back to the studio.

"What's up Anton? Your desperation is palatable. I recognize the signs. I could barely contain Susie. She was frantic to join your liftoff."

Anton doesn't answer. He goes to his desk, pulls open the desk drawer and shows Vanessa and Margret the full picture of his financial disaster.

"No wonder you took off like a rocket. Vanessa's right. You're on a ledge."

Anton sits at his desk, takes the marker he used to warn people off Vanessa's purse and scrawls in large letters "Studio Closed" on the back of the eviction notice. He walks to the door with scotch tape and sticks the sign to the door. Vanessa, Margret and Susie sit on the couch and consider the implications of a shuttered dance studio. Margret gets up and assumes command.

"Anton, this isn't the end. It's the beginning. Sit down and listen. Vanessa, take down the sign. Anton, call Susie. I didn't change my whole life to watch the catalyst for that change give up. Vanessa didn't get back on track to watch her life preserver drift away with the riptide. No Sir. We are Anton Dance Company, and we're in this together. You have assets, Anton. I have money, Vanessa has strategy with a gift for dance beyond compare, and you have a brilliant career ahead of you. Your choreography stuns, and your generous nature that shares all that you have is gold. Don't trash your assets."

"Yes, Anton. Margret's right. This is the beginning, and if there's one thing I learned in the service, it's that strategy and sticking together yield success. No more doing this all on your own."

Susie jumps into Anton's lap, but her attention is on Margret.

"Anton you created a company. A company requires capital. I offer capital. I don't think you grasp the depth of my pockets. I could buy this entire strip mall, and it would be chump change. So when I say I can help, I can help, and it's not a burden or sacrifice. It's an investment in my sanity, or as you would say, 'in my soul.'"

"It's true, Anton, you gave me, Margret and even Susie a

path forward. You made us official members of a dance company! Whatever we can do to keep that dream alive is essential for each one of us, and we're not going to allow you to crush our hope, let alone kill the dreams of all the other dancers that come to this studio to dance flamenco."

"I don't know what to say."

"You say, 'Thank you,' and that's the end of it. Vanessa and I will take over the business management, and you, Anton, the Artistic Director, will focus on making this dance studio a tour de force. I can bank roll the operation, and Vanessa can be the bookkeeper. Susie will be our mascot and cheer leader. We'll play to our strengths."

"The Three Musketeers Strategy 'All for one and one for all.' And we'll checkmate any naysayers."

Anton laughs.

"Vanessa, I guess that would be me. I concede. You and Margret win."

"We'll create a business plan, and we will succeed. Anton, you need a detailed proposal for your first event. Vanessa and I will give it legs."

"With the money from Margret, I'll pay these outstanding bills, back rent and create a budget for your first mainland event. Anton, I can hardly wait to see what you imagine for our first show!"

"Let's set a date. Anton, what's a reasonable amount of lead time for putting on a performance?"

"I think three months at the earliest, Margret. We have three dances started. The adult class can polish what we've started there, and the children can showcase a dance they have been working on. Yes, three months is possible."

Margret gets the ball rolling.

"I say we meet once a week to keep things on track. Any ideas on what day, or night we can meet?

"How about Sundays, early evening, at the Studio. I can have an event proposal ready."

"That works for me and Susie. We're just around the corner."

"Sundays are fine with me. We'll create a mission statement, and I'll have a legal agreement ready to spell things out. We'll keep it simple."

Anton is in shock. The whiplash from failure to opportunity overwhelms him. To ground himself, he opens his laptop and brings up a video of a flamenco performance to show Vanessa and Margret the type of band and singer he imagines for the show. Susie lies in Anton's lap and watches the dance company resurrect. Anton announces,

"Okay dancers, we're here to dance flamenco."

Anton puts Susie on the couch and goes to his music resource center on the bookshelves below the poster of his friend, Alvaro, who sweats and twists as his piston legs and boots hammer the floor. Anton selects the signature recording he used for his dance company in Cuba. He has already decided this show will celebrate his heritage and unite the two cultures he now embraces. Vanessa and Margret take their places. They face the mirror and wait for direction.

The Latin rhythm takes hold of all three dancers. Vanessa and Margret clap in complementary rhythms while Anton begins to dance. Vanessa, who sang and danced in high school, is inspired by the video she just watched and spontaneously begins to howl in a raw soprano voice. It's a song born of her joy and disappointments. Margret draws on her newly discovered passion for rebellion and substitutes powerful footwork rhythms for claps and finger snaps. Anton signals the women to take their places, and they dance the same dance they worked on before the collapse and resurrection of Anton Dance Company.

Anton stops the music and without words shows them a new-precise choreography to follow. Vanessa grasps it instantly. Anton patiently repeats the patterns slowly until Margret internalizes the choreography. The dance design firmly established, Anton starts the music again, and the women speak the universal language of Anton's choreography. Vanessa's voice weaves a powerful thread that tells a story of loss and compensation when Anton or Margret take center stage. A few people gather to watch through the window, as the Anton Dance Company brings life to the strip mall community.

SEVENTEEN

Luisa lies on the front porch and waits for Anton to come home. She licks her paws and belly and stretches out on the warm-cinnamon-brown cement. It's past her usual dinner time, but she naps in contentment.

Anton pulls into the driveway in his sleek-sports car and parks in front of his vintage garage. He apologizes to Luisa, now pressed against the front door, and, true to a hungry flamenco cat, meows loud and raw. Anton unlocks and opens the door, and Luisa races to the kibble cupboard.

"Luisa! You're a hungry girl! Hold on. Let me get the salmon. I'll have it ready in no time."

Luisa continues to wail.

"Luisa! I think you would be an excellent addition to our flamenco band! Here eat your dinner! I apologize. I stayed too long under my Sunset road sign. Eat up!"

Anton sips a Bucanero beer, heats up congri y ropa vieja,

sits with his Havana News on his laptop computer, clicks on Entertainment for flamenco updates and Sports for baseball. He finishes eating and moves to the living room TV. Baseball is on, and Anton is immediately invested. His favorite team is down three points. Anton studies the plays and understands baseball is a team of individuals playing specific positions. He understands baseball choreography.

Anton can't help himself and throws himself into a dance with the players and feels the adrenalin rush with each play. He leaps, slides and waves his arms and legs like an octopus. He chases the bases, as the baseball floats and lands in the stands where frantic outstretched arms push and shove to catch the ball. Anton stops his sport dance to watch the ball land. Unlike civilized American baseball fans, he sees a rare Cuban soccer-like frenzy similar to sharks circling a fishing boat. The weight of the rush causes the stadium bleachers to wobble, and a group of fans pile on top each other. A young man, bruised and bloodied where the ball slapped his face, stands victorious with his fist holding the baseball to the dismay of most of the group, but a younger boy cheers. Anton celebrates with continuous clapping and a few howls to animate his appreciation for the homerun that puts his team on the winner's board. The four players take their time around the loaded bases to clench the win.

Luisa, annoyed with Anton's disruptive choreography and noisy celebration, leaves the room. Anton settles back down on the couch, turns off the TV and thinks about his day. He is about to mount a flamenco show and is astonished that the money that was invisible in the morning is now apparent without limit due to Margret's generous commitment. And Vanessa is on board to keep the books. Anton shakes his head in amazement and wonders at the synchronicity of it all. Vanessa, a natural dance sensation, and Margret, a force of nature, are both becoming Latin in spirit. A dance company with enough support to proceed without limitation is beyond anything he could have imagined.

Luisa follows Anton to the bedroom and waits while he puts on his pajamas and slips into bed before she jumps up on her side and curls into a ball with her back to the pillow. Anton smiles as he watches Luisa fall asleep. He yawns and snuggles under the covers ready to join Luisa in dreamland. He remembers his Rosary on the side table, reaches over his head to pull the string of beads to his chest and turns out the lamp. Tomorrow, he will begin to contract the band, reserve the Civic Auditorium, ask Maria to organize and reserve an order for dresses plus all the other outfits once the designs are set. He suddenly feels panic at the immensity of this first event in America. He is a tiny fish in an enormous pond. He starts down the road of all that could go wrong, and the panic grows. Luisa feels his anxiety, stretches out a paw, gets up, comes to his side and lies down. Anton smiles,

"Luisa, you always forgive me when I come home late consumed with flamenco and jump around with TV baseball."

Anton rolls over and strokes Luisa's silky fur. He closes his eyes, and the panic fades. He slows his strokes and falls asleep with one hand resting on Luisa.

***

The simplicity of a bed roll on a hardwood floor, in front of a campfire in a fireplace, is Margret's happy place. Dinner from Antonio's Italian Restaurant is barely warm but still delicious. Margret contemplates the fire, and how it devours the wood and finally extinguishes itself if left unattended.

"Aren't we all like this fire? If Anton hadn't paid attention to my mechanical dancing, and suggested I go to the beach and watch the ocean, I'd be extinguishing myself in Mother's house."

Margret feels around for the framed photo of her Papa fishing and finds it at the edge of the bedroll. She draws an invisible fish over the photo with her forefinger.

"You, Papa, certainly fed me! Now you're feeding Anton and Vanessa too. I miss you. I wish you were here and could watch the show. It's going to be something! I'll ask Anton if we can dedicate it to you!"

Margret closes her eyes and presses the frame to her chest.

"A hug for you Papa, I miss Annie, and I feel a little quilt about Mother. I mean who is going to feed her? Her appetite is voracious. She gobbled bites out of me in her despair over Annie. Now she has no one to bite. She may starve."

Margret tries to think of one kind thing Mother did since Annie died. Nothing comes to mind. Not one kind word.

"I'll send her a bouquet of roses tomorrow. I can't let her starve."

A scraping sound catches Margret's attention. She listens to hear where it's coming from. The scraping is intermittent and it takes a moment for Margret to pinpoint the sound, another scrape, louder than the others, and Margret realizes it comes from the porch on the other side of the front door. She puts the photo under her pillow and goes to the window to see what creature can make such a racket. At the same time the creature goes to the window to look inside the house, Margret lurches backwards in surprise. A goat stands at the window and looks through the window with big glass-like eyes, flop ears and a sweet smile on its curious face.

"I guess I bought a barnyard."

Margret opens the door, the goat walks over and pushes Margret with her head. Margret laughs.

"You're a pushy broad. What are you doing here?"

The goat sniffs Margret, gives her another push and scrapes her hoof across the porch boards.

"Okay. Stop. Were you left behind when the goats-for-hire mowed the property? I'll call you, Tilly. Come, Tilly. I'll put you up in the barn tonight and find out who you belong to in the morning."

Margret goes back inside, puts on shoes and a jacket and returns to Tilly to lead her to her sleeping quarters in the barn. The hills are still pink from a cloudless sunset and the pungent smell of the meadow is a reminder of when she camped with Papa.

"Tilly, your entrance is perfect timing. I hope you're able to stay!"

Tilly follows Margret to the barn. Her short tail wiggles and twitches as she walks across the manicured grass that circles the flagstone deck around the swimming pool.

"Come on, Tilly. We're turning in early."

Margret considers the events of the day while she settles Tilly in the barn.

"A flamenco show, Tilly, you have no idea what this means to me. Hold tight, I'll open the stall with the run. You can eat the weeds."

Margret leaves the barn and returns to the peace of her living room campsite for a night of flamenco dreams.

***

Vanessa sits at the table and studies the book filled with how-to-corner-the-king-chess strategies. She's fascinated with the power the Queen has to tip the balance in her favor – whether it's to protect the King or take him down and win the war.

Vanessa considers the chess pieces and their roles. Every move they make is governed by the need to protect their side while engaged in the destruction of the opposing king and his kingdom of chess pieces. It's clearly a game about power, and how to keep it. She picks up a pawn and holds it up in front of her face. Vanessa's palm is open, and the pawn stands in the middle. Dull in design, it's the smallest piece, a sacrificial-foot soldier perched on her open hand.

"You poor sap. You're a mere pawn in a larger game. You're cannon fodder. You can't retreat. You can't even back up to get out of harm's way – one or two squares forward and an occasional vicious-diagonal-one-square capture but no wiggle room. However, once in a while, you do exhibit extraordinary hutzpah that leads to a fatally wounded king!"

Vanessa puts the little foot soldier down and picks up the castle.

"Umm, the only piece without a soul. Oh, the strategic moves you've seen inside the castle walls."

The rook catches Vanessa's attention. She puts the castle on the end square next to the rook and gently lifts the rook to examine the horse's head.

"Now you're the one I like the best. The power, beauty

and majesty of the horse combined with the bravery and strength of a knight, and the interesting pattern you create as you move into battle. Maybe you're the reason I signed on the bottom line – the romantic notion of the Calvary saves the day."

Vanessa touches the bishop's hat and chuckles.

"You sneak around, take confidences and sell them for political favor. Ah, in your mind God is always on your side, because you pay for the secrets."

Vanessa moves her fingers to the king hiding on the other side of the queen. She taps his crown and reminds him that he is the king. Feeble, but still the king, and, while he fiddles, his queen remains vigilant in her post. Vanessa laughs.

"I just don't understand what you, queenie, see in this king. Why don't you kick up your heels, leave the confines of the palace and settle in the country?"

Susie is bored and becomes impatient with Vanessa's chess musings. She prances to the door, sits below the door knob and waits for her courier to jump up and take her on a walk through the neighborhood.

"It isn't gonna happen, Madame. It's late, and I'm tired."

Vanessa pulls out the bed from the couch. She scoops up Susie and tells her to stop being afraid.

"The couch is harmless, Susie."

Vanessa feels Susie tremble against her chest. She squeezes Susie until she relaxes and puts her in the bathroom while she finishes making the bed. She pats the pillow in place, thinks about the harmless couch and retrieves Susie.

"Susie, I understand. It's irrational to be afraid of a fold-out couch, but it terrifies you. I have the same thing going on. It's irrational to be terrified of a flashback, but to me it's real and scary. I'll make you a deal. I'll be there for you, to help you get past the couch dragon if you'll be there for me when I start to panic. I want you to bark and break the hypnotism. I know it isn't real. I just need you to wake me up."

Susie cocks her head. In her eyes there's a flicker of understanding.

"Let's practice."

Vanessa suddenly freezes, begins rapid breathing and rushes for cover under the breakfast table on the kitchen side of the studio. Susie races over to her and begins to bark frantically. She gets louder and louder and races back and forth in front of Vanessa while she darts in and out to get her attention. Vanessa rolls over, laughs and grabs Susie.

"Susie you did it! You understood, and you did it!!! You're my rescue pup."

Susie is relieved to see Vanessa laugh. She licks Vanessa's face and prances in a circle obviously thrilled with this new game.

"Susie, I'm going to order you a service vest and see if the VA can make a certificate for me that will make your job official. You'll be with me at all times, and we'll break this terror up with shrill-little-dog barks."

Vanessa goes to brush her teeth, and Susie follows at her heels. They return to the now-a-bed couch. Vanessa climbs into bed, and Susie jumps up beside her, snuggles and stretches out along Vanessa's side. They breathe in a quiet rhythm and fall asleep.

EIGHTEEN

It's still dark. Anton jumps out of bed, dresses in sweats and dance shoes, tosses some kibble into Luisa's outside dish and pulls his knit cap down tight over his ears. He bounds out to his still-hard-to-believe-it's-mine-sports car and drives straight to Ocean Beach Park to witness the dawn. He parks outside the gate.

    A train's whistle sounds in the distance, and Anton sees the single headlight glide across the wetlands. He hears the coupled flatbeds, that carry containers, click and clack over the rails. He senses the weight of the train, as he walks under the trestle and heads to the beach. He turns and watches the freight cars string one at a time onto the tracks on solid ground, notices the dark hole in one where the door is open and the car is empty. He thinks of Margret and her breakthrough moment with the train and the young vagabonds. He watches the train disappear into the distance as dawn lights the massive wetland. Gulls fly overhead out to sea while ducks bob up and down on the ever changing wetland fed by fresh-river water and an ocean. A lone-bright-white egret struts on the edge of it all and brings meditative stillness to the sea, wind and underwater river current.

Anton removes his shoes and socks and tucks them behind the small wall that makes a feeble attempt to keep the tide at bay. He takes a long-deep breath and sprints through the soft-dry sand to the packed-hard sand from the ocean's tongues that stretch out and suck back on the ocean's edge. He stops and spreads his arms wide while he welcomes the light that seeps into everything and brings a sunrise that gives him a reason to celebrate.

The surface is sprinkled with small rocks that leave room for footprints. Anton looks down the empty shoreline and takes off in a run into the illusion of an ocean and a tideline that disappear into a pinpoint intersection. He gallops over sea stones and sand dollars until he vanishes into the illusion. The glow of the invisible sun, suspended in an infinite atmosphere, grows brighter until the glory of dawn is on full display.

Anton emerges from the pinpoint and grows in size, at the same time the marine layer skulks from the horizon across the foaming ocean and buries the churning sea and the leaping dancer in a damp-thick-blind fog. He lands where he started his exuberant chase down the coastline and bends over to pull a sand dollar from the seascape. He puts the exquisite skeleton into his pocket to save it as a symbol of good things to come.

At the still-empty-parking lot, Anton dusts off the sand, puts his shoes on and checks on his sand dollar in his pocket. The thought of Lupe's bakery makes his mouth water. He walks alongside the wetland to his car parked outside the park gate. The fog rolls along with him.

Anton pulls up to Lupe's and sees two young men walk into the bakery. He feels uneasy. Anton comes to the door and hears one man demanding money and sees the other man steal bread and pastries. Anton stops before he's noticed. He doesn't hesitate. He pushes the panic button on his fob, and the sports car begins to scream. He quickly disappears behind the building and calls 911. He sees the back door is open and comes in and yells "Police." He catches sight of the confused-scared-hungry-young men as they drop everything except the gun and run out the front door. Lupe is sheet white and cries. Anton locks the front door and goes to Lupe to reassure her.

The police arrive, and Anton unlocks the door. Both officers have their firearms drawn. Anton calmly explains what took place, and Lupe confirms that one of the young men had a gun. One officer looks familiar, and Anton remembers the day this officer told him to get his car fixed and called him Cuba-linga.

Anton feels his face flush and his muscles stiffen. The officers holster their guns and start to ask questions. Lupe is nervous and doesn't answer sensibly. Anton listens to Lupe's awkward responses and remembers his own difficulty with this officer. He steps in to protect Lupe.

"I'm happy to translate if necessary."

"It isn't necessary. . . Lupe, how long have you worked here, in this bakery?"

"What has that got to do with this robbery? Lupe owns the bakery. Maybe you want to eat one of her pastries to understand why she was robbed! There's a long line here every morning – before she opens!"

The investigative officer ignores Anton and continues to

question a nervous Lupe who struggles to understand. It's clear he has dismissed the robbery and has started to question Lupe's immigration status. The second young officer stands off to the side and listens. He looks uncomfortable.

"Lupe, I need to see your business license and residency card. And who does that sports car in front of your shop belong to?"

"Me."

"You're not Lupe."

"No, I'm not Lupe. I'm the Cuba-linga you stopped and told to get my car fixed. I did. I got a new car."

The officer instantly steps back in time and recognizes Anton.

"That's your car??"

"Si Señor. What else do you want to know about the attempted robbery? I witnessed it, and I can give you all the details. Lupe needs to take a moment to quiet her nerves and get back to baking. I'll tell you all you need to know."

"Okay. Let's get to it."

The junior officer goes to Lupe and offers to help her pick up the mess the would-be robbers made. The senior officer walks with Anton and writes down details of the event. Lupe fixes coffee and a plate of pastries for the officers. In no time, the police are out the door and on their way with crumbs on their uniforms. Lupe is relieved.

"Anton how did you stop the immigration questions?"

"I didn't. The car did. It astonishes me to see the power of an expensive automobile level the playing field."

"Your coffee and pastries are forever free."

"Lupe, I'll pay for my coffee and pastries! My reward was to watch my stock rise when that mean-streak policeman groveled the moment he heard the car is mine."

Lupe smiles, makes Anton a cappuccino and puts a pastry and napkin in a paper bag.

"Today, it's free."

Anton gives Lupe a hug and writes his phone number on a napkin.

"I'll see you tomorrow morning. Call me if anyone bothers you."

Anton sets his coffee and pastries on the roof of his bargaining-chip-luxury automobile and unlocks the door. He gathers his pastry and coffee prize and settles into his now heroic car. He takes stock of the sheer magnificence of this exclusive automobile. He sits in his leather covered throne with its cherry-wood-steering wheel and considers how the world works. Money talks and particularly when it's rolled up in cars. See a man driving an expensive automobile, and one immediately associates the man with worldly success. Margret's gift changed a Cuba-linga into a respectable citizen in the eyes of a bigoted policeman. Image is everything.

Margret and Vanessa sit on the bench in front of the studio and watch Anton slide into a parking space in front of them. Anton springs out of the car and bows to Margret. Susie, asleep under the bench, wakes up and sits at attention knowing Anton is nearby.

"Your humble servant owes you a significant thank you. Not only did you give me your car. You gave me the opportunity to save a humble bakery owner from a vicious robbery topped by a singular power play. I told the investigating officer to back off immigration, stick to the burglary and watched him scrape the sidewalk in awe that a scummy-Cuban immigrant could own such a valuable sports car!"

"You're a hero! Who knew that my once-upon-a-time chariot could elevate a dancer to civic superman! Can I touch you?"

Margret rises and touches Anton's forehead with her forefinger. Her lips purse, and a sizzling hiss issues through her lips. Vanessa claps her hands and laughs. She shouts "Bravo!" The people who walk in the parking lot experience whiplash when their eyes discover the source of the loud shout of admiration and the infectious belly laugh!

Anton unlocks the studio door and invites Vanessa, Margret and Susie inside with a bow and sweep of his arm. Vanessa and Margret, laugh, enter and prepare to dance. Margret is suddenly sober.

"Is the bakery owner okay? How terrified she must be to be robbed."

"Yes, she's nervous, but the real terror is the threat of an immigration investigation! She's documented, but it still terrifies her. The officer is so obviously prejudiced!"

"Tell her not to worry. Her pastries soothed the beast. A uniform, and I know because I wore one, intimidates, but a belly full of sugar sweetens the spirit inside and the situation harmonizes. He'll be back for coffee and forget about round-up."

"Vanessa, I hope you're right. Curious, on the way over, I thought our dance could incorporate this story, a kind of fusion-flamenco-ballet-tango-opera performance that expresses the emotions of a vulnerable-foreign shopkeeper."

"Oh yes! My father was such a champion of the vulnerable. He would be honored to know he supported a project that brought people together. He was awarded many international honors during his lifetime, but this one would top them all!"

Margret chokes back tears. Vanessa confirms the honor.

"We must dedicate the show to your father and demonstrate support for our diverse community!!"

Susie, who waits patiently while the discussion progresses, leaps onto Anton's lap and smothers him with kisses. Anton laughs, picks Susie up, holds her in front of his face and tells her in a serious tone,

"Susie, you just cast the deciding vote. We'll dedicate the show to Margret's father and honor his memory. Now we dance."

Anton, not one to sit still for long, changes his sweats into fitted black slacks, and a flowing black shirt tucked in at the waist. He trades his street shoes for sleek-leather boots. He drills the nails in the heels further into the soles with a series of untamed drum rolls. Vanessa and Margret, already dressed to dance, walk onto the floor and watch Anton begin to choreograph the foundation for the main performance of their upcoming show. They wait for his direction.

Anton capitalizes on Margret's vulnerability while she takes the tentative steps she always takes when she first begins a new pattern. He points to the middle of the room and tells her to play the shopkeeper who is busy putting her artisan jewelry store in order before she opens.

Margret is convincing as an immigrant shop keeper. She

lowers her eyes, slumps her shoulders and tenderly arranges her jewelry in the front window. Anton chooses gentle guitar music with flamenco affects to set the Latin character of the shopkeeper. Margret follows Anton's direction and opens the door of the studio with the idea that it is the entrance to the jewelry store. She flips an imaginary "closed" sign to "open" with a fan of fingers and turns back into the studio to tend her store. Her back is to the open door as she bends over a glass case with the valuable precious-gem necklace that she made last week. She unlocks and opens the case, puts the necklace around her neck and fastens it. She dances a solo tango around the store and shifts into flamenco footwork when she returns the necklace into the glass case. Her confidence in her steps increases, as she celebrates her shop and necklace. Completely absorbed in her joyful dance, she forgets to lock the glass case.

Anton gestures to Vanessa to go outside and observe Margret from the far side of the window while she arranges her jewelry. Vanessa's feet take flight, as she taps her heels in rapid succession and skips past the bench to her observation post. Her movements express freedom and stealth. She becomes invisible to Anton who now dances his way through the door and threatens the shocked Margret. He mimics a gun with his hand, brandishes it overhead then points it directly at Margret. In panic, Margret freezes. Vanessa, in response to the robbery, dances to the side of the studio and begins a shrill howl. Anton, with the remote, chooses a wild flamenco guitar to accompany Vanessa's vocal alarm.

At the same time, Anton, the armed and dangerous would-be thief, scoops up the exposed necklace from the glass case and dance-races to the door. He stumbles on the threshold as Vanessa dances through the studio back door to sing a sustained high C on the word "Police!" In panic, Anton drops the necklace and disappears into the small crowd of locals that has gathered outside the window wondering what is going on at Anton's Dance Studio.

Anton assures everyone it is simply a work-in-progress and invites them all to the upcoming show. He wishes there had been someone to film it all with his phone camera, so Margret could use the embryonic choreography as a tease announcement for the upcoming event on social media. The strip-mall crowd, grateful for the explanation, assures Anton they look forward to the event.

Back inside, Anton shuts off the music and shares his thoughts with Margret and Vanessa. Susie insists she's part of the creative team and bounces over to Anton. She sits and begs to be lifted up and held in Anton's kind embrace.

Anton outlines a rough sketch of how the performance might go, and adds the school dancers as police and witnesses. He explains how the flamenco band will add color and drama to his innovative approach to flamenco, support the different styles of dance and music and deliver a visual-audio-kinetic drama with an emotional wallop. Margret and Vanessa are spellbound, as Anton describes his creative vision. They are unsure how it will unfold on the stage of the Civic Auditorium, but they trust Anton to create a spectacular event beyond any of their wildest dreams.

NINETEEN

Vanessa gets up from her checkmate game, picks up her phone and calls home. A soft southern accent rolls into her ear, and Vanessa marvels at the charm of a Texas mom.

"Hello?"

"Hi Mom, I'm here with Susie and want to tell you the latest news."

"Oh darlin' I hope it's good. We can sure use some good news around here."

What's up? Is Dad ok?

He's havin' a hard time. I sure wish you'd come and visit.

"What's wrong?"

"What isn't wrong? First off, he's losing his mind. With the stroke he lost his mobility. Now it's his mind. I'm not sure I'm hangin' onto mine."

"Oh Mom, I'm so sorry. You and Dad have been in my prayers. Do you have help?"

"O mercy, yes! The house is crawling with help. The church has taken us on like family. It's like a-big-honey hive here dear, but sometimes I just want to scream, 'You all get out and go on home!' I just want to lie down on the couch and play dead, but then they'd call someone. They'd take me serious and prescribe pills and on it goes. Honey, sometimes too much help can be a curse."

"Well…I'm glad you're not alone."

"No, we're surrounded with do good folk. I need a few do bad folk to lift my spirits."

"What about your friend, Anna?"

"Anna? Oh Lord no. She was the last of the do bad folk, and now she's determined to shove me into heaven. Lord knows that's a barrel of boring fish. I just want to have a little fun. These do good folks just don't know how to have a good time. But then look what havin' fun did to your Dad. So maybe it's a good thing to be surrounded by a bunch of do goods."

"Mom, I gotta go now, but I'll call again real soon."

"Oh, Vanessa, please get down here. Your Dad talk's gibberish about you and that damn-dog Ralph all the time."

"Mom, you loved Ralph. We all did!"

"Oh, I know. I loved him, but it's all your dad gibbers about now, and it gets on my nerves."

"I understand Mom. I'll call next week. I gotta go. I love you. Tell Dad I love him. Bye now. . ."

"Please come and visit soon. We could all use something to look forward to! Love you. . ."

The connection is cut short when Vanessa holds the button down to shut off the phone. She sits down on her studio couch and holds her arms out to Susie.

"Susie, I swear I will never go back to Texas! I was so excited to tell Mom about the show and work out a way for them to come. Then Mom goes off the rails. I don't know how Dad stands it. Mom used to be so much fun. No wonder I signed up. See the world baloney! Bag of candy is right."

Vanessa curls up in a ball and smothers Susie. Susie begins to bark and tries to wiggle out of Vanessa's grip. Vanessa lets go and slugs the couch pillows in frustration. Susie barks and pokes Vanessa with her nose.

"It's okay Susie. Stop. No flashback here, just a taste of good ole Southern Discomfort. What was I thinking? Maybe three months from now, it'll be different."

Vanessa gets up and heads to the front door to pick up Susie's leash and take her out for a walk before her group class at the studio.

"Susie, I have to keep moving. I can't sit too long. Let's just stay happy."

Susie bounces to the door in agreement, and the two of them walk into the afternoon sunshine. A morning of butterfly-hand practice, a set-up of a bookkeeping system for Anton Dance Studio and Vanessa is ready for a walk to Old Town to explore downtown. Susie, too, is ready for fresh smells and new directions.

"Susie, this is a walk to Old Town downtown. Not Anton's house! Today, I'm the alfa dog. Follow me."

Vanessa and Susie walk in the direction of Old Town business district. Susie is delighted with the lush-floral landscape in front of quaint-historic buildings and prances joyfully ahead of Vanessa.

At the intersection, Vanessa sees a real estate office inside a charming yellow and green vintage cottage. Without thinking, she drags Susie back to the window with photographs of properties for sale. One in particular catches her attention. It's listed for $950k – a two story Mediterranean house, three bedrooms, three baths and a walled yard and close to Old Town downtown.

Vanessa checks the hours on the door of the real estate office. It's open. She picks up Susie and walks inside. A middle aged gentleman asks if he can help.

"I was wondering where the Mediterranean house that's for sale is located, and if I can walk to it. I'd love to have a look inside."

"Certainly, are you looking to buy a home in the area?"

"Truthfully, I haven't thought about it until I saw the photograph of this house displayed in your window. It caught my interest."

"Well, it's within walking distance on a beautiful-shaded street lined with large Italian Stone Pines. I'm alone here at the office. The house has a lock box, but I can give you the key, and you can bypass the box. You and the little dog can let yourselves in and have a look inside. I'll be here for a while so just return the key to me."

"Really? That's perfect. How far is it?"

"Walk to the intersection then go right, walk two blocks down and turn right on Lighthouse. The number is 164. You can't miss the house. It's a great location if you want to be near Old Town downtown."

Vanessa takes the key and carries Susie back outside. She puts Susie down on the sidewalk, clips on the leash, walks with Susie to the corner and down the avenue to Lighthouse. On Lighthouse Street, Susie takes over and dances on the strips of lawn between the giant Stone Pines until they arrive. The house is better than the photograph, and Vanessa is covetous.

Susie and Vanessa walk up three steps to the front door, bypass the lockbox and unlock the door. The house is empty. The polished hardwood floors, big windows, large fireplace, updated kitchen and bathrooms reveal the sturdy bones of a classic.

Time slips away, and Vanessa checks her phone for the hour. She needs to go to make the group class. She walks around the yard once while Susie runs and jumps off leash. She takes a moment to check out the two car garage. The yard is protected by well-established hedges and a rustic-rock-wall. Before Vanessa and Susie leave, they take a quick second look at the upstairs master-bedroom-suite fireplace, walk-in closet and bath with views of the back garden. There's a smaller bedroom at the end of the upstairs hallway with its own bath and fireplace. Wrought iron detail is on the staircase railing and the hallway balcony is fine craftsmanship. Blank walls throughout the house are perfect for large-scale art.

Vanessa hands the key to the gentleman waiting for her at the real estate office.

"How'd you like it?"

"Oh, we loved it."

Vanessa looks at Susie for confirmation. Susie runs in circles and barks.

"Oh yes, Susie and I like it just fine."

"It won't be on the market long."

"No. It will be scooped up in a heartbeat, I'm sure! Thanks for allowing us a peek at an exquisite house."

"You're welcome! If you're ever in the market for a new-old house, keep us in mind."

"You can bet we will!!"

"Susie, that's what we need. We need a home."

Vanessa and Susie power walk straight to the dance studio. They arrive in time to visit with other dancers, and Vanessa has time to change into her loan skirt, tank top and shoes. She laughs out loud while she buckles her dance shoes.

"I look at a $950k house, and I can't even afford my own dance wardrobe. Call me crazy."

Anton arrives, and the adult class of eight dedicated women of various sizes and shapes gather to warm up and learn new choreography. They are expected to practice what they learn each week on their own, and they do. As a whole, they are capable dancers. Under Anton's direction, they are inspired.

"Ladies, we have an event planned for the Civic Auditorium in three months. It will be our first real show and will require added rehearsals. Rehearsals are mandatory, so check your calendars and be ready to commit to the final two weeks of daily rehearsals here at the studio. The final two rehearsals and dress rehearsal will be at the Auditorium. We'll have a flamenco band with us on stage. It will be a full stage production with lighting and visual backdrops. We'll pull out all the stops! Maria is your go-to woman. She'll have all the information regarding dress orders, rehearsal dates and protocol. This is your show, so suggestions are welcome in the suggestion box on the desk. Anton Dance Studio spreads its wings! Just to let you know, we'll have one rehearsal at low tide at Ocean Beach Park. Ladies let's dance flamenco."

The adult class dancers are in shock. Anton is twice as animated as usual, and his "usual" is hummingbird pace. Maria smiles with added sparkle, and Vanessa tingles with enthusiasm. Anton reviews footwork for the class and explains that, in addition to a show case of their familiar dance number, they will also be part of the premiere Anton Dance Company featured performance.

Vanessa observes that the morale of the Anton Dance Studio has climbed the temperature gage and is red hot on the thermometer. She is "one of the girls" in this class and the female bonds are tangible. Vanessa glances over to the siesta couch. She sees Susie lean on the couch cushions and watch Anton take the class through the footwork and choreography for their showcase dance. Vanessa smiles and refocuses as she leads the group with her clear demonstration of what Anton tries to teach the class.

The forty-five minutes of intense concentration leave the women exhilarated as they gasp for air. They all caught a glimpse of what's to come as they prepare for the event. Maria takes over and briefs the women on a few performance details and promises an event calendar to share next week.

Anton goes to the siesta couch, picks up Susie and sits with an invisible shield around him, as the children arrive for their 6:00 p.m. class with Vanessa. Moms know that they are to drop off their children and leave. Vanessa addresses each child as a mature be-it-small individual, and they respond accordingly. One mother speaks briefly to Vanessa,

"You have no idea what you and this class do for my child! Thank you for sharing your talent and your compassion for my daughter. I know she is a bit chubby, but loves to dance. You give her confidence to live in her own skin and feel the joy of being true to who she is. I'm forever grateful."

Vanessa hugs the mom and whispers,

"And you have no idea what your daughter does for me! I too am forever grateful"

The mom senses Vanessa's sincere gratitude and tears up, as Vanessa tilts her head down to hide her own emotions. The mom continues to hold Vanessa in an embrace. Their stillness is in stark contrast to the flurry of activity around them. The daughter tugs at Vanessa's skirt while the mom disengages, squeezes Vanessa's hand and leaves.

Vanessa organizes the kids into two rows in front of the mirrors, and Anton gets up from the couch. The kids stand still and watch while Anton reviews their choreography and footwork.

"Dancers, you are small but mighty. I need all your attention on the details of your dance. Remember the art is in the details, so listen to every word your teacher, Ms. Vanessa, shares and follow her instructions with precision."

Vanessa takes over and drills the children until each child is secure in the dance. She turns on the music and runs the entire dance twice. She gathers the children together and congratulates them on a dance well done. Vanessa demonstrates butterfly hands in slow motion and encourages the children to curl and uncurl their fingers one finger at a time. She insists they practice at home to prepare for next week's lesson.

Mothers and two fathers stand at the door to collect their children. Vanessa greets each parent, thanks them for their cooperation and gives a heads-up about the upcoming show. Questions abound, and Vanessa tells the parents she will have paperwork next week with all the details.

The last child leaves and follows her butterflies out the door. The child's father claps his hands in a Latin rhythm as they walk to their car. Vanessa remembers her father jump up and down and shout from the soccer field sidelines, "Brava, Vanessa!" the time she scored the winning goal that determined the National Youth Soccer Championship.

Anton hands Susie to Vanessa and thanks her for inspiring the children to new heights with their flamenco practice.

"You are a gifted teacher as well as a phenomenal dancer! How did I get so lucky?!"

"Hold on, remember the Lotto tickets? Not so lucky!"

"Yes, and now I have Margret. She is beyond any lottery ticket, and you who is beyond any dancer I've ever seen. Don't be embarrassed. You are a freak of nature in a good way."

Anton rattles a tsunami of heels that slam the floor, and a spin that elevates him up, around and down with a butterfly dismal when he lands. Vanessa howls with laughter and answers with a quick flash of her butterfly hand, nonchalantly picks up Susie and walks out of the door.

Back in her studio apartment, Vanessa sits on her couch and reviews her day. The house she and Susie toured in old town is a testament to family. Vanessa picks up her phone and calls home.

"Hello. . ?"

"Hi Mom, can Dad talk at all on the phone?"

"Oh Honey, it's so good to hear your voice again – twice in one day!!! Honey, your dad talks gibberish. He thinks he's speaking sensibly, but it comes out gibberish. . ."

"Mom put him on the phone, please."

"Sure, Honey, it's hard to listen to. He was always so articulate. Now, it's incoherent babble. . ."

"Okay, Mom. Just put him on the phone."

"Yes, Sweetheart . . . just a little minute dear . . . here he is. . .its Vanessa…"

A string of mixed up words with inflection that makes no sense travels into Vanessa's ear. She listens as her father struggles to communicate with her. He babbles for a couple of minutes, and then there's silence, as he waits for her answer.

"Daddy, its Vanessa. I love you Dad. You are the best dad a girl could have! I can't believe how much fun we have together. I wish you could move out here, and I would take care of you and Mom. You could hang out with my dog, Susie. You would spoil her, and she would love you! Of course you would have to get in line behind Anton for her attention. She adores Anton. He's my flamenco teacher, and he helps me with my PTSD. Maybe you could learn to dance flamenco. It might help you walk or at least stand. Anyway,

I want you to know, I love you more than anything on planet earth!"

There's a long silence.

"Hello? Vanessa . . . Dad's crying. . . I have no idea what you said, but your daddy's crying. The only other time I ever saw him cry was when Ralph died. . ."

". . . Mom, give him a kiss for me . . . I gotta go. . ."

Vanessa hangs up the phone and buries her face in the throw on the couch. Susie pokes her several times with her nose and barks. Vanessa ignores her and lays down with her head covered in the blanket her Mom crocheted to celebrate her junior high school graduation. Susie senses this is different from her PTSD assignment. She curls up beside Vanessa and waits. . .

The sunset comes and goes, and Vanessa lies under the blanket with Susie by her side.

TWENTY

The pool is eighty degrees, and the flagstone is warm. Margret is stretched out on the oversize-natural-stone pavers in her tropical-print bikini while she stares at the water. Tilly nibbles the grass growing around the flagstone. Her short tail wiggles in delight.

The goat herd for hire moved on from ranch to ranch. Tilly isn't missed until a week later. Meanwhile, she nibbles her way deep into Margret's heart and secures permanent residency on "Tilly's" farm. Her amber eyes with the black rectangular pupils stare at Margret between bites of grass. This privileged-barnyard life is all new, and Tilly tries to trust what she sees. As a goat, she is remarkably present. She has decided Margret is her person, and that means twenty-four-seven security duty. Tilly is the best service creature ever, and Margret is thrilled to have a bold new friend.

Margret considers her morning dance with Anton and Vanessa. She's astounded that she is an official member of Anton Dance Company. The changes in her life are seismic, and Tilly lends solid ground to Margret's tailless kite.

"Tilly, you are my warrior guardian. However, there's an oversized elephant in my head . . . Mother."

Tilly stares at Margret for a moment then resumes her tasty nibbles.

"Tilly, I'm not sure you understand the gravity of the situation with Mother."

Tilly walks over and brings her face full front and peers into Margret's eyes."

"Well, I guess you do understand. Here's a question… do goats and elephants get along? You see, Tilly, I think I should bring Mother to this farm. I cannot in good conscience leave her at the mansion alone."

Tilly butts her forehead against Margret's forehead and breaks the spell.

"Hey, that hurt."

Tilly abruptly bounces sideways and looks for a rock to stand on. She ignores Margret and her elephant.

"There's my answer! Tilly, you know exactly how to handle an elephant!"

Margret gets up and heads to the house to change into street clothes for a trip to the title company to sign final documents for her farm and visit her mother for the first time since she packed her bags and left home. Tilly marches behind with a busy tail. Margret goes in the back door. Tilly prefers the front porch.

In minutes, Margret appears on the front porch dressed for her meeting in town and a powwow with Mother. Tilly stands and patiently waits for direction. Margret points to the Gorilla and tells Tilly to "load up." Tilly bounces in a crooked path to the Gorilla, shakes her head and dances around the vehicle while Margret opens the back and shows Tilly where to jump in.

"Tilly, I'm so glad you're on my team. You're so confident. It gives me joy and courage to hang out with you. I can hardly wait to see Mother's face when you walk in the front door with me!"

Tilly sits on the bench seat behind the driver's side and waits for instructions. She must have hired out to a number of ranches for fire maintenance, as her peaceful demeanor indicates she is used to travel that takes her to unfamiliar places. She looks out the window then puts her head down for a nap. Margret drives to the title office and finishes the final paperwork for the purchase of "Tilly's Farm." Margret honors her goat today, because Tilly has shown her a way to confront Mother and bring her into the camp.

Margret pulls up in front of the gates at the entrance of Mother's mansion. Tilly jumps onto the front passenger seat and looks out through the front window. Tilly's nose smudges the glass, and Margret laughs.

"Tilly, are you ready? You're about to meet your match."

Margret gets out and jumps the fence to push the button on the back of the black box that controls the electric gate with its false sense of security. The heavy gate opens slowly. Margret watches Tilly tilt her head and follow the movement of the panels. She climbs back into the Gorilla, before Tilly can climb onto the dashboard. Margret and Tilly pull up to the broad expanse of steps, at the front entrance, just as Mother opens the front door to investigate the security breach.

Mother slams the door closed and locks the house down. Margret, not surprised, but still never expecting to be locked out by her own Mother, sits in her Gorilla to consider "what next?" Glancing around the landscape, she sees Mother's sacred rose garden that stretches from back to front of the one entire side of this semi-transparent mansion. An impish grin curls Margret's mouth as she climbs out of the Gorilla, opens the passenger door for Tilly and leads her to the ultimate floral feast.

Mother is a devout practitioner of all natural pest and disease control for her garden. Tilly is free to eat all the roses without consequence. She mows the rose bushes with her busy lips while she flicks her ears and wiggles her tail to signal her delight. Tilly sometimes stamps her hooves in frustration that she can't eat everything in front of her all at once.

Margret sees Mother's distorted face pressed up against the glass wall that divides the rose garden from the living room. Horrified, Mother sees the four-legged-invader devouring rose hips, rose buds, and the new leaf sprouts on her historical-championship-rose bushes. Margret watches Mother frantically press the switch to draw back the glass wall. In her panic, Mother has forgotten she locked down the entire house when she saw Margret and her Gorilla at the front steps. The override is on the other end of the house, inside the garage. Mother is forced to stop and think. She disappears from view and goes to the garage to release herself from her own prison. Meanwhile, Tilly continues to enjoy the delicate rose banquet and indulges herself on a particularly delicious rose bush. Meanwhile, Mother is in lockdown somewhere in the vast mansion in search of the switch that unlocks the palace.

Margret's satisfaction, as she watches Tilly do damage to Mother's precious rose garden, is less about revenge and more about destruction of an obsessive passion that robbed Margret of shared time with her mother. After Annie died, Margret wasn't allowed to garden, because everything Margret used to do with Annie caused her mother pain to watch. At first it was out of a desperate need to stop the anguish from the loss a child. Later, it morphed into an insane-sadistic cruelty fueled by alcohol. Mother lost Annie. Margret lost Annie and her mother. Each rose that Tilly enjoys gives Margret a pleasurable subconscious return to a childhood of fun when she used to play in the garden with Mother and Annie.

This strange reverie is broken when Mother emerges from the back corner of the house with a loaded shotgun. Margret runs straight into to the line of fire and tackles her mother before she has time to do any harm. Tilly, unsure if Margret is okay after she threw her own mother to the ground, trots over to investigate. Mother struggles to get up, and Tilly pushes her face into Mother's face to see what's going on. Mother continues to struggle to escape Margret's hold, and Tilly, as Margret's protector, gives a head butt to Mother's forehead and knocks her cold.

Tilly resumes eating her smorgasbord of roses while Margret drags Mother over to the shade under an arbor covered with climbing roses with oversize yellow blossoms. The insanity of the scene is softened by the sea of tea rose blossoms in every color gently bobbing up and down on a light breeze. Margret watches Mother's unconscious face melt into soft folds of well-fed skin and a sweet smile – something Margret hasn't seen since Annie passed.

It is in this moment that Margret finds her release from years of abuse by her Mother. She kisses her mother's cheek, puts Tilly in the Gorilla and returns to the arbor to wait for her mother to regain consciousness.

"Where am I? What happened? Margret? How long have I been asleep?"

". . . a long time Mother."

"What's going on? I thought I saw a goat in my rose garden!"

"You did. You saw, Tilly, my goat."

"You have a goat?"

"Yes."

"That's not possible. Where have you been? You really have a goat?

"Yes. Her name is Tilly."

"Where's your father?"

"He's passed Mother. Annie and Daddy are dead."

"Who's Annie? And stop calling your father Daddy. It's disrespectful. He's Father. I'm Mother. Who's this Annie?"

"Annie is your favorite daughter, dead or alive, and my little sister."

"Strange, I don't remember her. What's happening?"

"I don't know Mother. Maybe all the booze you consume day and night has softened your brain. Maybe your brain is pickled."

Margret starts to laugh, and Mother joins in.

"I love pickles! What's your father's shotgun doing here

in my rose garden?"

"You tried to shoot my goat! I tackled you, and Tilly knocked you out."

"I tried to shoot Tilly? How could I? I love goats. Who doesn't love goats?"

Margret listens to her mother in awe and disbelief. She realizes she hasn't shared time with her mother sober since Annie died. She realizes her mother's grasp on reality has been permanently altered by alcohol and dementia. She sees this soft-skinned woman, disoriented and forgetful, in a new light. Mother is back in another form, and Margret is mystified.

"Mother, let's get you out of this garden and into the house. We have a lot to discuss."

Mother leans on Margret. They get up together and walk slowly to the glass wall that opens to the living room. After Mother is settled on the couch, Margret leaves her mother to move the Gorilla into the shade for Tilly. Mother insists on joining her. She wants to introduce herself to Tilly. Mother doesn't remember that she tried to shoot her.

Tilly is happy to see Margret and Mother. She carries no hard feelings. Mother is thrilled to see Tilly. She had a goat as a child, and Tilly brings back all the joy with her floppy ears, glass-like eyes and curious presence.

"Where did you get this awful truck? Tilly needs a van with a bed. Right, Tilly? I can see you need an advocate for animal rights, Tilly."

"This awful truck is a Gorilla. She's the top-of-the-line-off-road vehicle, she's mine, and Tilly loves her. She's rugged and footloose like me and Tilly. Climb in, Mother. I'll take you for a drive."

Pleased with the opportunity to be near Tilly, Mother accepts Margret's invitation and her help to climb aboard the Gorilla. Tilly, endlessly curious, nibbles Mother's colorful shirt while she sits on the bench beside Tilly. Margret chauffeurs Mother and Tilly to "Tilly's Farm."

"Here we are kids."

Margret smiles at her own goat joke. Mother and Tilly have enjoyed a playful journey to the farm – two "kids" on the back seat of the Gorilla.

"Where are we Margret?"

"We're at 'Tilly's Farm' Mother. This is where we live. Just a moment, and I'll help you out."

Margret jumps down and comes around to open the door for Tilly and Mother. Tilly leaps out and bounces to the front porch. Mother backs out and carefully steps onto the running board before she steps onto the gravel driveway. She straightens, turns around and sees a parklike scene of a goat-mowed meadow shaded by historic oak trees. The breeze carries the perfume of chaparral with a tinge of ocean air.

 Mother stands still.

"Margret I'm lost. I don't know where I am."

"You're home Mother."

"That's impossible. Where's my house? Where's your father? Where's Tilly? I'm all mixed up, Margret. I'm ready for a cocktail. Let's have a cocktail."

"I don't drink, Mother. Let's go inside."

Margret guides her mother through the meadow to the front porch. Tilly impatiently paws the wood planks then bounds over the steps on a run to see Mother.

"Tilly! I wondered where you were! What a lovely farm you have. Margret, isn't Tilly's farm splendid?"

"Yes, Mother. I'm pleased you like it."

"Can we stay for a while? Let's sit on the porch and have a cocktail together."

"I don't drink, Mother."

"Stop saying that."

"I'll take you around back and show you the barn where Tilly lives. Let's go."

Margret helps Mother navigate the uneven terrain and shows her the pool and barn. Mother is childlike in enthusiasm but hungry and thirsty. Tilly, too, is ready for food and water, and she eagerly enters her private quarters in the barn.

"Oh Tilly, I could live here. I love the smell of hay and an old barn. Unfortunately, I have to get back to my house and my roses, but I'll come again soon."

Margret locks Tilly in and helps Mother navigate her way back to the Gorilla. As she helps her mother onto the Gorilla front passenger seat, Margret considers her options. She can take Mother back to the glass palace and lock her into her bedroom for the night, or buy camping gear for Mother, and they camp in the barn with Tilly. She settles on a camp overnight with Tilly to ease into the obvious necessity of twenty-four hour surveillance for Mother. All the inebriated days masked Mother's cognitive decline. Mother's newly enforced sobriety unveils another story, and Margret's change of heart is timely.

"Mother, let's get an early dinner to go, and I'll bring you home."

Mother is relieved to have Margret make the decisions.

"I'll have a cocktail, when I get home."

Mother nods off, and they drive in silence to town. Margret does a drive through and orders burgers, fries and sodas. Mother smells the food and wakes up. Margret continues on to the sporting goods store. She locks Mother in the Gorilla with her take out meal and hurries into Dan's Sport Chalet for a sleeping bag and pad for her mother. The salesperson recognizes Margret.

"How'd the sleeping bag work for you?"

"Excellent. Do you have another one like it? I need another sleeping bag and pad for my mother."

"How fun to camp with your mom. I wish my mom would do that with me."

"Maybe she will one day. You never know."

"Oh no, not my mom, She can't stand camping!"

"Don't be too sure. You never know . . . you never know . . ."

Margret carries the new sleeping bag and pad and loads it into the back of the Gorilla. She climbs into the driver's seat and eats her take out while she drives.

"Margret, you know you mustn't eat while you drive. It's dangerous."

Margret laughs.

"So is running into the line of fire of a loaded shotgun!"

"Who would do that?"

"Someone trying to save a goat"

"Who would shoot a goat?"

"I have no idea, Mom."

"Who are you calling Mom?"

"You Mom, like Saul to Paul you have been born again with a new name."

"That's nonsense, I'm Mother."

"From this day forward you are 'Mom' to me, and we're going camping together."

"Camp?"

Mom is quiet in her confusion. Margret parks in front of the farm house and takes Mom, the pad and sleeping bag into the house. She sets up a bed next to her campsite by the fireplace.

"Where are we?"

"We're home, Mom. You live here with me and Tilly now."

"I do?"

"Yes, the big house is for sale. I'll move all your roses here. You'll have your own room, bathroom and forty acres as long as it is safe."

"I don't understand. Where's Tilly?"

"I understand that you don't understand, and it's okay. I'm in charge, and you are safe. Tilly is in the barn, and we'll visit her in a minute. It's time you know that the game has changed, and it's better for everyone. No worries. You might even learn to dance."

Mom is tired and looks for a place to lie down. She sees Margret's cozy nest and lies down for a nap. She feels something hard underneath her and pulls up the framed photo of her husband."

"Who's this fishing and why is it in this sleeping bag?"

"It's Daddy, Mom."

"Yes! Father loved to fish and camp with you! He was a wonderful man. And oh did he ever love you!! Where is he?"

"He's gone, Mom."

"Oh."

Mom gets comfortable and falls asleep. Margret is astounded at the change in her mother's nature. She pulls her cellphone from her back pocket and calls her personal physician. He makes recommendations, and Margret begins the journey of caring for her mom. She contacts Sandy, the real estate woman who handled "Tilly's Farm," to ask if she would handle the sale of the glass palace. Next, she calls her lawyer, a long-time associate of her father, to acquire power of attorney and a health directive for her mom. She also calls an estate sales agent to begin to divest the vast collection of furniture and art that belongs to her mom.

Margret sits on the floor next to her napping mom. She appreciates the simplicity of her new home and experiences an odd sense of peace to hear her mother gently snore. It's like a tsunami or a wildfire destroyed what was and leaves nothing but what is. The shock leaves a blank canvas, and Margret can paint whatever picture she wants. Margret embraces this new situation with bold strokes and paints the new picture with bright colors. She loves her new palette and intends to make the most of what she has.

TWENTY- ONE

Anton is still in shock from the whirlwind of events that now place him as head of his embryonic dance company. He's filled with gratitude for Vanessa and Margret and excited to bring Anton Dance Company to the same professional level he experienced in Cuba. He stops to pick up his usual *Bucanero* beer for dinner and his soda and chips for his evening reverie under the Sunset Road sign.

Tonight the sky is reminiscent of Port Havana at sunset, and Anton feels a sting of homesickness. He checks the time and sees 7:00 p.m. in California is 10:00 a.m. the same day in Cuba – and the perfect hour to call home. He dials his mother to share all the head spinning news.

"¿Hola?"

"Hello?"

"Hola, Mamá…"

"Hello Mama."

"¡Anton! ¿Cómo estás mi hijo?

"Anton! How are you?"

"Mamá estoy bien. Te echo de menos. Los extraños a todos. Tengo una gran noticia."

"Mama I'm fine. I miss you. I miss you all. I have great news."

"Tengo una nueva compania de baile y un espectaculo en tres meses."

"I have a new dance company and a show in three months."

"¡Bravo hijo!"

"Bravo son!"

"¡Mamá, quiero que toda la familia vea el espectáculo!"

"Mama I want the whole family to see the show."

"¿Es posible?"

"Is it possible?"

"¿Quieres ver el espectáculo?"

"Do you want to see the show?

"¡Si! Todo queremos ver el espectáculo."

"Yes! We all want to see the show."

"Esta bien, mamá, puede comenzar a reunir documentos de viaje. Visas y pasaportes."

"Okay mama, you can start gathering travel documents. Visas and passports."

"Si, Anton. ¡Gracias!"

"Yes, Anton. Thank you!"

"Llare de Nuevo cuandoenga las fechas exactas. Ese bien mamá. ¡Te quiero!"

"I'll call again when we have the exact dates. That's good mama. I love you!"

The connection is not clear. Anton says goodbye and starts his car for home. He thinks about his Mama riding in his sports car with the top down. The show will be in mid-November, so the sun will still be warm, and Mama can feel the wind in her hair like a young girl.

Luisa is at the door and ready to go in. Anton carries his left over chips, empty soda can and *Bucanero* into the house. He tosses his trash in the waste basket under the sink and obeys Luisa's demand to fill her dish with the usual kibble topped with canned salmon. Anton is eager to watch baseball and skips dinner.

Tonight he's focused on ideas for his dance company and takes notes on particular moves he would like to include in the choreography. He particularly likes the homerun swing linked to the catcher's signs to the pitcher, and the runner taking his time running the bases after a homerun hit. Baseball is all about the art of the steal, so the game suits the libretto. Anton makes sketches and notes. He almost forgets who is playing on TV. It is the ballet of baseball that catches his attention at the moment. He uses the moves to tell the story of the immigrant shopkeeper, and, by the end of the game, he has a skeleton dance sketched out on paper.

After an evening of baseball, Anton is usually ready for bed. Luisa anticipates "good night" and goes to the bedroom and curls up on her side of the bed. Anton continues to create more choreography. He closes his eyes and sees the show happen before him.

The show opens. The children and adults present dances with the Flamenco band. This is the warm up act for the Anton Dance Company. He sees his flamenco-tango-rock-opera fusion unfold on the Civic Auditorium stage with a rear screen projection of an Old Town downtown jewelry store. He storyboards the dance, and each scene has a new image of precious gems. The professional lighting will highlight the colorful dancers on stage. Anton makes a list of other professionals to hire for the show: a lighting director, a stage manager, a still photographer, videographer, professional male flamenco dancers for group scenes and the flamenco band.

Before Anton goes to bed, he makes notes of possible show schedules with tentative dates. He lists a program for the event with bios for the professionals, and plans free refreshments before the show to bring the audience together. A Cuban food truck is another addition as well as coffee, water and sodas. He takes time to quiet his thoughts. He changes into pajamas and settles his head on his pillow. His go-to-for-peace Rosary is always at hand. He says prayers for every aspect of the show and wonders if he has fingered enough blessings on the people who will make this show come to life. He realizes there's not enough beads and runs through his Rosary three times. At last, he places the Rosary back on the night stand and closes his eyes with a peaceful smile.

Dawn arrives, and Anton jumps out of bed eager to get to the beach to practice some of his dance sketches on the packed sand. He parks in his usual place, gets out and goes to his trunk to put his sweats on over his dance clothes. He doesn't notice the three men that watch him from a picnic table near the wetlands. Anton carries his phone and keys in his sweatshirt pocket after he locks his car. He's preoccupied with dance routines when one of the three men approaches him and asks for money. Anton is surprised, says "no" and continues his walk to the beach. The beggar follows him, and the other two draw closer. Anton takes off running. He runs into the dunes and disappears from view. He runs effortlessly and leaves the three men in confusion about where their mark went.

Anton waits hidden in the dunes. He tentatively ventures out to the vast-empty stretch of isolated beach with no one in sight. He begins to practice his new routines. The undeterred malcontents appear on top of a dune and see Anton doing cartwheels on the hard sand. Anton rolls along facing the dunes. He suddenly sees the beggar and company and takes off running again. This time he runs straight into the vanishing point of the tide and cliff. The malcontents consider the distance and turn back to the parking lot. Anton feels intense anxiety and doesn't trust that the men will leave him alone. He considers calling Vanessa or Margret, but is concerned they might run into the same three thugs.

Anton weighs his options. Stay in the dunes or return to the parking lot. He incorporates the fear and uncertainty he feels into his dance ideas for his jewelry theft in his flamenco story. He changes the scary situation into art. Anton imagines he's a weak antelope chased by a hungry cheetah. He lays limp on the sand and waits for the cheetah to clamp onto his neck. The cheetah is suddenly distracted by a hyena, and the weak antelope gets up and runs back to the herd. It's an important story insight Anton would have missed if his morning had been tame.

Anton returns to the parking lot. He starts his car, and the engine purrs while Anton revisits Kenya, and the proverbial elephant (the three bullies) crowd his imagination. This prehistoric Mammoth threatens and frightens until he disappears into the sea without drama. Anton embraces the opportunity to expand his creative expression. He uses his present day challenge as a catalyst for choreography.

Anton stops at Lupe's for his usual pastry and cappuccino. He asks her if there have been any more problems with immigration. Lupe laughs.

"Oh no, the officer and his partner come every morning for coffee and pastries. Can you imagine? They study Spanish now!!! What a curious world! We should all have such an expensive car!"

Anton high fives Lupe, hurries out the door and drives to the dance studio.

Margret is first to arrive.

"Hola, Anton! I can't wait to see what you have boiled up in your pot of creative juices!"

Anton laughs,

"And I can't wait to see how you and Vanessa interpret the moves! You seem anxious. Is everything alright?"

"Ha! I just moved my mom to "Tilly's Farm" and her mind is mush. I found a caretaker for today, but I need a long-term-care team to keep her out of trouble. The beauty is that we found a happy place together, and I want to have her with me to make up for lost years. Oh, and I want her to learn to dance Flamenco! It saved me, perhaps it can save her!"

"That's a great idea! A flamenco class for seniors, Anton's Dance Studio is a community center!"

Vanessa and Susie arrive.

"Howdy, what's in store for us today?"

Margret jumps in.

"Anton went to the beach again. You can bet it's a limb twister."

Vanessa adds to the repartee.

"Foot and hand grinder."

Anton places Susie on the siesta couch, kisses the top of her head and laughs,

"Stay, Susie! Vamanos dancers!"

Vanessa hurries to the loan closet, and Margret stands in front of the mirror directly in front of Anton to catch every nuance. Vanessa straps on the size seven flamenco shoes, twirls her skirt and shows off her butterflies. Anton is impressed,

"Perfect, you can teach a special class on butterfly art."

Margret chimes in,

"We'll advertise. Learn to be a butterfly, hummingbird or both at the Anton Dance Studio."

Vanessa laughs, and Anton gets serious. He puts on a CD of flamenco guitar. Anton's feet warm up, he hovers like a hummingbird, snaps his arms and legs and claps his hands in energetic rhythms.

Anton leaps to another level. The first and second bases are loaded. He stands sideways to the mirror, lifts his leg and he swings his arm around like a rag. He stretches his leg to the farthest reach to anchor his body against the mound, and heaves an imaginary hardball ninety-five miles an hour into the strike zone where the opposing team is lined up to wait for their turn at bat. Each player warms up for their opportunity to smash the ball into another dimension. Anton's drum line of heels hits the hardwood floor without mercy, his arms swing and the whole weight of his body hurls itself into the throw.

Margret and Vanessa are stunned and terrified at the sheer force of Anton's hundred and fifty percent engagement, as he shows them what being bullied at the beach can do to a person's psyche. Anton doesn't stop to show Margret his choreography or pretend that he is aware that he has left them behind. Anton has entered a level of consciousness that offers him an extraordinary power of expression, and he intends to stay on this playing field.

Margret and Vanessa recognize the game has changed, and much more will be demanded of them as this flamenco show evolves into its final presentation. Anton struggles to calm down mentally and physically and return to earth.

"Excuse me. I need a moment to collect myself."

Anton walks outside for air. The small-white clouds drift slowly across the blue. Anton watches them and breathes to match their gentle roaming. Moments later he re-enters the dance studio ready to develop the pieces of the new work into art. Anton faces the mirrors, and Margret stands behind him to follow his choreography. He shows Margret the dance for the jewelry store owner. Margret follows with accurate steps but lacks assurance.

"Excellent Margret, hold on to the insecurity. This is an immigrant bullied with immigration issues. Her posture is tentative. As you inspect your precious handcrafted masterpieces in the cases, you grow more confident and proud of what you have accomplished. The necklace of precious gems is the pinnacle of your artistry, and you are filled with joy. You unlock the case, put on the necklace and dance with complete abandon. When you see two young men enter the store, you put the necklace back and forget to lock the case."

Margret listens to Anton as intently as she watches his steps.

"Are you ready? Now that you have the steps along with the story, lay your own experience over it. As you dance, relive a time when you experienced great happiness after a difficult struggle. Take a moment to find that emotional doorway."

Margret listens to the guitar music while Anton and Vanessa clap flamenco rhythms. She relives the first time she went fly fishing with her father and watched him cast his line, tipped with a colorful-tied fly, over Wyoming's Snake River. She relives the beauty of the light that sparkles on the running-water surface, and the earthy smell of the rocky shallow under her feet on the river's edge. She sees her father's face as he turns to smile at her when a fish jumps high out of the water to capture the buzzless fly.

The emotional doorway is wide open. Margret dances like the river she smells, and the fishing line she sees float through the air. Each turn-bow-leap-tap and land grows in intensity. When the fish jumps into the air, the footwork Anton showed Margret becomes a dance of pure joy, and her fingers spin the silky goo of a perfectly roasted marshmallow stuck on the end of a willow branch. Her feet sing like drums, and her skirt flashes up-down-around to display legs like forest trees – strong and well rooted. Her arms reach out like an embrace of a dear friend, and she puts the priceless necklace around her neck. Her hands circle in a graceful flurry around her head until she can no longer hold them up.

When she sees the two young men enter her store, she is nervous and embarrassed. She hurries to replace the necklace under the glass. She forgets to lock the display case. Her movements are rushed, graceless and weak like a young-frightened antelope separated from the herd. Margret is limp at the end.

Anton is the first to high-five Margret.

"Stunning, you set a perfect tone! Brilliant! You may not like the beach, but you have the power of a breaking wave.

Vanessa gives an extra high, high-five and shouts,

"Brava! Wherever that came from is beyond the beyond! Flamenco saves you!"

Margret laughs.

"I think I've got it . . ."

Vanessa confirms,

"You own it!"

Anton, Vanessa and Margret see the writing on the wall, and it is all good. Anton's dance company in Cuba taught him that your performance is only as good as your weakest link. No weak links in this dance company. Margret moves aside, and Anton pushes ahead.

"Vanessa, you're up. We rehearse here as if we are on stage at the Civic Auditorium. What I gave you the other day was a rough sketch. Now we need to set the choreography."

Anton positions himself on stage left close to the wall of mirrors. Vanessa stands stage right as an observer. Anton reminds Vanessa that she is watching an armed robbery. He asks her to dip into her past, momentarily forgetting her PTSD, to relive a terrifying event as she dances her part while Anton dances his.

Vanessa begins a slide into an internal place of terror, as Anton adopts the dance of the aggressive armed-robber that threatens the immigrant jeweler. Like a predator, Anton steps into the store, and, with a gun pointing at the jeweler, steals the precious necklace he saw the jeweler place in the unlocked case. The flamenco guitar music intensifies, and Vanessa reaches a tipping point. Instead of disappearing backstage and reappearing singing a high C siren, she throws herself under the desk terrorized by the suicide bomb that just destroyed another marketplace.

Susie races to Vanessa, barks and pokes her with her nose, as Vanessa has trained her to do. Anton turns off the flamenco guitar music. Susie continues to bark and poke Vanessa to break her flashback. Vanessa crawls out from under the desk. Anton helps Vanessa stand, and Margret is there to steady her.

"It's okay Susie. It's okay. No bark."

Margret is amazed.

"How did Susie know what to do?"

Vanessa reaches down, picks up and hugs Susie.

"I trained her. I wasn't sure it would work, but she did it once on her own, and I saw the possibility of giving her the job. I don't even care if I have a flashback. Susie can fix it. I can't tell you the relief. By the time of the show, I should be so well rehearsed I'll be immune to the triggers."

Anton reassures Vanessa.

I know you're still shaken. Let's take a break then move on."

"I don't need a break. Let's continue."

Anton restarts the music, and Vanessa picks up at the point when she witnesses the armed robber threaten the jeweler. Vanessa's shrill high C siren shocks the armed robber and forces his retreat. The choreography is more precise, and Vanessa has no hesitation in taking it to the next level. Her ability to internalize the moves layered with authentic terror, now neutralized as a trigger, gives Margret goosebumps.

"Vanessa, all potential victims and police departments should be equipped with your other-world-high-C alarm. Your performance makes me shiver."

"This is enough for today. We have a foundation set, and you two dancers have gone beyond my expectations!"

Margret is eager to establish dates and have consistent information for the dance studio, and anyone else that is part of the production.

"Are we still on for Sunday at five to settle logistics?"

"Yes."

"Vanessa, does that still work for you?"

"Affirmative."

TWENTY-TWO

Vanessa is engaged in a solitary chess strategy when her phone rings. Her ring tone is a flamenco guitar clip that always makes her smile.

"Hello?"

"He's gone Vanessa . . .he's gone…"

"Mom?'

"He had another stroke, and he's gone! I can't believe it. He was doing a little better, but now he's gone. . ."

"Mom, are you okay? Is there someone there with you?"

Vanessa hears her mother sobbing.

"Oh mom, I'm so sorry. I'm so far away. Is anyone there with you?"

"No, it just happened. I was in the kitchen. I went into his bedroom, and he was gone. He's just gone. . . I can't stop crying. I'm the Rio Grande . . . a river of tears . . . he loved the Grand Canyon. He wanted to go there again, but it was just too hard . . . why didn't I take him? . . . Vanessa??"

"Mom, call the church and ask the priest to help you. I'm doing much better. I'll call the VA and see if I can get permission to travel. For now, call the church and talk to your priest. The priest will know what to do. Mom, get someone over to the house to be with you."

"I'll call the church . . . I'm so sad…"

"Yes Mom. Call the church. I'll come as soon as I can."

Vanessa hangs up, picks up her wallet, puts a leash on Susie, walks out of her studio apartment and heads to strip mall liquor store. She walks in and goes straight to the snacks. She buys a package of small-powder-sugar donuts, sits on the bench outside Anton Dance Studio and eats all six – one right after another. Her dad loved these donuts, and Vanessa finds comfort while she eats them. Susie senses the somber atmosphere and sits quietly in Vanessa's lap while the powder sugar sprinkles onto her fur.

Vanessa watches the cars pull in and out of their parking spaces, people go in and out of Glenn's Market, and people go in and out of the liquor store. It's a steady stream of humanity doing their daily activities. Vanessa thinks about how much time she missed with her dad, because she joined the Army, went to Afghanistan and came home a mess. She was so excited to think of the possibility that he could see the flamenco show, meet Susie, Margret and Anton and witness her victory over PTSD. She doubted after their last conversation that any of this would happen, but she had hope.

Vanessa is compelled to walk to the Episcopal Church in Old Town downtown with hope that the sanctuary is open.

When she arrives, she hears the organ. She chokes up, enters and sits near the organ consul. Dad loved Sundays, and church was a big part of that love. While she listens, she studies the ascending dove in the stained glass window. Susie sits under the pew with her nose resting on Vanessa's tennis shoe.

Vanessa gets up, as the organist begins to pack up and close down the organ.

"Thank you for allowing me to listen to you play. I love to hear organ pipes breathe music into a sanctuary. Something about the breathing makes the music come alive."

"Thanks for listening. I agree. There is nothing like the King of Instruments when it breathes. It's alive."

"Your music soothed my troubled heart."

"You're welcome here anytime,"

Vanessa half smiles, picks up Susie, walks out of the sanctuary and carries peace into the busy downtown. She remembers the real estate office and wonders if the Mediterranean house is still on the market. She and Susie head towards the intersection. Sure enough, the middle aged gentleman is in the office, and the picture of the house is still taped to the window.

"Hello there! Good to see you and your little dog again!"

"I'm pleased to see you, and I'm surprised to see that the Mediterranean house is still on the market."

"Me too, you ready to buy it?"

Vanessa laughs.

"Yeah ... in my dreams. . . thanks for allowing us to see

it. If I ever buy a house in the area, I'll be back! Oh, in three months, Anton Dance Studio and Anton Dance Company will perform at the Civic Auditorium. If you're interested, I can bring more information."

"Yes. Please do! Are you a dancer?"

"I am! I'm a member of the Anton Dance Company! It's going to be an amazing event. I'll keep you posted!"

"I look forward to it! My wife and I did ballroom dancing for years. She died two years ago, and I haven't danced since."

"Oh, I'm so sorry for your loss. Maybe the show will get you onto the dance floor again. It's so much fun to dance."

"You're right about that."

"Thanks again for your kindness. Susie and I are off to dance."

"Have fun."

"Yes."

Vanessa skips down the stairs and stumbles on the bottom step. She remembers saying to Margret "flamenco saved you" as she heads face first towards the cement. Sure enough, Vanessa gets her feet back under, lands upright and acknowledges flamenco saves her. Headed home, she thinks of her dad. She was in Afghanistan when her mom called to tell her about her dad's stroke. She sees herself start down the dark road of bad memories. She stops walking and, literally, turns around in a tiny full circle. When she resumes her walk home, her mind is turned around to the present, and the day is filled with brightly colored houses and gardens full of flowers. Vanessa dances a few steps down the sidewalk.

"Yes! Flamenco saves me!"

Back home Vanessa unleashes Susie and gives her a dog biscuit. She pulls out her phone from her back pocket, sits with her eyes closed for a few minutes then calls her mom.

"Hello . . .?

"Hi Mom, how are you doing?"

"Oh Vanessa, I called the church, and I'm certainly not alone anymore. They handled everything and are completely in charge. I'm able to rest a little. The priest came over and talked with me, and you know what the church meant to your dad. Everyone has been so thoughtful, and I'm grateful. You know I had no idea what to do. Thank you for telling me to call the church!"

"Are you alone or is someone with you today?"

"I'm alone right now, which is kind of a relief, but someone will bring dinner tonight and stay awhile to visit. It's the strangest thing. You're with someone every day for forty years and then they're gone. You wonder where it all went. All that time. A lifetime together . . . then they're gone . . . all that's left are photos, a closet full of clothes and shoes. It's the shoes. They really get to me. One church lady told me it was the shirts. It's the strangest thing . . ."

"Mom, I know it's all new to you, but what do you think of moving here. We could live together. We could share a house here."

"Honey, I have never lived anywhere but Texas!"

"I know, but it's nice here. I think you would like it. You wouldn't be alone, and I could help if anything went wrong…"

"I'm too old to move."

"Mom, you're not too old. You're too scared."

"No, I'm not scared. I've never been afraid of anything except scorpions!"

Vanessa laughs.

"You'll be happy to know there are no scorpions here!"

"Honey, that's so sweet that you would live with your old mother, but your old mother is Texas all day, every day. I can't imagine a move to California."

"Mom, you're not old. I know it's a new idea, but consider it. It might be fun."

"I like the word fun. I haven't known fun for a long time. I just get sad when I think. I'm going to consider it, because you didn't say 'think about it,' if that makes any sense!"

"I understand, Mom."

"You do? At least one of us does!"

Vanessa and Mom laugh.

"It's such a relief to laugh. Thanks, Honey for making me laugh. One more long face, and I'll shoot myself or them. Yes! Moving is scary as a scorpion in a hurricane, but I'll consider it. I guess Texas can get along without me . . ."

"No, Mom, you can get along without Texas!"

"I'll consider it."

"I gotta go, Mom. I love you."

"Bye Sweetheart. Thanks again for making me laugh . .

. your dad loved to make me laugh, God bless him . . . now you have the job!"

Vanessa and her mother are quiet. Vanessa gently whispers,

"Bye mom. I love you."

Vanessa ends the call and sees Susie stare at her with a cocked head.

"Susie, I think your Grandma might move to California!"

Vanessa sits down to her chess game and studies the board.

"I play solitaire chess, and I lose! How is that even possible? Come on Queenie. Step up! Be the power player you're designed to be!"

Vanessa sees an opening and moves a lowly pawn to checkmate the King.

"Ha! Take that!"

She laughs and looks at the time on her phone.

"Yikes! The business meeting for the show is now!"

Susie races to the door. Vanessa gathers the notes she made through the week and picks up Susie's leash. They arrive at the studio and see Anton and Margret have already started the meeting. Unleashed, Susie runs to Anton who catches her right before she lands in his lap.

"I apologize. The time got away from me!"

"That's okay. We got a lot done on logistics and, to bring you up to speed, Anton secured the Auditorium for four days! He also contracted the players for the flamenco band, hired three professional male flamenco dancers for the featured performance, a lead singer, a lighting professional and a set designer to transform the stage! Get ready California Central Coast!"

"I have a surprise too. I talked with my colleague and friend in Cuba who is a Flamenco dance artist extraordinaire, and he will join us!! I couldn't believe it when he said 'Yes!' He has an international reputation and is well known in Cuba. This is a great honor to have him come."

"With all the pieces in place, I will start to market ASAP. I have a ton of ideas, and, by our next meeting, you will see some interesting digital applications."

Vanessa brings out her notes and lays out her spread sheet to show how she'll be tracking expenses and income. She starts to explain the categories and stops mid-sentence. She lays her head on the desk and sobs.

"My father died today."

Margret reaches out and gently strokes Vanessa's back. Anton lifts Susie up off his lap and places her next to Vanessa's arm. Her head down and face hidden, Vanessa pulls Susie into her chest in a firm embrace. The crying slows, evolves to heaves and then a painful silence.

Margret whispers,

"I'll order pizza. Vanessa you stay right there and hold on to Susie. Anton what kind of pizza do you want?"

"Veggie is good and sodas."

"I'll order the large-special-veggie-deluxe, and we can stuff ourselves with cheese, mushrooms, artichoke hearts and whatever else they want to put on a veggie pizza. Vanessa you just cradle that little furry-fluff ball. We're here to see you through."

Vanessa pulls herself up and sits. Her nose is runny, and Anton jumps up to get a tissue. Margret is on the phone to order pizza, and Susie stays still in Vanessa's continued embrace. Anton puts on classical guitar music, and they wait in silence until the pizza arrives. Anton finds paper plates and napkins. Margret and Anton eat, and Vanessa drinks a soda.

"I apologize. It hit me like a cement truck. When I shared the spreadsheet and heard the details of the show, I realized Dad will miss the whole event, and it broke me. My Mom kept repeating "He's gone. He's gone." But it didn't get real 'til now. The curve balls just keep coming."

"Hey. No need to apologize. When my father died, I lived in shock for months. In some ways it still isn't real. I relive his presence every day in small ways. I have a special photo of him fly fishing, and that's how I keep him near me. I'm glad we have each other for support. Family is a big word and expands when we allow others in. What would I do without you and Anton? No, never apologize for a broken heart."

"Margret's right. Your wounded heart is our wounded heart. We live in a dance community, and one person's dance is everyone's dance, and, happy or sad, we all take a bow together. I can still smell my father's cigar. Life is rich, because we share. Vanessa, the way you dance is an inspiration to all of us. You can dance your way through."

Vanessa tries to soldier up, but the weight of her pack these last few years brings her to her knees. She curls up on the siesta couch and watches a parade of memories. She pulls into herself, curls into a tighter ball until even Susie is locked out. The solo classical guitar is the only audible sound in Anton's Dance Studio.

Anton and Margret finish the pizza, give bits of cheese to Susie, sit on the floor and silently support Vanessa. Anton gets up and goes to the studio door. He turns the "open" sign to "closed" while the late afternoon fades into evening. Margret helps Anton put Vanessa into his car to take her home. Anton locks the studio front door while Margret climbs into her Gorilla.

The strip mall is quiet. Anton remembers when Vanessa showed up on the bench outside his studio with her bottle of tequila in a bag, her surly attitude and her extraordinary ability to mimic choreography. A wave of compassion for Vanessa washes over Anton. He starts his car and takes Vanessa home to her studio apartment. Vanessa gets out of the car, and Susie follows her to the door. Vanessa turns and gives Anton a thank you with a flamenco butterfly, opens her door wide and disappears into the apartment.

Vanessa walks to the couch, forgets Susie is under foot, trips and falls to the floor. Her center is rocked to the core with her father's death. Her mom is guilty over a missed opportunity to take a trip to the Grand Canyon. Vanessa is guilty about a lifetime of postponed opportunities to spend time with her father. She rolls over and stares at the ceiling. He was always there for her, quiet and in the background. Now, he's gone for good. He couldn't believe she signed up to wear a uniform and was horrified when his fears were confirmed, and she came home broken with severe PTSD.

Vanessa continues to lie on her back on the floor. One memory stands out. She remembers the drive to California to go to Disneyland, and her mom wants to stay at the Disneyland Hotel. She sees her dad's jaw tighten and hears his voice get firm. "We'll stay at a hotel on the sand, in Huntington Beach." She sees a photo of her dad with a tall surfboard on the California beach. He looks happier than she's ever seen him look except when Ralph came into the room, she made a goal in soccer, or her mom wore a dress, and they went out to eat dinner and dance. Vanessa sees her dad show her how to dive under the waves and, after the waves break and roll over, how to come up for air. She hears him say, "This is a life lesson, Vanessa, never fight the waves. Just dive down, swim in peace and pop up when the rough stuff passes over."

TWENTY-THREE

"Margret, are you still here? Where are you?"

"I'm here, Mom. I'm in the kitchen."

"What are you doing?"

"I'm cooking, Mom. I'm making dinner."

"Oh."

Margret scrambles four eggs, toast stays warm in the oven, and peas are in a sauce pan on the stove. The table is set for two.

"Mom, are you hungry?"

"Yes. Where's Tilly?"

"She's in the barn, Mom."

"Where are you?"

"I'm in the kitchen. Where are you, Mom?"

"I don't know."

Margret gets two plates from the cupboard. She plates the eggs, toast and peas and carries them to the dining table. Mom sits on the new couch in the living room and watches the fire.

"Here, Mom, let's sit at the table by window and watch the sunset."

Margret escorts Mom to the table.

"Thank you, Margret. You're a wonderful cook."

"That's a stretch Mom, but I like the sound of it. I'm not a cook. I much prefer to do the dishes."

"I'm so glad to be here with you, Tilly and that handsome man that comes every day."

"You mean, John, the ranch manager?"

"Yes! That's him. He loves roses too."

"Not as much as you and Tilly! But he did do an amazing job transplanting all your roses! Mom, I have a lot of planning to do for this flamenco show. Do you want to be in here with me or spend time in the barn with Tilly?"

"Tilly!"

"Okay. I'll take you out to the barn and come back in a couple of hours. I'll bring the pastels, and you can draw."

"Thank you, Margret!"

Mom and Margret walk arm in arm to the barn. Inside, there's an area arranged for art projects. Some of Mom's drawings hang on Tilly's stall door. Tilly is thrilled to have visitors.

"I'll be back in a couple of hours. There's the intercom, if you need anything. Do you want some music, Mom?"

"Oh yes! Let's have Willie!"

"Willie?"

"Nelson, Willie Nelson!"

Margret hugs her mom, puts Willie on the boom box next to her Mom's collection of CDs and gives Tilly a pat on the head. Mom gets down to drawing, and Tilly watches Mom with great interest then returns to nibble her full bin of hay.

Margret returns to the living room and sits in front of the fire to gather her thoughts. She marvels at the shift in her relationship with her mom. It's a mystery she isn't able to solve, and she doesn't try.

"I have two hours to spend. I'm certainly not going to sit here and waste them on bad memories!"

Margret gets her laptop and pulls up a video of Anton's friend, Alvaro, performing in Cuba.

"And I thought Anton was incredible. This guy, Alvaro, is insane!!!"

Margret shifts to her marketing plan for the flamenco show. With this level of talent, Margret is inspired to pull out all the stops. She makes lists of who to contact and columns for dates when contacted, follow ups and commitments. Margret is a pro, and nothing escapes her eye for detail. She inputs Anton's contacts and coordinates all the elements that make for a flawless production. Two hours fly by, and Margret remembers Mom and Tilly. She closes shop and hurries out to check on the artist and her goat.

The barn door creaks opens, and Tilly lifts her head off Mom's lap. They both nap on the straw bedding, but Tilly wakes up with Margret's entrance. Mom continues to snooze while Margret studies Mom's new pastel drawings.

"Wonder why I didn't get any art genes? These are good! Okay Mom, time to go to bed."

"I'm in bed."

"Yes, you're in Tilly's bed, and now it's time to move to your bed."

"Tilly's bed is my bed."

"Yes, it's super cozy, and so is your bed. Let's go. You can play with Tilly in the pasture tomorrow. Now it's bedtime. Your drawings are amazing!"

Mom gets up, brushes off the straw and looks at her drawings.

"I want to do a portrait of you to go with Tilly. My two best friends."

"I'd love that, Mom."

Margret and Mom walk back to the house linked at the elbows. Mom's bedroom is off the kitchen with a view of the pool and the barn.

"Mom, maybe you want to dance flamenco."

"Me?"

"Yes, you! The way you've taken to Tilly, I'm thinking you might take to flamenco."

"I do love Tilly!"

"Mom, consider it. . . Sweet dreams."

Margret tucks Mom in, leaves and locks the door.

Morning comes, and Margret wakes with the idea to take a ride on her mountain bike. There's permanent help for Mom, and the ranch manager has Tilly handled, so Margret feels free to explore the countryside.

"Let's get out of here you highway flyer!"

The morning is full of sunshine and the smell of freshly mowed alfalfa from the ranch next door.

Margret eyes the dirt-fire road ahead.

"What the hell, it's a dirt bike!"

At full speed, Margret barrels up the dirt road and bounces over shallow ruts. She struggles to stay on her bike. The road climbs a gentle hill shaded by mature oak trees. There, all alone, a goat grazes by the edge of the road. Margret slams on the brakes and stops. The goat looks up, sees a friendly face and marches over to investigate. Her ears and tail flick and wiggle while curiosity takes her fearlessly up to Margret and the bike.

"Oh my God, you're Tilly's twin! I wonder if you got left behind like Tilly did. No worries. Stay here. I'll be right back!"

Margret, filled with new purpose, rides the road like a bull rider, and, by the grace of God, arrives safely at the intersection of the paved road to home. She races down the middle of the road to "Tilly's Farm," jumps off her mountain bike and runs inside for the fob to the Gorilla. Mom is eating breakfast.

"Mom, Tilly's twin is just up the road. Let's go get her!"

"Tilly has a twin?"

"Yes! No time to explain. Let's go!!"

Mom jumps up ready for adventure. Margret is already out the front door and running to the Gorilla. Mom's attendant watches with surprise. Margret and Mom load into the Gorilla and speed down the driveway and onto the paved country road. Mom is exhilarated.

"Margret is this you ... you're a wild gypsy!"

"Yes, Mom, and isn't it fun!"

The wind rushes through the open windows, and Mom claps her hands and shouts,

"Olé!"

Margret laughs and sings,

"Old MacDonald had a farm E-I-E-I-O ....hold on tight, Mom!"

Margret makes the same sharp turn onto the dirt road and speeds over the ruts and bumps until she reaches the bend where she left Tilly's twin. She stops the Gorilla, gets out and scans the valley for a wandering goat. No goat in sight. Margret shrugs off disappointment, turns around and walks to the driver's side of the Gorilla. As she climbs in and tells Mom Tilly's twin is gone, she feels a nibble on her pant leg.

"So where did you come from?"

Tilly's twin climbs into the Gorilla and settles on Mom's

lap.

"Tilly, how did you get here?!"

"No Mom, she's Tilly's twin."

"Tilly has a twin?"

"Not a real twin, but they look alike."

"What's her name?"

"Gypsy!"

"Oh yes, yes Gypsy. She's one of us!"

Margret smiles at Mom thinking of herself as a gypsy.

"Let's get back to camp, Mom"

The ride home is as wild as the ride out. Tilly and Gypsy are instant friends, and Mom is happy to spend the day in the barn. She draws with pastels or works in the garden and tends her roses. Margret finds her dance bag and changes into her black Anton Dance Studio tank top and flamenco skirt.

"We need a signature outfit for Anton Dance Company! And merchandise to sell at the show. Gypsy branding! The Gorilla is the new gypsy cart!"

Margret climbs into her Gorilla and arrives at the studio at the same time Anton unlocks the door.

"I thought you would be whirling around practicing your beach choreography."

"Not this morning. I'm helping my mother get a visa and passport for travel to see the show. I hope she can get the documents in time. I hoped to get the whole family over here, but it's down to just my mother."

"Your mother will come to the show?"

"Yes! She's my biggest fan!"

"That doesn't surprise me! You are the darling of every mother, which reminds me . . . my mother moved in with me, along with two goats. Now she thinks she's joined a gypsy camp. I suggested she dance flamenco. Can Anton Dance Studio seriously handle a flamenco dance class for seniors?"

Vanessa, who came through the front door minutes after Margret, joins the conversation.

"I wondered the same thing! I'm trying to convince my mom to move here and thought a flamenco dance class could keep her dancing. She loved to dance with my dad."

Anton is onboard.

"Excellent. We have two seniors to start. We need a minimum of six to make it viable and a teacher…Vanessa?"

"Oh yes! I'm happy to teach, and I know a real estate salesman who might be interested in the idea!"

"I'll make a flyer and post it on social media and our website. 'You old goats get out here and dance!' What do you think?"

Anton is taken a back.

"I'm not sure 'old goats' is the best image."

"You're right. I was thinking of my mom and my goats with their hard hooves."

Vanessa weighs in,

"People aren't old, they're seasoned. Bill it as, 'Stay young in every season. Anton Dance Studio is for all ages.'"

"I'll take it. Anton what do you think?"

"Yes! Perfect. Let's dance."

The three principal dancers of the Anton Dance Company get into character. Each dancer is dressed to dance and primed to tell a story. The flamenco guitarist fans across chords while heels and toes tap and pound out drama. Nothing exposes the soul like a serious and talented flamenco dancer with a story to tell.

Anton directs Vanessa and Margret to take up at the jewelry store robbery. Vanessa dances from the back of the studio on a shrill high-C siren POLICE!! Anton stumbles in surprise, drops the precious necklace and races out of the store in terror. At center stage, outside the store, his legs jackhammer the floor in frustration. He creates a solo display of choreography that amplifies anger, confusion and disappointment with his failed attempt at armed robbery. Margret remains frozen at the jewelry case, and Vanessa circles around the hopeless thief with an unrestricted high-C siren. Anton stops the dance drama.

"Perfect. Now here's the choreography for the police. There will be a swarm of dancers in sync for the show, but for now I will demonstrate the basic choreography. The police arrive on the scene from the front left and right sides of the stage with castanets sounding like machine guns while three male dancers rattle the establishment in lockstep flamenco dance moves based on baseball's art of the steal. The bandit escapes, and the police devolve into an immigration interrogation of the store owner about her immigration status. Here's the choreography for the swarm."

Anton gathers his arms, tipped with castanets, into a straight pillar against his body with legs marching, and his head whipping left and right. He swings his arms from side to side in military precision. The castanets play continuous drumrolls. Anton's moves are reminiscent of military drills, as he changes from pursuit of the thief to intimidation of the victimized Latin-jewelry-store owner. Anton is happy with the way the choreography develops.

"The dance is only as good as the technique that enables it. Let's spend some time on technique."

Vanessa and Margret appreciate the shift of focus and ask detailed questions about various sections of the choreography. Anton goes over the nuances of the castanets and patterns in footwork, arms and hands. Vanessa watches, and Margret films sections that demand precision. Anton selects several flamenco dance videos on YouTube to illustrate technique.

"Anton, thanks for taking apart some of the sections and showing us more technique. I know I grasp the choreography easily, but the details give me fits, and I definitely have to practice."

"Thank God, I have my phone and can film this tornado! It takes me twice as long to process new choreography even with my reference video."

"No worries. You both are professional in your talent and approach to learning. I am exceedingly proud of Anton Dance Company. I can't wait for Alvaro to meet my dancers! Believe me when I tell you he will be impressed!"

Margret quips,

"If we impress Alvaro, I'll fall down dead and wake up in heaven!"

Anton and Vanessa laugh, and Susie barks at hearing a playful tone in the studio.

"I hope you don't ascend until after the show. We need you! My friend Alvaro will be happy that I have such a creative and talented team."

The dance trio closes up the studio, and each dancer goes their separate way. Each one still laughs while they know the next couple of months will demand total commitment to the art of flamenco.

TWENTY-FOUR

Anton is filled with more ideas for the choreography after the morning practice with Vanessa and Margret. He opts for a late afternoon at the beach to release his restless imagination.

The ocean is a pot of un-tamed waves that roar, churn and twist over each other. It is the relentless flow of salt water whipped into millions of tiny bubbles and pushed by the undercurrent that makes this beach unsafe for swimmers. The wind blows against the layers of a choppy sea and shoots mist over the backs of the powerful tumblers.

Anton stands ankle deep while he faces the ocean and deep breathes the sea-fresh air. The contagious energy of the massive force that spreads over the sand then slips back out beneath the next inward surge exhilarates. The tide rises faster than Anton anticipates. A bigger wave rushes over his feet with unusual force, and pulls him down to his knees. A rock trips his effort to stand back up, and another wave swoops in and buries him. Anton tumbles around. He is captive in a riptide. Occasional signs up and down the beach warn swimmers to beware of danger, but there are no lifeguards on this remote beach to protect the naive, visitor.

Anton is tossed around like a piece of unattached seaweed carried out to sea on a stream of rebellious current. He is helpless in Neptune's grasp. A panic builds, as he is unable to free himself from the rapid-flow ocean channel that ferries him away from a cove-less shore to the deep ocean beyond the waves. Anton tires in the cold water. He feels a desperate need to swim against the current, but he wisely lets go. He floats aimlessly until the riptide spits him out. He bobs up and down, far out at sea and way to the left of where he started.

Anton recognizes the danger he faces and waits for some sign that signals safety. The cold is an equal danger as the waves that pummel him and dull the will to live. He resists his desire to give up and begins to swim the long distance to shore. He is exhausted and doesn't dare to look beyond his tired strokes. With his head down, he plows ahead breathing every other stroke.

The ocean here is a death trap for swimmers, and a mecca for wind surfers. Today because of the wind, a wet-suited-wave jumper plays in the ocean where Anton struggles to stay afloat. The windsurfer rips toward a wave, and, as his sail lifts him up into the air, he catches sight of Anton and recognizes that the swimmer is in serious trouble. He lands on the ocean, checks his speed, comes about and pulls up next to Anton. The windsurfer quickly unhooks his sail, boom and mast from his board while choppy swells continue to wash over him. He slides his windsurfing equipment into the sea and holds onto his board.

The windsurfer trusts his wetsuit and his own physical fitness. He puts his life jacket on Anton and tells him the only way they will survive is if they use every ounce of strength and paddle straight to shore. He tells Anton to hold on,

"It's your life you're holding onto to so hold tight!"

Anton, now dressed in the wind surfer's life vest, musters enough strength to climb onto the board and stretches out flat. The windsurfer lies down on top of Anton to protect and warm him, and they both use their arms to paddle toward the shore. They stroke in rhythm like a four legged sea turtle on a raft, until they float to shore on the tide. The sea seems reluctant to let them go, but they are finally able to walk out of the churning water and flop exhausted on the shore.

Anton sees the rocks they barely missed, and the slow setting sun that saved them from darkness. He shivers out of control.

"I'll replace your sail, and I thank you a thousand times for putting your life at risk to save me. I'm forever indebted to you."

"Save your breath. We need to get you someplace warm!"

They slowly walk up the beach to the wetlands and parking lot. The only vehicles in the lot are the windsurfer's truck and Anton's sports car. The windsurfer pulls a blanket out of his truck and wraps Anton in a bundle of wool. He hands Anton his shoes that they stopped to pick up near the retaining wall close to the train trestle.

"You're brave to bring a car like that to a remote beach like this! I'd be looking over my shoulder the whole time. Beat up truck like mine, no problem."

Anton's reminded of the bullies and smiles while he shivers.

"Yeah, it can be a rough neighborhood. But here we are, and you saved my life! I can't thank you enough!"

"That's what lifeguards do. I grew up on the beach, was a lifeguard in high school, joined the Coast Guard after high school and now work in the surfing industry."

"I, at least, want to replace your equipment."

"Forget it. Like I said, I work in the industry and get stuff sent to me all the time to test. How'd you get caught in the waves anyway? You definitely aren't dressed to swim!"

"I'm a flamenco dancer and came here to work out some choreography. I was standing in the high tide, and a wave knocked me down. Before I knew it, I was in a riptide and headed for China."

The windsurfer stretches out his hand,

"My name's Will. Those little rogue waves are deceptive."

Anton grasps Will's hand with both of his hands.

"I'm Anton, thank you many times over!"

"Forget it. Let's get you into your car and on your way. You were fortunate that I decided to go wind surfing this afternoon. It looked rough and cold. I almost didn't go! You head home, have a warm bath and some hot soup. You could still be in trouble if you don't warm up inside."

"I'm certainly grateful you decided to ride the wind today!"

The two men wave each other off, get in their vehicles and drive away. Anton is still in shock. The near death experience sinks in, and all the "what ifs" terrify him. The heater on full blast isn't able to thaw the chill, as he confronts his mortality. He pulls the dashboard tray out and fishes for his Rosary. Anton's hands are numb and still shake while he kisses the cross. He continues to drive, but his shaking increases until he is forced to pull over. Parked on the side of the road, he calls Vanessa,

"Hello?"

"Vanessa?"

"Anton??"

"Vanessa, I'm sorry I missed the adult class and children's class. I hope Maria had a key, and no one was locked out."

"Anton, where are you? Your voice is shaking and slurring! Are you okay?"

"I'm on the side of the road to Ocean Beach Park. I almost drowned."

"Drowned???"

"Yes, I was knocked down by a rogue wave, locked into a riptide and carried out to sea. A windsurfer saved my life, but I can't stop shaking. My hands are blue. I'm shaking so much, I can't drive."

"My God, Anton, how terrifying. Stay there. Turn the heater up all the way. I'll call a car to bring me to where you are. Do you have any dry clothes?"

"No everything is wet. I have the wool blanket the windsurfer wrapped around me."

"Take off the wet clothes and stay wrapped in the blanket. I'll bring some dry clothes. Get out of the wet clothes immediately. Put your bare feet up to the heater to keep them warm."

"Okay. Thank you Vanessa."

"I'll be there right away. Don't try to drive."

Vanessa's military training kicks in. She's well aware of how dangerous hypothermia is and calls a car to take her to Anton. Fortunately, there's one available in the neighborhood, and she gets to Anton in minutes. She thanks the driver and gives her a generous tip from the cash she stuffed into her pocket after she made the call for the car. Vanessa goes to Anton's car and sees he's asleep. Vanessa pounds on the driver side window.

"Anton! Wake up!"

Vanessa knows drowsiness is a dangerous symptom of hypothermia. She continues to pound the window. Anton doesn't respond, and Vanessa is determined to wake him. She knows the consequences if she doesn't. She looks around for anything she can use to break the window. It's dark, but she has her phone flashlight. Twenty feet away is a medium size rock that could work. She runs, grabs the rock, returns to the car, slams the rock full force against the window and shatters the glass. Anton still doesn't wake up.

Vanessa reaches through the window and unlocks the door. The alarm goes off, and Aton remains unconscious. Vanessa shakes Anton and tells him to wake up. He's groggy and slurs his words. She has no idea what he's saying. The shivers stop, and Vanessa begins to fear for his life. She presses the starter and restarts the car. The heater is still on and begins to blow hot air again.

Anton's feet must be warmed up. She lifts both feet and holds them in front of the heater. Next, Vanessa rubs Anton's hands to keep the circulation going. He did manage to get his clothes off and wrap himself in the wool blanket. Vanessa continues to talk and encourages Anton to wake up. She half wraps him in another blanket she brought along with a hoodie and sweat pants. She pulls the socks over his thawed feet. Finally, her efforts begin to have an effect. Anton opens his eyes, and Vanessa calmly explains the situation. She tells Anton he needs to stay awake and put on the sweat pants and hoodie.

"What happened? Who broke the window? Why am I naked? What's going on?"

Anton tries to get out of the car, but Vanessa convinces him to stay where he is and put on the hoodie and sweat pants. She knows from military training that the most important thing is to stay calm and be gentle with someone in hypothermia. Anton's confusion is intense, and he struggles to understand what's happening.

"Anton you nearly drowned. We need to raise your body temperature. I broke the window because the door was locked. You were asleep and wouldn't wake up. Is there anything in the trunk I can use to cover the window?"

"What are you doing in my car? I need to get home and feed my cat."

"We'll get home and feed your cat, but we have to cover the window first. Can you open the trunk?"

Anton fumbles around and pulls the lever to release the trunk. Vanessa reaches over and locks his door then slides out on her side and checks the trunk for anything that can stop the damp air from coming into the car. A roll of duct tape catches her attention. She grabs it, closes the trunk and opens the passenger side door. She takes the mat from the floor, circles around the car and tapes the mat on the outside of the car to cover the hole. Anton is awake, but still confused. He tries to get out of the car, but his coordination is impaired, and he can't get his legs to work for him.

Vanessa hasn't driven anything since her tour in Afghanistan. She is terrified at the prospect of driving, but she is aware that Anton must get into a warm bath as soon as possible. She goes to the passenger side of the car, reaches over and unlocks Anton's door. She takes his legs, gently lifts them over the center and places them on the passenger seat with his feet above the floorboard. Next, she goes around to Anton's side of the car, the driver's side, opens the unlocked door and lifts and shoves Anton up and over onto the passenger seat. Anton's confusion is amplified, and he tries to resist, but with no coordination in his legs he's helpless.

Boot camp and Afghanistan made Vanessa a fit survivor. She steels herself for the drive to Anton's house. She knows the stress of driving could trigger a flashback. Vanessa sits in the driver's seat and tries to quiet her mind.

"Anton, we'll be home in a few minutes. Everything is going to be okay."

The heater does a good job and warms the air in the car. Anton responds, and the shivers are back. It's a sign his body now works to heat itself.

Vanessa pulls onto the road, and Anton gradually becomes alert. The immediate danger is mitigated, but Anton still needs to submerge in warm water to raise his body temperature and stop the hypothermia. Vanessa passes oncoming traffic one by one, and each vehicle tests her ability to stay in the moment. She rounds the corner of Sunset Avenue and takes a deep breath. She turns into Anton's driveway, and there's Luisa waiting for dinner.

"Here we are Anton. Luisa demands dinner, but a warm bath is first on the list."

"Can you come in and make sure I don't drown in the bathtub. Where's Susie?"

"Susie's home, I didn't know where things were headed. I figured it best to leave her in charge of the home front. Can you get out of the car on your own?"

"I think so . . ."

"I'll bring the wet clothes, and, no, I won't let you drown in the tub. You turn on the heat, and I'll run the bath. I'll feed Luisa too. Enough talk."

Anton definitely comes around, goes straight to the back door and unlocks it. Vanessa is right behind him to make sure he can navigate the stairs. Luisa howls for dinner. Inside, Vanessa drops the wet clothes at the washer, goes to the bathroom and runs a warm bath. Anton turns up the heat and is eager to submerge himself in warm water.

"Vanessa, I've never been so afraid in my life, and, then after a while, I didn't care anymore. If that guy, Will? If he hadn't been out windsurfing, I'd be gone. And if you hadn't come to my rescue, I'd be gone again. I don't know how to thank you."

"Thank me by getting into that bath to raise your body temperature!"

Anton obeys and heads for the bath. Luisa paces back and forth and howls in front of the cabinet door that hides her food.

"I fed Luisa. I'll be in your living room. Shout out, if you need anything."

Vanessa sits on the couch. Finished with her dinner, Luisa stares at her from under the coffee table. Vanessa closes her eyes and dozes. She wakes with a start.

"Anton, are you all right in there?"

"I'm in the kitchen. Do you want anything to eat? I put a frozen pizza in the oven."

"I fell asleep. Do you have any soup?

"Yes, I saw you dozed off, so I gave you the same blanket that saved me"

"I wondered about the blanket."

"Soup is vegetable noodle. Do you want some?"

"No, thanks, pizza is plenty, but it's a good idea for you to have the soup."

Anton carries a tray to the living room with pizza and soup. Vanessa and Anton eat, and Vanessa can't help but notice the irony.

"Here we are eating cheese pizza and soup in your living room, and, not too long ago, I was drinking tequila from a bagged bottle on the bench outside your studio. I guess we were destined to save each other. Do you believe in destiny?"

"I guess I do. What else could explain the synchronicity of things? I mean what else explains Will windsurfing over me, at the exact moment I'm about to drown, and you knowing what to do with a frozen-flamenco dancer?"

"Is that destiny, chance or coincidence?"

"How about a three-in-one-beautiful-divine mystery directly connected to my Rosary!"

Anton laughs, and Vanessa continues to ponder.

"There were so many times in Afghanistan I had to wonder how it is that I'm here in this God forsaken barrenness, at war with itself, while others at home and around the world are shopping for Christmas at the mall. It's surreal."

"That's the perfect word for the pictures of this world. That's why I finger my Rosary and say little prayers. Yes, I guess I do believe in a kind of destiny, and the power of beads. Superstition perhaps, but today, I have to say, I believe a divine love coordinated my survival."

"Amen to that! And the show must go on. That's it! The show must go on regardless of what show it is. There you are! I hesitate to bring it up, but a studio-rehearsal event at the beach? Are you still okay with doing that? I do love the idea!"

"Absolutely, I want everyone to roar with the ocean, and feel the primal force that we will bring to the Civic Auditorium. I want everyone to feel their feet in the sand!"

Vanessa claps her hands and shouts,

"'Bravo!' Thank God you didn't die today. I want to dance flamenco on that stage and see the audience on their feet, clapping and shouting 'Olé!'"

"No doubt you will."

Vanessa gets up with the tray and carries it to the kitchen. Anton follows her and continues to thank Vanessa for everything.

"One more synchronicity . . . when you showed up in front of my window, drunk as a bar sponge, you brought a force of nature with you that swooped me up with Margret, and later Susie, and brought us together as family. I'm grateful for that fateful day."

"Yikes! That reminds me, Susie is at home wondering where I am! I have a lot to explain. Wait until I tell her what happened. She'll cling to you more now than she already does!"

Vanessa jumps up. Anton goes to the door, opens it and bows as Vanessa hurries away.

"Hasta la vista, Señor Anton, stay warm!"

TWENTY-FIVE

Vanessa sits with a cup of tea, studies her chess board with the ongoing game of solitary chess and wonders why she's so solitary. The loss of her father and almost losing Anton to the ocean unsettles a fragile peace.

"Hello…?"

"Hi Mom, it's your favorite daughter, Vanessa!"

"Sweetheart, you are my one and only favorite daughter! I'm so glad you called! You know, I've been thinking a lot about what you said, about moving to California, and I can't believe it, but I think it's a good idea.'

"Really…?? I thought I was going to have to cajole or beg you! What changed your mind?"

"You did. You asked me to consider it. The word "consider" is so gentle, such an invitation to ponder the idea, that California wormed its way in and bumped out Texas!"

"That's quite a bump!"

"Yes it is, and I'm ready to move anytime you say 'Come on, Mom!'"

"Come on, Mom, before you change your mind!"

"I can't stand another day of 'poor me' . . . your dad and I had so many good times. I don't want to gum it up moping around here wishing the recent past wasn't what it was. No, I'm ready for the present. I want to build a future on a new adventure. Child, I'm so happy you opened your door to me. I'll sell the house here, and we can find something in your neighborhood!"

"Seriously ...?"

"Dead serious, well, maybe not dead, but yes, serious."

"I'm amazed! Not long ago, Susie and I went for a walk to Old Town downtown. I happened to look at a real estate office window and saw a fabulous old-Mediterranean-style house for sale. I don't know why, but I asked if it was within walking distance, and if I could see it. This middle-aged salesman said 'sure' and gave me the key to let myself in to tour the house with Susie. Mom, it is crazy wonderful with an old stone wall around a big back yard."

"Child, ask that real estate salesman to email me photos and all the details on the property. If you like it, I know I'll love it. You, Dad and I have always loved old houses in historic towns."

"Mom it's listed at 950k. Is that a problem?'

"Sugar, money is no object. Your Daddy left us a Texas fortune. I only wish he was here to see the place. Now, I'm going to cry for a few minutes then stop the tears and buy a new-old house that he would love."

"Mom, you're a classic! I think "consider it" should be engraved on your grave stone!"

"I like that. Just hold off a few years, so I can enjoy what I've considered!"

Vanessa and Mom laugh again, and this time they laugh until tears are streaming down their cheeks. Suddenly, Mom goes quiet.

"Sweetheart, you have no idea what it feels like to laugh again. I thought I would never even smile again, let alone laugh. Let's get that house going. I love you to the moon and back – and that's a hell of a lot of love!"

"Bye, Mom. I can't wait to have you here!"

"Bye, Sweetheart."

Vanessa puts her phone down on the table, looks at her chess board and smiles.

"No more solitaire. Mom is one hell of a chess player. Susie, we need to go for a walk."

Susie leaps up and runs to the door. Vanessa takes the leash and clips it onto Susie's collar.

"Susie you're about to have a grandma's love and affection smother you. You'll have three people who adore you. How will you choose who to run to? Oh yeah, I know, Anton."

Off they skip to old town, and the real estate office that holds such promise. Vanessa looks at the window that still displays a photo of the classic Mediterranean house, and there, beyond the photo, sits the lovely gentleman that encouraged her to buy a house someday. He catches sight of Vanessa and gets up to open the door.

"Well hello! And what brings you to my neighborhood again?"

"A very special Mediterranean house listed still for sale in the window."

"Your stopping by is timely. There's been a flurry of interest lately, and one offer is pending."

"If it isn't too late, my mother would like all the details on the house via email. She lives in Texas, but my father recently died, and she wants to move to California to be with me. I told her about the house."

"It's never too late 'until the fat lady sings' and I haven't heard a note."

"I'll give you her email and phone number. In her words, 'Money is no object. Daddy left us a 'Texas fortune,' whatever that means, and she's ready to buy something."

"My guess is a Texas fortune is a lot of cash, and she has no worries. I'll email her ASAP and follow with a call to discuss the property. I hope it works out for you and your mom."

"Me too, and Mom loves to dance. I'm scheduled to teach a senior flamenco dance class. Maybe you'll join us."

"That sounds fun."

"It is, and so is my mom. Come Susie, we have a dance class to teach."

Vanessa and Susie walk down the street. Vanessa again appreciates the colorful houses and creative gardens. Susie appreciates the lawns. It's a town that works for dog lovers and dogs. Vanessa hopes the house purchase will work out and leaves it up to her mom and the real estate agent.

"Susie, we need to hustle. I want to arrive early for dance today."

Vanessa starts to run with Susie in tow. Susie speeds up and overtakes Vanessa to lead the way. Home in minutes, Vanessa changes into her new-black-flowing-flamenco skirt, tank top and shoes she secretly ordered with "Anton Dance Company" printed on the tank top. She enjoyed being a soccer star in high school. This new tank top reminds her of her days on the championship team. This little "Anton Dance Company" tank top restores a large measure of innocence.

When Vanessa and Susie arrive at the studio, Susie runs to the couch and wiggles her way to Anton and wakes him from a short siesta.

"It's good to see that you're resting. Yesterday was a nightmare. I hope you had pleasant dreams today."

"Yes! I chased yesterday away with a dream rehearsal at low tide."

"I'm happy to hear that! Such a rehearsal is beyond my imagination!"

"Maria is organizing the rehearsal details with parents, and Margret said she would ferry dancers to and from the beach. Some can go in the Gorilla, and parents are volunteering to get students to the beach. Margret is checking for low tide and following up on all the insurance requirements. I spoke with Lupe, and we'll stop at the bakery for coffee and Mexican pasteles after the rehearsal. Maria has all the permission slips for the children and written details for the adult class. It's happening!"

"I hope you'll tell the classes what you want to achieve with this rehearsal."

"Definitely, and I love your new outfit! 'Anton Dance Company' on your tank top is inspiring!"

"Margret has some ideas for fonts and image, but I wanted to give myself a boost and wear it now! I'm no good at waiting."

Anton claps his hands, and Vanessa lifts her skirt to her knees, does a drum roll with her feet and shows off her new dance shoes. Maria arrives with arms full of paperwork, fabric samples and tape measures for dress orders. Adult students arrive ready for instruction. Anton gathers the adult dancers together and briefs them on the beach rehearsal.

"Good afternoon dancers. Today I share more details of the special beach rehearsal. Maria has the time and place, list of parents who volunteered to drive and release forms. Also, I have a sign-up sheet for coffee, cappuccinos, hot chocolate, hot cider and pasteles when we stop at Lupe's Panaderia on the way back from the beach."

Anton continues his announcements to the adult class.

"The reason for this mandatory-special-outdoor rehearsal is to take you to a primal experience so that you can translate it into your expression of flamenco, and allow your soul to govern your choreography. You'll learn to layer your dance with honest emotion. I want to share my favorite rehearsal spot, and show you the freedom you can find when you allow your spirit to soar with the wild sea birds, and the restless ocean while you do variations on the basic flamenco moves over the hard sand at low tide. I want you to dance with nature and celebrate flamenco in a new way. This has nothing to do with how well you dance. It has everything to do with how far you are able to let go and move from the inside out. I want you to listen to the sound of the sea, to watch the waves as they tumble into and over each other, to smell the beach perfume, touch the ocean wilderness and move with the rhythm of the natural world."

The adults are silent as they listen to Anton's revelation of where and how he finds his inspiration. His speech emphasizes how serious Anton is when he shares flamenco and reveals his personal aspiration to develop a world class flamenco dance company. The dancers are profoundly affected. No one wants to let Anton down.

"Dancers take your places. We will review choreography and technique. From here on, we focus only on the dances we will perform at the Civic Auditorium."

The dancers move through their choreography with fresh intention. At the end of class, everyone buzzes with enthusiasm. A few dancers ask Vanessa to show them, again, some of the more difficult patterns.

Everyone checks in with Maria and signs up for Lupe's Panaderia while they wait in line to be measured and shown fabric samples for the dresses, shirts and pants they will wear for the performance. Makeup, hair and finger nails are all part of the show and coordinated to present a seamless whole. The adult class ends, and the children are due any moment.

"Anton, you shared an inspired description of what you hope we gain from our day at the beach. You're brave to face the tide again."

"It's small compared to what you endured – and what

you face every day. I'm grateful you have Susie to pull you out of your terror. Of course she's not big enough to pull someone from the waves, so I'll let you have her most of the time."

Vanessa laughs.

"It's a friendly battle to keep her. Her heart is all yours!"

Parents and children arrive, and Maria meets them at the door to answer questions and hand out release forms. Vanessa greets the students and prepares them for Anton's talk about the special beach rehearsal. Parents are encouraged to stay and listen to Anton.

"The beach rehearsal approaches, and I want everyone to have some understanding of why a low-tide-beach-dance experience is part of our preparation. At the core of the idea is the opportunity to experience nature's extraordinary dance floor. The packed sand offers our bare feet a fresh sensation that travels all the way to our head, and we feel a surge of energy that infuses our body with happiness. I want every dancer in this class to understand that they are unique and valuable to the whole performance. I want every dancer in this class to explore moving in new ways and feel the freedom of jumping over rocks and stopping briefly to bend down for shells and sand dollars. My only requirement is that you listen and watch everything around you and shout "Olé!" because you feel so happy! Now, let's practice shouting 'Olé!'"

Anton's enthusiasm is contagious. Parents and children shout,

"Olé!"

The room comes alive. The children wave goodbye to

their parents and follow Vanessa. The pep talk accomplishes Anton's goal. He raises the performance bar, and the children are aware that they are part of something special. They understand that they are being asked to give their best effort, and they want to make Anton proud.

"Anton thanks for making my job so easy today. The children were absolutely on fire and focused . . . an uncommon combination."

"I hope we all come together for a peak performance. To have all the elements come to together in full bloom is an art in itself, and my job is to set a strong pace and build to the end."

"I hear an urgency in your voice I never heard before."

"It's a make or break moment for me."

"Well, you've carefully planted many seeds, and they seem to have taken root. I will do everything I can to make the event your success. I think your dancers feel the same way. You gave me my life back, and I've never really told you what that means to me. I was in so much pain, and I tried to drown in alcohol. You gave me purpose and an art form that broke me out of self-pity. People shout "Olé!," but for me flamenco offers a way to bring my whole body into a fight for freedom from despair. This performance at the Civic is an opportunity to release the glory that is in each one of us. It's no longer just about me or you. It belongs to all of us. We won't let each other down!"

Anton gives Vanessa a hug and holds on long enough to steady his emotions.

"Vanessa, you're a rock in a big ocean."

TWENTY-SIX

Margret is buried in paperwork for the Civic event. She covers her face with her hands and rubs her eyes to get a sense of relaxation after so much time on the computer. Fortunately, she has a view of the ranch and can adjust her eyes back and forth to keep her vision healthy. Today she notices an important-overlooked detail. Margret likes to think out loud.

"We need a hook line name for this community event that reads on the larger reach of social media. Something that says the event is an important cultural milestone. Note to self, bring this up with Anton and Vanessa at today's rehearsal!"

It's time to settle everyone into a groove at the farm. Margret goes to Mom's room and knocks on her door.

"Hey, in there, are you ready for eggs and bacon?"

"Sure am."

Mom's assistant opens the door. Mom is dressed in jeans,

cowboy boots and a flannel shirt – ready for a day on the farm. Margret is relieved to see things are handled, and she's able to get in twenty minutes of a mountain bike ride before she dresses for dance.

Margret puts on a warm jacket over her hoodie and takes her mountain bike for a spin down the road to the fire-break and a tough climb up "Goat Hill." Beyond where Tilly's twin "Gypsy" appeared is a lookout spot that has a view of the entire valley. Margret pulls over and stands next to her bike. She feels powerful and free.

"I hope to God, I don't see another stray goat. I'm such a sucker for orphans!"

The air is fresh with the smell of fall-meadow grass mixed with dry leaves. Margret checks the time and takes one "long" minute to survey her new life in the wild. She enjoys her new identity as a mountain biker and considers a membership in mountain bike club. She gears up for a burn-it-downhill challenge, and rides hell-bent-for-leather home. She stops at the barn, dripping sweat and feeling the adrenalin.

"Hi Mom, Tilly and Gypsy!"

"Where have you been? You're soaked! When I die be sure to bury me next to Tilly and Gypsy! I love my girlfriends!"

"Show me where. Your girlfriends may last longer than you or me for that matter. We'll have it spelled out in the trust."

Margret laughs at her present circumstances and is happy that her mom loves "Tilly's Farm."

"Mom, I'm off to flamenco. I'll be back this afternoon.

Anything you want from town?

"Yes, chocolate chip cookies for me, and raisins for Tilly and Gypsy!"

"You got it."

Margret changes for dance. She jumps into the Gorilla and speeds into town. She stops for cookies and raisins, and grabs crackers, cheese, potato chips and three sodas for a spontaneous celebration with Anton and Vanessa. She is set for the event campaign and can't wait to share her marketing innovations. She also wants to get Mom started in flamenco with private lessons if Vanessa is up for it.

"Hello amigos! I warmed up on my mountain bike. I'm ready to rock the house."

Anton and Vanessa are outlining a senior flamenco dance class.

"Margret, is your Mom still interested in flamenco?"

"Vanessa, Mom doesn't know one day from the next, but she's up for anything. I hope you'll consider private lessons. A senior class would be great, but she needs to start ASAP. I hope she can do both. She's sure she's a gypsy."

"If Anton is ready to put it into the schedule, I'll teach both. I can't wait to meet your mom!"

"Vanessa, start anytime you want. Just let me and Maria know what you set up. It's time to dance."

Vanessa and Margret move to face the wall with mirrors and leave room for Anton to show them what he wants to see happen in the next hour.

"Next week, we begin to rehearse for two hours every

morning. All part of how we set the pace for our peak performance."

There's no nonsense in Anton's tone. Margret and Vanessa glance at each other and acknowledge a kinship in how far away they are from being true professionals in the world of music and dance.

Anton starts and wordlessly expects Vanessa and Margret to follow. Feet, hands, arms, legs and head swirl around his flexible torso, while his powerful finger snaps keep a steady rhythm. He stops frequently to correct weak technique. The pace demands commitment.

"Up to now, the dance is focused on the drama of theft and immigration. I want to end the show with the spirit of fiesta. I want to shift to mutual respect and celebration. The flamenco band will initiate the shift, and the singer will lead the way."

Anton puts on a CD of his favorite flamenco guitarist and singer and pushes ahead with the rehearsal. Nothing escapes Anton's attention. He expects perfection. He demonstrates the choreography for the fiesta. It's acrobatic and alive with homeruns and stolen bases animating the moves. Vanessa and Margret silently beg for mercy, and the rehearsal finally ends. Margret drips sweat, but she is determined to get a quick approval on where she's headed with marketing.

"I know we're spent, but I can't wait for our Sunday meetup to share a marketing plan and get approval. We need a title for this signature event. Can we take a minute and come together on this?"

Vanessa, equally challenged by the rehearsal sighs,

"Yes."

Anton, animated by exertion, gives an enthusiastic,

"Yes!"

Margret recharges thinking about marketing strategy.

"Okay! Titles..? What are we calling the show? Everything starts with the title."

Vanessa is quiet then spontaneously blurts out,

"*La Vida*! Considering Anton almost died from an incident at his recent solo beach rehearsal . . ."

"What . . ?"

"Margret, Anton got caught in a riptide, was saved from drowning by a wind surfer and nearly died again from hypothermia!"

"What? Obviously you're not kidding!! Why didn't I know about this?"

"It just happened after our last rehearsal at the studio. Fortunately, I live in the neighborhood and could get there to help in the emergency. I planned to tell you after this rehearsal, but the title popped out before the terrifying story!"

"I'm still in shock. I have nightmares. I'd be dead, if Vanessa hadn't been close by and hadn't known how to treat hypothermia."

"My God, Vanessa, you saved everything! Without Anton, we're all dead in the water!"

"I guess that's why *La Vida* came to mind for a title. It sums it all up, from the day I sat on that bench with my tequila to drown out Afghanistan, to the day you stumbled, and flamenco saved you, to the day Anton's father died, and

Anton came to America...from the day each of us was born ... the journey ... *La Vida* is universal. Everyone can identify."

"Vanessa, it's perfect! Flamenco is life! *La Vida!* I love it! Anton?"

"Yes!"

"That was painless! Thank you for indulging me. The rest can wait for Sunday."

The *La Vida* title inspires Margret with more ideas of how to promote the show. Margret, Anton and Vanessa are in sync on and off the dance floor.

"Anton, is it okay if Margret brings her mom for a private lesson before the children's class?"

"Certainly."

"Margret does that work for you? I'll arrive a little before four. We can do a forty-five minute private lesson. The studio charges $75.00 for privates. If she likes it, we can expand it to a group lesson. When my mom moves here, she can join too."

"And perhaps, when my mama arrives from Cuba for the show, she can be a guest dancer in your class. She knows flamenco and will add Cuban sizzle."

"We could use some Cuban sizzle!"

"Vanessa, your mom is moving here? You mentioned it, and now it sounds like it's actually happening!"

"Yes, Margret, and she loves to dance. She's working out details on buying a house in the historic downtown neighborhood."

"Mothers unite! I never dreamed Mom would be under my roof with two goats for company, but there you are, and it's wonderful!"

"I can't wait to see these two fierce women tell their stories with castanets, finger snaps, stamping heels and fans. This class will be rich in soul. What a privilege to teach the patterns and technique with people who have a history to share."

Margret and Vanessa clap their hands together, and Vanessa affirms there's definitely a place for Anton's Mama in her class! Margret excuses herself and takes off to activate the promotion now that the title is set. Vanessa picks up Susie who waits patiently and heads home to call her mom. Anton, still energized from rehearsal, takes time to work on some of the choreography that is embryonic.

"Hello . . .?

"Hi Mom, I'm home from dance, and we have a flamenco class for seniors planned. You'll love it!"

"I trust you all the way. The house is in escrow!"

"Mom, I can't believe it! You'll be a California girl dancing flamenco in a month. Just in time for *La Vida!* That's the name of the Anton Dance Company performance and is also the title for the whole event. Margret, you'll meet her, is doing a big promotional push. She wants to put Anton Dance Company on the map. It's so exciting!"

"Sweetheart, you sound happy. I hope the PTSD is under control, and you take all your meds. I do worry about you."

"No worries Mom. Between the VA and AA, I'm covered. My meds have been reduced, and AA is my ground floor. Susie and flamenco are my anchors, Anton is an exceptional teacher, and Margret is a good friend. Truthfully, I've found my tribe, and I couldn't be happier."

"Thank God! Dad is smiling, and I'll leave it there, or I'll be a sobbing mess. I've scheduled movers for the day after escrow closes. I'll donate most of our furniture except for a few treasured pieces. I purged a lot of stuff over the last few years. Most everyone ends up in a 12 x 12 foot room at the end. It feels good to let go. Besides, it's a fresh start in California. We'll decorate the house with the latest designer everything. I can't wait!"

"Mom, you're going to love California. After the show, we'll take a vacation to see the highlights of this state. I look forward to a road trip!!"

"Honey, I can't imagine a better tour guide . . . and maybe I'll get a dog, so Susie can have a pal too. My God, did I actually say that out loud? I think I've gone crackers, but it's a good kind of crazy."

"Mom, I'm glad to see you embrace this adventure. The last decade was unbearable, and you made it through intact. Now it's time to celebrate."

"Yes! I'll call the minute escrow closes! Thanks, Darlin' for looking out for your mama."

"I can't wait to teach you to dance flamenco!"

The phone conversation ends in laughter. Vanessa begins to mentally pack and realizes how little there is to do. Her life is small. Even her dog is small. In Texas everything was big – house, dog, money. Now modest Anton Dance Studio, little dog and solitary chess are her orbit.

"I wonder how it will change with this big flamenco show, a big downtown house and big dog if Mom buys her favorite kind of giant-furry purebred."

Vanessa chuckles.

"I better bone up on my chess strategies to prevent total wipeout from Mom."

Vanessa picks up her *Teach Yourself Chess* book and opens to the chapter on strategic play. A yellowed clipping from *The New York Times by Robert Byrne* that analyzes the win of *Hikaru Nakamura, the youngest American to win an international master title,* falls onto the table near the chess board. Vanessa scans the article and declares out loud to Susie,

"This kid was thirteen years old! I love this. '*He played the tricky opening with a sure hand, parrying a threatened counterattack deftly; he attacked single mindedly in the early middle game and won cleverly and efficiently in the end game.*' Who needs more? That's it. That's my new strategy for life!"

Susie cocks her head and runs to the door. Vanessa laughs.

"Susie you have no beginning or end game. You're all about the middle! Okay, let's see if we can sign up our real estate agent for Anton Dance Studio flamenco. That's a middle game action."

Vanessa and Susie walk to the real estate office in Old Town downtown. The door is open and Susie trots in ahead of Vanessa.

"Well hello there! I'm sure you know that your mother bought the Mediterranean house. Escrow closes in a month, and she plans to move in the day after. Congratulations!"

"Yes. I do know, and I'm over the moon. I hope you'll join us in a flamenco dance class for seniors."

"I certainly will. Your mother is a hoot and a half, and it turns out we both love to dance."

"That's good news. If you belong to Rotary or any other organizations that have senior citizens, please spread the word. I'll have flyers next week and will drop some off."

"Vanessa, you have brightened my world. I look forward to meeting your mother and to learn how to dance flamenco. I've watched a few YouTube videos, and flamenco is what I need!"

"Olé! I can't wait to have you in the class."

Susie and Vanessa step outside the real estate office, start down the steps when a pickup truck runs a red light and tee-bones a small passenger car turning left. Smoke rises from the intersection. Vanessa grabs Susie and heads for the shrubs on the side of the real estate office. Vanessa is back in Afghanistan. Susie barks and pokes Vanessa to no avail. Vanessa trembles and runs to the alley with Susie tucked up tight to her chest. Susie, desperate to stop Vanessa from her strange and scary behavior, bites Vanessa.

"Susie, you bit me!"

Vanessa realizes she was caught in a flashback, and Susie bit her to stop the panic. Vanessa starts to cry and hugs Susie in gratitude. Susie, happy to have peace restored, licks Vanessa's face.

"Susie, you saved me, again!"

There's no one around to witness Vanessa's panic. She's relieved she escaped the embarrassment of being seen as completely bonkers. Vanessa takes stock of what happened, sees it for what it is and isn't and continues her walk home with Susie still in her arms. Vanessa has a new perspective on her flashbacks. She no longer sees her condition as inevitable and feels liberated.

Vanessa arrives at her apartment and looks for the self-guided meditation information she picked up at the VA. She sits in her chair and begins to practice the guidelines. To her amazement, she feels relaxed and peaceful after ten minutes of meditation. She considers visiting a yoga studio to learn more. It seems such a contrast to flamenco, but the relaxation and flexibility it offers interests Vanessa.

"I could use some of this mindfulness thing. It could take my chess skills to a whole new level. Susie, have you ever considered meditation?"

Hearing her name, Susie jumps to attention.

"No, it's definitely a human thing. You, Susie, are an in-the-moment-action-kind-of-girl. Speaking of being in the moment, let's get boxes and start packing!"

The liquor store has perfect boxes to pack for a move. Vanessa leashes Susie, and they walk to the backside of the liquor store. A pre-squashed stack of boxes is piled next to the cardboard-only bin. Vanessa helps herself to four medium sized boxes. She pinches them between her fingers on each hand and starts back to her apartment with Susie's leash looped over her wrist. As she rounds the corner, a man runs down the sidewalk, chased by two policemen, slams into her and grabs her around the neck with one arm. He drags Vanessa, the boxes and Susie to a car and, with his other arm, he keeps a gun pointed at Vanessa's head. Vanessa is totally present and leans on her military training. The police take a position behind parked cars and warn the man to drop the gun. With Vanessa as a hostage, the man is emboldened. He tells Vanessa to drop the boxes, take the keys from his pocket, open the car door and get in. Vanessa complies while still connected to Susie by the leash. The man starts to back through the open car door after Vanessa. He ducks and tries to push Vanessa onto the passenger seat. Susie slips along unnoticed on the floor boards. Suddenly, Vanessa becomes the warrior she was trained to be. At the man's most vulnerable moment, as he ducks to get into the car, she takes the keys and stabs him in the eye. Blood floods out of his eye, blinds him and in agony he lets go of Vanessa and drops the gun. In a catlike move, Vanessa jumps out of the car, on the passenger side, and drags Susie with her. Crouched over she runs, and the officers move in to capture the wounded-liquor-store thief.

Vanessa continues to run and hides behind a parked car. The man is in custody, and the police make every effort to assure her it's safe to come out. A female officer approaches Vanessa with a blanket and offers to wrap her and Susie up. Grateful, Vanessa accepts the offer.

"You won't believe my day. I'm an Afghanistan war veteran with severe PTSD, and this morning, I witnessed a truck run a red light and cream a small car and now this!"

"You handled the situation perfectly. Are you okay?"

"I'm amazed I didn't imagine I was still in Afghanistan under fire and hide under a car."

"Are you sure you're okay?"

"This blanket helps."

"We need some information from you then I can take

you, the dog and the boxes home. Do want anything from the liquor store?"

"You know what… I'll take a pack of those small-white donuts."

"Comfort food, you got it!"

"How do you handle this job?"

"I'm not sure I do, but I'll buy two packs of those donuts, one for you and one for me!"

Vanessa thanks the officer, gives her the information she needs, declines the ride and walks home with powder sugar on her chest just above her heart.

Inside her apartment, Vanessa unfolds her bed from her couch. She pulls down the shades and makes her usual nest. She climbs into bed with her clothes on, reaches out to Susie and invites her up. She practices her new mindfulness and falls asleep. It's the first crisis she's met without a complete or even partial collapse into delusional panic.

TWENTY-SEVEN

Anton is troubled. The choreography is strong but disjointed. He still doesn't have a coherent program that can carry the production to peak performance and close the show with maximum excitement. He wants the building to shake with the audience on their feet while they shout "Bravo!! Olé!"

The studio desk is covered in production notes and program ideas. Anton shoves it all away to make an ordered list:

LA VIDA Saturday, November 12th

1. Flamenco band guitarists play music in foyer.
2. Ushers escort audience guests to rows and seats.
3. Flamenco band takes its place on stage behind closed curtain.
4. Lights dim on and off.
5. Welcome audience.
6. Show opens with Alvaro, band and singer.
7. Children's two dances. Recording with lights.
8. Adult class two dances. Recording with lights.

9. Alvaro performs solo with flamenco band and lights.
10. Alvaro and Anton dance an improvisation with flamenco band and lights. Vanessa and Margret join the spontaneous dance.
11. Anton Dance Company La Vida with flamenco band and lights.
    Last scene of La Vida is fiesta and acts as an encore. House on fire!

Pre-show tapas, sodas, wine and beer on court yard in front of auditorium, i.e. Cuban food truck. Anton muses,

"This is good start. The beach rehearsal should be one week before we move to the Civic for final rehearsals and show. This will allow everyone to breathe the wild sea mist and feel the power of the waves."

Anton finishes his program and notes the time. It's two o'clock, and Sunday baseball is in the park. Anton Dance Company and Studio business meeting is at five o'clock, at the studio.

"Hello…?"

"Vanessa, do you want to meet for a picnic at the park?"

"Sure…you wouldn't believe the afternoon I had yesterday!"

"Good! You can tell me at lunch. There's usually a food truck there."

"Okay. You can have your vegan hotdog. If I want something else, I'll bring it."

"I play baseball at two. We can have a picnic at one and then go to the business meeting at five. I'll call Margret and see if she wants to join us. We could have pizza before the meeting."

"Anton that sounds terrific...I definitely need a picnic and pizza!"

"Good! See you at one."

Vanessa is happy Anton called. She picks up her phone and calls her mom.

"Hello...?"

"Yes, Mom, I do have friends! Anton asked me to have a picnic in the park. And you have a friend too! Mr. Real Estate told me you're 'a hoot and a half', and he can't wait to meet you. He's up for the flamenco class, too!"

"That's wonderful, Sugar. You sound a bit giddy, like a girl with a crush!"

"Oh, no Mom, Anton's just a friend, but a very good one. I think Margret's coming to the picnic too! I remember I told you I had no friends, but now I do!! I just wanted you to know, I'm on my way back to normal!!"

"I'm happy for you, Sweetheart. Hang on to normal. Me, I'm a crazy Texas native, nothin' normal 'bout me! I can't wait to dance flamenco!"

"I love you Mom. I love abnormal! Got to go, I'm packing!"

Vanessa fills a few more boxes with closet storage, dresses in jeans and hoodie and heads to the park. Susie trots along beside her.

"Giddy? Maybe I am giddy, but it's all about freedom from PTSD and fewer meds. Susie would you say I'm giddy?"

Susie ignores Vanessa.

"Forget it. You're the giddy one! Anton at the park, how does it get better than that?"

Susie hears "Anton" and picks up the pace.

"Vanessa, I'm over here!"

Vanessa sees Anton, waves and makes her way to the bleachers. Susie prances and pulls to get ahead. Only a few of the team members are there early, and Anton breaks away to meet Vanessa half way.

"Hola! I'm glad you decided to come."

"So am I. It's good to get outside."

"Margret said she would meet us for pizza. Are you hungry? The food truck is down the street.

"Let's go! Susie can eat a plain dog. I'll get one with everything, including sauerkraut!"

The trio walks to the food truck. Anton orders three hotdogs (one vegan) potato chips and sodas. The food truck isn't busy, and the steamed hotdogs slide through the window in a hurry.

"Vanessa, eat here or head back?"

"Eat here."

There're a few picnic tables with bright red umbrellas. Ketchup, mustard, relish chopped-onions, jalapenos and sauerkraut are on a shelf at the end of the truck. After loading their hotdogs with all the extras, Anton and Vanessa sit to eat while Susie searches for scraps under the table. Vanessa lays pieces of a plain hotdog on the ground near Anton. Susie eats her hotdog and curls up at Anton's cleated feet. Baseball is a serious game at this park.

"What happened yesterday?"

"Where do I start? My mom bought a house in Old Town downtown, and I went to see the real estate agent, because I think he might enjoy the senior flamenco class. I got thumbs up on the class, the house, and I think he likes my mom. Anyway, as I was leaving a truck t-boned a car in the intersection, and I lost it. But no one saw me panic. Susie actually bit me to pull me out. I came through the flashback to normal right where I was!! It was incredible. I felt like my problem was no longer inevitable, and I could be free. I could be in the present, stay in the present and not go halfway around the world to revisit hell."

Anton offers a high-five to Vanessa. She meets his hand with hers and celebrates.

"It gets better. I got home and decided to go to the liquor store to get more boxes to pack for the move. As I come around the corner of the building with boxes and Susie, an armed robber, chased by police, runs into me and takes me hostage. He locks my neck in his arm, drags me to his car and holds off the police with his gun pointed at my head. He tells me to take his keys out of his pocket and back into the driver's seat. My neck is still locked in his arm. I do as he says while Susie stays close. The gun is still pointed at my head while he backs into the car. His backside pushes me over towards the passenger seat. He's vulnerable when he bends down with the vice grip still on my neck. At the moment he slides into the car, I stab him in the eye with the car key. Blood goes everywhere, and he can't see. In extreme pain, he drops the gun and surrenders. Susie and I escape out the passenger door."

"What amazes me is I didn't leave the crisis. I acted like a trained soldier in a dangerous situation, and I did my job. No flashback. No panic. Truthfully, it was just cold-blooded-self-defense. The officers had to let me know when it was safe to come out from behind the car, but I wasn't freaked out!"

Anton offers another high five, and Vanessa feels a tingle when her hand lays against Anton's in celebration.

"I'm happy that you escaped without injury and kept your cool. Susie deserves a lot of credit. Should I buy her another hotdog?"

Vanessa laughs.

"Another hotdog might make her sick. Get her an ice cream!"

Anton buys a vanilla-ice-cream cone. Susie licks the ice cream and looks adoringly at Anton. The ice cream is a forever promise. Anton scratches her behind the ears. In the distance, people start to fill the bleachers and some of the players warm up. Anton takes Vanessa's hand as they walk to the baseball diamond. When they near the field, Anton goes into baseball mode and warms up with players he hasn't seen for a while. Vanessa and Susie head to the bleachers. Vanessa is as star struck as Susie and still in shock at what happened. She pretends everything is still as it was, just friends.

Anton plays short-stop, and his team wins the game. Vanessa is struck by how he shuts out every distraction. He plays baseball with the same intensity he dances, and the team begs him to play every Sunday. Anton shares news of the upcoming show and encourages everyone he greets to join the audience for *La Vida,* at the Civic Auditorium,

November 12th. Vanessa stands back and watches Anton with butterflies in her stomach. Anton waves her over and introduces her to the group. Susie, not to be ignored, insists Anton pick her up and basks in the attention from the charmed crowd. Anton guides Vanessa away from the baseball diamond and waves goodbye to renewed acquaintances.

"See you at the show!"

His fans cheer with double thumbs up. Anton turns his attention to Vanessa.

"Ready for pizza. . ?"

"Yes! Wow what a game! You play baseball like you dance flamenco!"

Anton laughs.

"Baseball and Flamenco are my soul food!"

"Pizza's mine!"

Vanessa reaches out to carry Susie, and the trio walks to the Pizza House on the far corner of the strip mall. Anton keeps an eye out for Margret. The parking lot is full.

"I don't see the Gorilla. Should we wait outside or get a table?"

The Gorilla appears at the corner, and Margret shouts,

"Get a table! I'll park the Gorilla on the street!"

Anton laughs.

"There's my answer!"

He touches Vanessa's elbow and, once again, guides her through a crowd. Most everyone watches football on the big screen TV. There's one booth in the back corner that opens up. Anton sails through the throng and settles Vanessa and Susie at the table. Vanessa slides to the back of the booth to make room for Margret who is at the door looking for signs of Vanessa and Anton. Vanessa waves just as Anton catches sight of Margret and points to the table. Anton orders two beers and a soda. Margret heads to the booth.

"Hi! This place is packed!

Margret sees Susie tucked up against Vanessa.

"Good thing I didn't bring Tilly and Gypsy!

"It's OK. She's my emotional support dog."

Margret laughs, and Anton arrives with the drinks. Margret sits next to Susie and Vanessa. Anton takes the seat opposite. Except for the noise, it's a perfect booth for a meeting.

"Will this work, or do we need to go to the studio?"

"Anton, I've been cooped up with my computer, Mom and goats. I love this. If it's okay with you and Vanessa, let's please stay!"

Vanessa and Anton give thumbs up while the crowd roars at a touchdown. Margret takes a swig from her glass of beer and pulls her computer and papers from her big leather bag. It's obvious she has every detail handled. It's who she is, and she's proud of it.

"Okay gang! Next week, on that same TV over that bar, there will be an ad for *La Vida*. I've contacted every form of media, and we are on schedule to hit the air waves at the same time. I have a local filmmaker and crew lined up to film the event from dress rehearsals to the end, so we'll have a professional documentary to promote our story. I figure Alvaro's stardom deserves the attention, and the Anton Dance Company needs to capitalize on his guest appearance. I have fliers and posters ready to distribute at the beach rehearsal. They can be shared with the community.

"Margret, this is way beyond my wildest imagination! You are a force of nature on and off the dance floor!"

"Now you know why I wanted to stay here and celebrate my release from the detail-desk!"

Margret unbuttons her jacket and takes it off. She stands up and displays a prototype black-fitted-red-ribbed-tank top with "Anton Dance Company" printed in bold-red letters. A man across the pizza parlor shouts "Olé!" and raises his beer in a toast. Margret with pent up energy releases her enthusiasm with a rattle of her heels against the floor. Soon everyone is shouting "Olé!" and "Bravo!" and toasting Margret, and the booth in the back. Vanessa and Anton burst with laughter while Margret parades around the room and passes out fliers!!

Suddenly, Anton jumps up on the table and begins to dance in his cleats. The sound electrifies the crowd. Some of the baseball team players are there and call out "Bravo, Anton!" Anton is transported to Cuba and brings the crowd with him with finger snaps and footwork.

Vanessa, in the corner, sings a high C and composes a passionate-flamenco song on the spot. Margret dances through the crowd back to the booth, and Anton fires his legs like engine pistons, and his arms like bull whips. Anton abruptly slows his pace and casually steps off the table. Margret, out of breath, announces,

"This is a spontaneous preview of "La Vida!" See you all

November 12th at the Civic auditorium!"

The crowd is wild and shouts for more. Anton, Margret and Vanessa wave them off with a dismissal flip of hands. People are buying them drinks, and the pizza Margret orders is on the house. Flushed, Margret sits in the booth.

"I didn't expect this for a meeting!"

Anton and Vanessa laugh.

"Margret, I think the meeting is over. Let's eat pizza!

"No, no Vanessa. No time to relax. We must keep the momentum and get ready for the beach rehearsal this week."

Vanessa reports that all the bills are paid and accounts are up to date. The dresses for the adult and children's classes are due to arrive in the next week and a fitting schedule is being set up by Maria. She also confirms the senior flamenco class will begin next week with a private lesson for Margret's mom, and a group lesson with Vanessa's mom, Margret's mom and the real estate agent. Vanessa is set to go.

Anton reports that the choreography is in place, and he's set for the beach rehearsal, rehearsals at the Civic as well as the final dress rehearsal. Alvaro has confirmed his arrival date on November 9th and will need a hotel room. Anton's mother still tries to make arrangements to come and will stay with Anton. All event personnel have been contracted and will arrive early for the three final rehearsals at the Civic. The flamenco band will need hotel rooms for the three Civic rehearsals and show. The lighting team and stage manager will need hotel rooms as well. He shares printed copies of his program, which Margret has already incorporated into her program design. Anton is on fire.

Margret reports that every aspect of marketing is detailed

and scheduled. Three vans will be on call to handle logistics, and a photographer and videographer will film the beach rehearsal for documentary and promotional purposes. Margret's experience with her father's international biochemical company and her personal resources elevate Anton Dance Company to world class status with Anton Dance Studio to benefit from all the attention. Margret is serious.

"We need an MC. I think we should ask the Mayor. She's popular, visionary and an excellent speaker. What do you think, Anton?"

"Excellent choice."

Vanessa confirms the idea.

"Margret, you're a born impresario!!"

The Pizza House is ready to close. Vanessa, Margret and Anton are reluctant to end the meeting, but recognize it's time to wrap it up. Anton and Vanessa laugh with good nature that belies an underlying nervousness that this event is a big undertaking. Only Margret laughs full throated and knows this is just the beginning.

"Hey, can I give you two a ride home?"

"I would love a ride in the Gorilla! I'm just a block away, behind the palm trees."

"Me, too, I decided to walk to the park today, so 'Yes' to the Gorilla. I'm three blocks away in Old Town neighborhood. I secretly want to trade the sports car for the dirt-eating-off-road primate!!"

More laughter as the three amigos and Susie climb into Margret's motorized chariot and experience the power and luxury of a Gorilla. It's the kind of ride you never forget after a meeting at The Pizza House and sets the stage for an unforgettable premiere of *La Vida* and the Anton Dance Company.

TWENTY-EIGHT

A ten vehicle caravan travels the highway to Ocean Beach Park through a thick marine layer. The early morning fog begins to clear with the sunrise. The cars turn onto the one lane road and drive along the edge of the wetlands to the empty parking lot. Headlights bounce against the gray surroundings. Excited children, parents and teachers bundle up against the damp chill and wait for Anton to gather the dance students for the beach rehearsal. Thermoses of coffee and hot cider circulate in paper cups to warm the troops. The serene marshes with bobbing ducks and sea fowl are a stark contrast to the excited children and restless adults.

    Anton mingles with parents. He glows with an internal fire that ignites his soul when he smells the sea and hears the seagulls squawk. Maria tallies the attendees and offers extra sweatshirts and jackets to anyone unprepared for the cold. The atmosphere is one of fiesta without Mariachis or bonfire. It's a celebration of primal and spontaneous movement. Anton hopes each dancer will catch the fever.

The film crew has already arrived and documents the arrival of the cars loaded with parents and dancers. Margret introduces herself and shakes hands with the director.

"Hi film crew! Thanks for being early and documenting the arrival! You are all pros, so I leave it up to you how you want to record this event. You already have the general design, so again, have fun while you capture this wonderfully-weird rehearsal. If you need to get close-ups, rely on your still photographer and work it out in post-production. We won't stop. I'm your contact person. If you have questions, talk to me. Let the cameras roll, and I'll catch up with you for the edits."

"Sounds great Margret, I can see this isn't your first rodeo."

"No, I've done a lot of PR work with film and video. Your reputation precedes you. I have no doubt you will do a super job."

"It's great to work with someone who knows what they want. We'll stay out of the way and capture every aspect of this rehearsal. Hopefully, you won't even notice we're here. That's our specialty."

"Wonderful. And remember the visit to Lupe's Panaderia after the rehearsal. Once you've captured the panaderia on film, go ahead and have as many pasteles and cappuccinos as you want. Breakfast is on us!"

"Yes, the crew looks forward to warming up after this morning's take on the notoriously wild-cold-windy Ocean Park Beach!

Maria signals everyone to walk under the trestle, out onto the packed sand and around the lapping edge of a temporary ocean lake dammed by a sand bar. The sand dunes stretch out in both directions, and the tide is low. It is a perfect day to dance on the beach.

True to their word, the film crew disappears into the background, and no one feels intimidated or restricted by their presence. With three film cameras and two still cameras the rehearsal is covered.

Animated, Vanessa walks with the children and encourages them to stick together and listen to instructions. Parents have been recruited to chaperon the children and keep them safe should they stray. Everyone is asked to remove their shoes and socks and place them near the small retaining wall that pretends to hold back a surge of high tide.

Margret forces a smile and groans when her bare feet feel the gritty-cold sand. Fortunately, her spirit is undaunted by her distain for the beach. She chatters with the adult students that are in shock for the most part. She empathizes and tells them to listen to Anton and embrace the wild.

The group moves along the beach against the steady breeze. A large troop of seagulls and pelicans watch the scrum of people approach and time their departure to the nearest human advancement. On the north side, in the dunes, is a large driftwood structure that faces down wind. The children rush to explore the handmade building, and, with Vanessa in the midst of them, they line dance around and through the elaborate-driftwood structure. Wild laughter and screams of joy issue out of the primal fort. Anton's plan to unleash the soul works.

The adults gradually awake to the sheer majesty of the sunrise, and although some are less than thrilled, as their toes wiggle in the cold sand, they all seem to relish the joy of the children that rush around like a flock of snowy plovers. Margret encourages the adults to swing their arms, jump up and down and clap their hands to warm up. Even Margret begins to breathe deeply, close her eyes and taste the salt air.

As they tramp along against the wind, the adults keep their heads down and stick together. Margret breaks out in front and starts to clap a flamenco rhythm and little by little the adults open up to the possibility of spontaneous movement. One parent suddenly yells, "Olé!" and starts to run in a circle around the group and then out to the broad expanse of packed sand left exposed by the low tide. Other parents, inspired by the freedom of one, begin to chase each other and jump ahead to explore the swirl of low tide while it rushes around some of the larger rocks that shelter sea anemones and starfish in small tide pools.

The children rush out to join the adults on the packed sand dotted with strands of seaweed, small rocks, shells and an occasional prize sand dollar. Hermit crabs scramble to hide in the seams of the larger rocks covered in grassy-green moss. The sun melts the mist, and the wind pushes the marine layer out to the horizon. The waves in the distance stay outside the boundary established by the moon's divine command "thus far and no further." The ocean's roar and spray surrounds the dancers while the washing machine of waves stays off shore and sends only wide puddles of bubbles in swathes of water that alternately surge and recede on the edge of Anton's favorite dance floor.

An adult straggles and wanders upon a bank of driftwood. He carries dry-bleached branches through the soft sand to the edge of the packed floor and starts to build a house. The children catch sight of his project and swarm around the foundation with driftwood they gather from the nearby pile deposited in the ocean's driftwood bank. The adult directs the children, and soon a respectable driftwood shelter stands against the wind. More adults join the project, and the one room house expands into two rooms. Children imagine themselves as pirates and deposit their sea floor treasures into the house. Flags of seaweed warn distant ships to stay clear of the island. The pirates and the natives start to dance, and the building takes on new significance. One child starts to build a sand castle near the tide pools, and a gaggle of children race to help. To look from the outside in, this group of humans that rush from place to place appear as natural as the birds they scare off with the wild shouts and shrieks of laughter. Anton could not have wished for more. Anton, Vanessa and Margret corral the group, and Anton talks over the waves.

"Let's begin the rehearsal. Each of you knows the choreography from your studio dances. Take any part of that dance, and group by group come out and share your interpretation. Margret and I will clap, and Vanessa will sing. Maria will organize the groups. As you dance your routine, be the sea, be the seaweed, be the tide, be the waves and move in any way you want to share your interpretation."

The period of play before the rehearsal excites the dancers, and the adult class is eager to experiment. Margret claps, Vanessa sings improvised flamenco songs, and Anton calls out,

"Be the seaweed!"

The first four adults coil, uncoil, bend, whip and straighten like seaweed washed ashore in the tide. Each dancer gives a unique interpretation of the same class routine. Groups of four parade across the packed-sand-dance floor. Parents and children stand to the side and clap and shout "Olé!" and

"Bravo!" as they move down the shore with the dancers. Together, everyone moves like a giant centipede that mimics waves, wind, birds and sand crabs.

Anton, Margret and Vanessa continue to call out, clap rhythms and sing. At the end of the line the dancers circle back and join the audience while the next group of four moves down through the tunnel of people that stand on the sidelines. No one is left out. The adult dance grows in intensity, and the words of the songs give new impetus to ways to share the dance routines. One dancer flips, spins and runs full speed ahead. Another sways gently side to side and claps while her feet take exaggerated steps. Some dancers are shy, some are bold, and all are committed to trust their own expressions of a shared theme.

When all the dancers from the adult class have danced their first routine, they line up in groups of four again to experiment with the second dance routine. So far the overall impression is one of serious improvisation. Now, with the second dance routine, Anton shouts,

"Celebrate La Vida! Viva la fiesta!"

The adults abandon their groups of four and take to the dance floor in mass with even more wild expressions when Anton shouts,

"Be sea birds!"

They move in swarms, wave arms and squawk like sea gulls. An occasional dancer pulls out and moves into stealth mode to celebrate pelicans! Vanessa sings a celebration song, and all the adult dancers join up. They keep their routine going but with wildly different interpretations. At last the momentum is spent, and the adults stand breathless. One parent calls out,

Where's the piñata?! Where's the candy?!

The adults laugh, and the children race about while they wait for their turn.

Anton calls the children's class together, and Vanessa prepares to lead them. Maria brings them together into one group and explains, again, that they are to do their dance routine for each dance, but bring their own interpretation. Margret begins to clap, and Anton joins her with castanets. The children go wild. They barely include flamenco routines and mostly run and jump over clumps of seaweed and remnant driftwood. Anton calls out,

"Be waves. Be the ocean!"

The children spontaneously bond together with their arms linked and make lines of lashing waves. They break apart, join together, and break apart again. Anton shouts,

"Be birds!"

The children run together in a flock and chase the tide as it rolls in and out. Anton notices the tide stretches further inland and decides it's wise to wrap up the rehearsal.

"Okay dancers and parents, the tide is rising. To be safe, let's join up and walk, run or dance to the parking lot! There's more hot cider and coffee in thermoses. Let's go! Wait by the vehicle you came in, and we'll load up and go to Lupe's Panaderia for pasteles!

Margret stays with the adults, and Vanessa continues to lead the children. This requires her to race to the front of the troop and keep the children focused on the trek to the parking lot. Parents are relieved to have the dance teacher take on the rowdy youngsters. Margret is great with the adults. She talks about the show and listens to parental concerns.

She assures them their kids will have a great experience at the show and reminds them promotional materials are in her Gorilla to post around the community. Again, Margret doesn't let a moment go by without purpose. She is definitely a skilled PR person.

Anton stays behind and keeps an eye out for stragglers. He shepherds the kids that are distracted by the driftwood houses and watches the incoming tide carefully. Although still a safe distance away, he takes no chances and wants everyone out of Neptune's reach. A straggler from the adult class approaches Anton.

"This was extraordinary. I've never experienced a dance rehearsal at low tide, but it makes perfect sense! Years ago I danced with a ballet company. We certainly could have used something like this to loosen things up. I love flamenco because of the spontaneous aspect, and today you threw away the lid and let the pot boil over! It was particularly wonderful for the children. They experienced self-expression in a whole new way. I think this idea will have long term benefits. I think everyone here came away with a liberated soul. I'd say you accomplished all that you set out to do with this creative approach to an upcoming performance. Everyone is ready to take it to the limit!

"Thank you for sharing your appreciation. I wasn't sure how it would work, but it turned out better than I could have hoped."

"Well, I'm thrilled to be a part of the show, and I can't wait for November 12th. I'm sure it will be a great success!

"Thank you! And now to Lupe's!"

Anton and the last of the stragglers round the bend under the train trellis and witness a parking lot busy with animated dancers and parents that load into vehicles. The noisy crowd is a distinct contrast to the isolated quiet of the wetland sanctuary. The trail of motorized transportation on the narrow road out of the park reminds Anton how rare it is to have a free and expansive dance floor all to one's own use.

Lupe's Panaderia is ready for the onslaught of this noisy flock of seabirds dressed in sports clothes of all stripes. The hot drinks and pasteles are the perfect cap to Anton's beach rehearsal. Margret leans into Anton and confesses,

"Maybe all the biking on dirt trails, and the cut on my chin prepared me for a whole new perspective about the beach. I loved every moment after my feet got used to the tickle of wet sand!"

Anton and Margret laugh.

"Seriously, Anton, thank you for giving me another soul experience. I can't wait to tear up the floor at the Civic. We all want to make you proud!"

Anton gives a high-five to Margret. She catches his hand and briefly holds it, then shakes it.

"None of this would be possible without you, Margret. We all should be thanking you!"

"Anton, It's enough just to hear the Mayor dedicate this event to my Dad. If Anton Dance Company becomes what I think it will, and I have a part in it, I'm beyond satisfied. You completely changed me, and I will always be grateful."

"Here's to flamenco and beach rehearsals!"

Anton and Margret toast each other with cappuccinos. Vanessa, now busy with parents and children, sees Margret and Anton celebrate. She disengages and joins Anton and

Margret to acknowledge the successful rehearsal. Margret notices Anton's heightened attention to Vanessa and watches his face light up, as Vanessa approaches. Vanessa, on the other hand, seems indifferent to Anton's body language, and Margret relaxes. Vanessa gives high-fives to Anton and Margret.

"We did it! Susie will never forgive me for leaving her at home!"

"Margret and Vanessa, you deserve those Anton Dance Company tank tops! You are lifetime members! Here's to *La Vida*.

The three cappuccino cups touch, and Margret watches for any further signs of affection from Anton towards Vanessa. The morning is free of any other hints of special feelings, and Margret is reassured.

The film director comes over to Margret.

"Thank you for choosing our team to film this extraordinary rehearsal. I look forward to the show. After I witnessed this wonderfully-weird rehearsal, I can only imagine what's in store for us at the actual event!"

"Thanks so much for filming today. You really were invisible! Call me when you're ready to edit. I can't wait to see what you captured with your cameras! I hope you got enough to eat and drink. If you stop for a real breakfast, put it on our tab."

'Thanks Margret. It's great to work with you. Talk about a pro! I'll let you know when we're ready to edit. I know you need it ASAP to promote the show and dance studio."

Margret and the director shake hands. Parents and children are ready to leave, and some of the adults need to get to work. Margret makes sure everyone has what they need and offers extra pasteles as they go. Vanessa checks in with Lupe and asks her to keep a running tally until the very end, give her the total and she'll pay the bill. Anton talks with parents. He finally breaks away.

"Lupe! Thank you! You are the perfect hostess for this madness! Lupe's Panaderia is a big hit!"

"And Anton Dance Studio and Dance Company is the talk of the town! Everyone loves you!"

"Everyone is high on your pasteles and cappuccinos! If you want to set up at the Civic before the show, we would love to have you!"

"That sounds good. November 12th, yes?"

"Yes."

"We'll be there!"

Vanessa hears "We'll be there."

"You'll be where?"

Anton confirms.

"Lupe's Panaderia will be part of the food before the show at the Civic!"

"Fabulous! Lupe you'll have to save a bunch of pasteles for the dancers for after the show!!!"

"Yes, yes! I will have extra pasteles for hungry dancers!!"

Margret hears laughter and comes over. Everyone else has cleared out of the Panaderia to go about their day. Margret celebrates.

"I'd say the rehearsal was a huge success! I can't wait for the show!"

Anton gives high fives to Margret and Vanessa.

"Wait you will, and you won't be disappointed. Alvaro will blow us all away."

Vanessa comments,

"Maybe, he'll get so many 'Bravos,' he'll want to stay and join Anton's Dance Company!"

"That would be a miracle. He has his own dance company in Cuba!"

Margret ponders.

"You never know . . . you never know."

TWENTY-NINE

"Hello?"

"Hi, Jeff this is Margret from Anton Dance Studio and Anton Dance Company. It's been a few days since we did the edits. I wondered where you are with the film.

"Margret! I was just about to call you! We'll wrap it up this afternoon. It looks terrific! Not only are you great at PR, but your edit instincts are spot on!"

"Thanks Jeff. I hope I wasn't too much about little details. I thought maybe I drove your team crazy!"

"No, on the contrary, Margret. Everyone appreciated the input. It made the project easier and better! With your permission, we now have a great demo to show other clients!"

"I'm relieved to hear it. You never know . . . you never know . . . if unsolicited suggestions are well received. You guys are super to work with. I look forward to the documentary of *La Vida*. It's certain to be a spectacular, one of a kind, flamenco-dance event!!

"I can't wait to be there, and my team is ready!"

"Thanks so much, Jeff. It's great to have real pros to depend on. And, yes, feel free to share the beach rehearsal video any time after the 12th."

"Same back to you, Margret. See you for the dress rehearsal and performance. I'll check in a couple of days before the first rehearsal to be sure we have all we need to do your event justice."

"Thanks, Jeff. I can't wait to see the beach rehearsal video, hasta la vista!"

Margret hangs up and feels relieved. One major project to cross off her list.

"I need an assistant! This is getting crazy!"

Mom is in the kitchen and hears Margret talking to herself.

"Did you say you need an assistant? Can I help?"

"Mom that's sweet. You certainly can help! You can help me make lunch! I'm starving!"

Margret and Mom put together peanut butter and jelly sandwiches and sit on the porch to watch Tilly and Gypsy graze on the front pasture.

"Mom, I hope you remember you have a private flamenco lesson with Vanessa at 3:00 today."

"I do?"

"Yes, you do, and we need to leave a half hour early to

get there in time."

"Dance flamenco?"

"Yes, Mom, you watch me all the time around here, and you said you wanted to be a gypsy, so I signed you up! I ordered skirt, tank top and shoes for you. You can start getting ready to leave around 2:30."

"Will you help me get ready? I haven't worn a skirt in years. . ."

"Yes, I can help you. It's 12:30 now. You can walk with Tilly and Gypsy back to the barn and work on your art pieces for an hour or so. When it's time to get ready, I'll come out, bring you back to the house and help you get dressed."

"That sounds wonderful dear. Do you want to do art with me in the barn?"

"No, I need to work on marketing the show. I have a ton of work to do."

"Do you want me to help you?"

"You already did! You helped me with lunch! I'll call John to see if he can help you with Tilly and Gypsy, and a walk by your roses on the way to the barn."

"Oh yes! John, he's so good to Tilly and Gypsy! Maybe he wants to dance flamenco."

"You can ask him. You never know. . ."

"I will. He's so handsome!"

Margret calls John and tells him the plan. She can see him give thumbs up as he walks over to Tilly and Gypsy to take them back to the barn. He heads towards the porch, and

Margret walks Mom down the porch stairs and out to meet-up with John and the goats.

"Thanks, John. Mom wants to ask you something."

Margret whispers in Mom's ear. Mom lights up.

"John, would you like to dance flamenco with me this afternoon?"

John is prepared for anything.

"I would love to dance flamenco with you. I can't today, but I'm sure we can get it on the dance card sometime. Maybe you can teach me."

"Oh yes! I think I have a lesson today. I'll show you what I learn. I've never danced flamenco before, but Margret thinks I would make a good gypsy!"

"Margret's right. You're a natural, and you have two wandering goats to prove it! We'll have to train them to pull a cart – a little gypsy wagon!"

"Yes Mom! You could drive the cart into town and sell bouquets of roses!"

"Oh, I do like the thought of being a gypsy and dancing flamenco!"

"Okay, Mom, you're on your way to the barn with John, Tilly and Gypsy. He'll bring you back to the house at 1:30. I'll help you get dressed for dance, and we'll leave for the dance studio at 2:30."

Margret leaves Mom with John and heads back to the house to work on marketing the show. To put Anton Dance Company and Dance Studio on the map pushes Margret to dig deep and think outside the box. She's got an embryonic dance company and fledgling dance studio to shove onto the world stage.

"Thank God for Anton and Alvaro. They alone are worth the price of admission. I'll see if I can get a TV station to do an interview when Alvaro gets here. Heck, this is a rocket-launch town with the Space Force base just down the road. Five-four-three-two-one . . . we can do this!"

Vanessa arrives at the studio early for Margret's mom's lesson. Anton is resting on his siesta couch when he hears Vanessa knock on the studio door. He jumps up and hurries to open up for Vanessa.

"Hello!"

"Hi! I'm here for Margret's mom's private lesson. I hope I didn't disturb you!"

"No, no I was resting. I went full steam on my workout this morning. I think this show might do me in. I forgot you have the senior lesson before the children's class."

Anton reaches for Vanessa hand and pulls her into the studio. Susie bounds ahead and dances around Anton's feet. Vanessa, in a state of sudden panic, eases her hand back and picks up Susie.

"I can see my affection makes you uneasy."

"You noticed."

"I did, but I think you like me!"

"I'm not sure it's the best idea."

"I think it's a great idea!"

"It makes feel like I want to throw up."

"Well that's a start!"

"No seriously, I'm all mixed up, and Margret adores you. I wouldn't do anything to break that friendship. I mean we're the "three musketeers" and the show is just around the corner and . . ."

"I understand."

"You do?"

"Yes."

Margret arrives with Mom, and sees Vanessa and Anton talking.

"Margret! Vanessa and I were discussing some ideas for your mom's lesson."

Anton takes Mom's hand and bows.

"Margret tells me you're a gypsy! I have special affection for gypsies! Let me introduce you to Vanessa. She will be your instructor.

Anton leads Mom over to Vanessa then takes Susie to the siesta couch. Margret follows Anton to the back and sits down at the desk.

"Thanks Anton for such a gracious welcome for my mom. She is obviously charmed."

"You're very kind Margret. I'm happy to see this senior dance class start. Flamenco can do great things for seniors. Do you want to get a coffee while Vanessa teaches your mom her first steps?"

"Sure! I can bring you up to date on the marketing. I want to arrange a TV interview with you and Alvaro when he arrives."

"Let's get coffee."

Anton and Margret leave in the Gorilla. Vanessa shows Mom a basic step, and Mom is completely focused on tapping her toes and heels with alternating footsteps and a double heel tap thrown in every third heel tap.

"Bravo! Mom, is it alright if I call you Mom?"

Mom answers without looking up.

"Yes dear, I like it. It makes me feel like I'm part of a growing family!"

"I see where Margret gets her looks and her determination. The Anton Dance Studio outfit looks great on you, and I think you'll have this whole dance down before the end of the lesson!

Mom laughs without looking up. She continues her step pattern without error, albeit at a snail's pace.

"Margret and I are twins, and we have twin goats, Tilly and Gypsy."

"Mom, I'd like you to speed up the pattern some. I'll do it with you. I'll clap, and let's see how fast we can go."

"Oh yes! Let's do it!"

Vanessa increases the speed incrementally, and Mom stays right with her.

"Wow, Mom you're a natural."

"I should be. I'm a gypsy!"

Vanessa and Mom laugh. Vanessa is the first to get serious.

"Okay, now I up the ante."

"I love to gamble. Gypsies love card games."

"Mom, you're a riot!"

Mom watches her feet and continues her steps without looking up.

"Mom, let's raise the ante. You have to look down then look in the mirror to watch yourself dance."

"I'll try."

Mom's head pops up, and she zeros in on her reflection in the mirror while she keeps a steady beat with her feet.

"Mom, you're fantastic! Can you reach down and pick up your skirt while you dance? Show a little leg!"

Mom grins, lifts her skirt to her knees and swings it left and right while she keeps the beat with her feet. Vanessa shouts,

"Olé! Brava, señora!"

Mom, smiles at herself in the mirror. Vanessa slows the beat then stops. Mom follows her lead, stands still and waits for the next instruction.

"I think you are the best student I've ever had!"

"Thank you dear. I think you're the best instructor!"

"Okay, since you like to gamble, I'll throw in arms and hands to up the ante again."

Vanessa stands in front of Mom, faces the mirrors and

raises her arms up and down from her side to over her head. Mom follows her. Vanessa then turns around and shows Mom how to curl her fingers in and out while she turns her wrists to the inside and then the outside. Mom follows her. They stand, face each other and raise their arms up over their heads while they twirl their hands at the same time. They practice together then Vanessa steps away and claps a rhythm while Mom watches herself in the mirror

"Mom, here goes . . . add your feet while you move your arms."

"I think I reached my limit, dear. I can't get the double beat in."

"Try it again. I'll stand in front of you, do the steps and raise your arms up and down. That's it, you got it!! Now we'll add some music, so when Anton and Margret return you'll show them your dance!!"

"Did Margret and Anton leave?"

"Yes, they went for coffee, but they'll be back ASAP."

"Oh, he's a catch!"

"He sure is!"

Vanessa clicks the remote, and one of Anton's favorite flamenco guitar songs fills the studio with Latin soul. Mom beams with happiness.

"Okay Mom, follow me."

Vanessa faces the mirror. Mom stands behind Vanessa, copies her footsteps, raises her arms up and down and twirls her butterfly hands. The guitar music, along with the singer, inspires Mom and Vanessa to move forward and back. Mom spontaneously picks up her skirt, flings it from side to side, shows plenty of good-looking leg and continues to keep a steady beat while she moves around the room. Vanessa whistles and shouts,

"Bravo! Olé!"

Anton opens the studio door, and Margret is stunned to see her mom dance! Anton quickly partners with Mom, and they dance around the room to together with continuous basic footwork. Anton claps, and Mom flips her skirt clear to the end of the song.

"Oh My God, Mom, you dance flamenco!"

"I sure do, and I love it! Vanessa is wonderful, and he's a catch! Can I do this every day?"

"Mom, we'll have a weekly class, but you can practice every day at home when Margret gets Masonite and puts it on the floor. You'll have plenty of opportunity to practice!"

"Vanessa's right Mom, you and I can practice every day on the front porch. We'll teach John how to dance flamenco too! Now, it's time to go home, feed Tilly and Gypsy and tend your roses."

"Yes, let's go. I can't wait to show John my dance!"

"Thank you Vanessa. You obviously did a spectacular job teaching Mom! Anton and I had a great mini-meeting. He can bring you up to speed on what's in store. Alvaro will take no prisoners!!

Vanessa and Anton stand side by side at the door and watch Margret and Mom load into the Gorilla. Margret backs out, and Mom leans out the window to shout,

"Olé! Vanessa and the catch!! See you next week!"

Vanessa and Anton wave back. Vanessa goes to the siesta couch and curls up with Susie. Anton sits at his desk.

"I know where Margret gets her energy! Mom is a riot, and can she ever dance! This senior class is going to keep me on my toes, literally!"

"It sure looks like she loves her new dance instructor."

"She loves the idea of being a gypsy that's for sure! How was coffee with Margret?"

"Good. We discussed the show and a TV interview with Alvaro when he arrives. Vanessa, I do understand your concerns, and I will keep my hands to myself. I haven't been interested in a relationship for a long time. It feels wonderful to experience a spark."

"I wish I could say the same. I feel dread, terror and nausea."

Anton laughs.

"I have to say I've never experienced this kind of response to my affection, but then I've never known anyone with PTSD, and I've never known anyone that can dance like you."

Susie waits for an opportunity to play with Anton. She bounces off the couch and leaps into Anton's lap.

"Well, Susie's love and affection is consolation. I hope we can still play chess, eat hot dogs and pizza and dance flamenco."

Vanessa gets up from the couch and puts a leash on Susie for her walk home. Susie is hesitant to leave. Vanessa gives her a little tug.

"Yes. Like Mom said, 'You're a catch'."

Anton walks the pair to the door and watches them leave. He walks back to his desk, sits down, opens his desk drawer and sees his Rosary. He gently touches the beads closes his eyes and smiles.

THIRTY

At first glance, it would appear that Margret is overwhelmed with the ambitious plan she has created to put Anton Dance Company on the world stage, but truth is she relishes every moment. As a young woman, she helped her father on so many occasions communicate with government officials to host company events around the world. The Anton Dance Company is small potatoes.

However, one element has her laser focus, and that's Alvaro with his established-international reputation. Her mission is to take advantage of his star power to build a reputation for Anton and his fledgling dance company. Her motive is pure, and this gives her an edge. She truly believes in Anton and, with Vanessa in Anton's dance company and her own dance breakthrough, she's convinced the upcoming *La Vida* is worthy of all the attention she can garner. She's been in touch with Alvaro's all-in-one publicist and personal assistant, Angelica, several times, and each contact leaves her more impressed. Now, Margret knows she must raise the bar and convince Alvaro that he's landed in a very big pond as the biggest fish.

"Angelica, speaking . . ."

"Hello Angelica, this is Margret with the *La Vida* production."

"Hello Margret! You are kind to give such attention to Alvaro's arrival."

"Anton is honored to have Alvaro on the program. He has asked me to be sure to take care of all his travel needs. If possible, and not too much trouble for you, I would like to have all the details of Alvaro's itinerary in place this week. This will ensure that we have a proper welcome to celebrate his arrival."

"That's wonderful, Margret, I just finalized his travel plans, and I can email you the itinerary this afternoon. I only wish I could be there to see the show!"

"Angelica, thank you, again, for all your help with Alvaro's travel. We'll have to squeeze another event onto Alvaro's crowded calendar and bring you over here to celebrate with us!"

"That sounds wonderful. It would be a pleasure to meet you and see the California Central Coast!"

"We'll work on it!"

"Yes! I'll send the itinerary and look forward to meeting you in the future!"

"Muchas gracias, Angelica!"

Margret hangs up the phone, takes a deep breath and draws a line through item one on her today list. With two hour dance rehearsals every day, and running a household and farm, Margret is a fanatic about time management.

Vanessa is considerably more relaxed. She moves from assignment to assignment without a ripple, and she and Susie take frequent breaks to stroll through the neighborhood. Dance class teacher, bookkeeper for the dance company and studio, and the two hour dance rehearsals everyday hardly faze her. She continues to make it all look easy.

Anton is still the hummingbird despite all the help with the studio and dance company. His siesta couch is his refuge when he hits overload, but *La Vida* is his dream come true, and he works tirelessly to bring it to life.

Alvaro is the new piece in the puzzle, and the "three Musketeers" are determined to make his time on the California Central Coast a peak experience.

Margret sits at the studio desk and settles down after a grueling two hour dance rehearsal. Vanessa continues to practice some particularly demanding foot work in front of the mirror, and Anton sorts through CDs of flamenco guitar music.

"Anton, I'm in touch with Alvaro's assistant, and she sent me his itinerary. He arrives at 11:00 a.m. at the local airport. It's the morning of the first rehearsal at the Civic Auditorium. I arranged for our film crew to document key moments throughout the rehearsals leading up to the show. Do you want to capture his arrival at the airport, and do you want to use the Gorilla to pick him up?"

"Yes to both questions, and what do you say to all three of us arrive in the Gorilla to give him the ride of a lifetime?!"

Margret laughs and claps her hands.

"Vanessa, will you stop a minute with the footwork! You never missed a step in the whole two hours! I watched you!"

Vanessa, laughs, stops and turns to face Margret.

"Do you want to go with us to the airport, in the Gorilla, to welcome Alvaro?"

"Definitely, what a moment . . .!"

"Anton, it's 'yes' to the Gorilla ride."

"Great. If Alvaro sees the cameras, he will probably give them a little show. That's who he is!

"Perfect, that's exactly what we need for getting a buzz going on social media and clips for our documentary!"

"Margret, my mom arrives tomorrow. Could you bring your mom to the senior class the day after tomorrow? I know it's close to the show, but I want to keep the momentum. I'm going to bring my real estate friend,` and Mom would make three seniors, and Anton, if your mama arrives in time, it would make four!!"

"I found out yesterday my mama is unable to travel. Her passport is delayed, and she won't have it in time to arrive for the show. I tried everything in my power to see if I could help expedite the process, but it's a firm 'No'. She also mentioned she isn't feeling well, so this might not be the best time to travel anyway."

Vanessa and Margret are shocked.

"Oh no, Anton, you must be terribly disappointed. You were excited to see her and share your life here with her. Vanessa had her scheduled to show our seniors how to dance flamenco! Bureaucracy can be cruel!"

"I'm disappointed yes, but when Mama says she isn't feeling well, I listen. She is never sick and never complains, so after the show I will visit Cuba and surprise her!! Maybe we'll all go to Cuba and put on a little show for Mama!"

"Oh yes! I would love to go to Cuba and meet Mama! We could close the studio for a week and have a vacation! I'll look into travel requirements for Susie!"

"Anton, Vanessa is on board and so am I. Cuba here we come! If *La Vida* is the success I think it's going to be, they'll roll out the red carpet!!"

Anton laughs.

"How am I so fortunate to have my two primas flamenco artists so loyal to their Artistic Director?"

Margret responds,

"Maybe it's because you saved us. You made our life so much better in every way! Anton we love you, and that's why. Simple!"

"Well … that explains it! The feeling is mutual."

"I'd like to stick around all day, but my mom arrives today. I'd better be ready!

"Hopefully, I'll see you this afternoon. The dresses arrived and Maria plans to distribute the clothes and check everyone's kits for make-up, earrings and hair accessories to be sure the classes look professional. Margret, if you want to make a plea for active efforts to bring friends and family to the show, you're welcome to make an announcement."

"I'd love to. I want to see the dresses!"

"Come Susie. We need to pack a few things, and your

new Grandma can't wait to meet you!"

Anton escorts Margret, Vanessa and Susie to the door.

"Thanks again for all you two are doing to make this show a success."

Susie doesn't want to leave and tries to hang back. Anton scoops her up and hands her over to Vanessa.

"Like I said, she has a terrible crush on you!"

Anton laughs.

"The feeling is mutual!"

"Vanessa, jump in the Gorilla. I'll give you and Susie a lift home."

"Thanks Margret! It's always fun to be with you and your Gorilla!"

Anton stands in the studio door, waves and calls out,

"Hasta la vista, mis amigas!"

Margret rounds the corner and pulls up in front of Vanessa's apartment.

"Here we are . . . can I ask you a question?"

"Sure. . ."

"I know Susie has a crush on Anton . . . do you?"

"You mean like everyone in the Anton Dance Studio!"

"That's true, but I mean do you see how he looks at you?"

"I know he likes me as a friend, but I doubt it's anything

romantic. Besides, I'm off the field. I'm so messed up even the thought of a relationship makes me panic."

Margret laughs.

"I know what you mean. I just wasn't sure you realized he's crazy about you."

"Maybe I haven't noticed because, with all the other freak out things on my radar, a relationship is the last thing I can handle."

"Well, get used to it girl, because it's coming for you!"

"Hopefully, I can dodge the arrow."

Vanessa and Margret laugh. Their bond is in tack. Vanessa sighs with relief as she unlocks the door to her apartment. She looks around the room.

"Susie, I have no idea why I said I have to pack! There's nothing here to pack. Probably take us thirty minutes to load up what's here and move it to the house."

Vanessa turns on her computer and is about to play virtual chess when the phone rings.

"Hello?

"Hi Sugarcane!"

"Hi Momma! I was just about to play a practice game of chess. I'm preparing for battle. No more chess-for-one after you arrive!"

"That's right Sugar Pie. I take no prisoners. I want to let you know I rented a car, so we can get around town easily. I'll arrive at your place around noon, and we can see Jackson after lunch and check out our new digs!"

"Jackson?"

"Yes, the real estate salesman!"

"What a cool name."

"Yes, and he's a delightful man. He said he signed up for the flamenco dance class."

"Yes, and we have the flamenco class the day after tomorrow."

"I can't wait. It'll feel wonderful to dance again . . . that is if I can stop the tears long enough to smile. It's been rough these last few days, but I'm ready dear. I really am ready to put Texas behind me."

"Mom, you'll love it here. It's a fresh start. Dad would want that for you."

"Okay. That's enough. I don't want to cry anymore. I cry at the smallest things."

"Mom, I can't wait to see you!"

"Ditto that my dear. I'll see you tomorrow at noon."

Vanessa hangs up and remembers the dress fittings at 4:00 p.m. at the studio. She texts Margret to remind her and heads over to Glenn's Market for a deli sandwich before going to the studio.

Anton sees Vanessa pass by the studio window, hurries to the studio door and calls out,

"Vanessa!"

Vanessa quickly ties Susie to the news stand, waves to Anton and disappears into Glenn's market. She wants to surprise Anton with a soda and chips. She waits in line to order a sandwich. Five minutes pass before she's able to check out. She takes her chips, soda and sandwich and goes to meet Susie at the news stand. As she approaches an older woman leans over, talks to Susie, unties her and picks her up to hug her. Vanessa watches in horror.

"Oh, you found my little girl, my "Zippy". I lost her a few months ago, and here she is! I know it's a silly name. My granddaughter named her. My daughter gave her to me to keep me company. I was recovering from pneumonia, and I was alone all day. I wouldn't have made it without her. I can't believe I found her. I thought she was gone forever!"

Vanessa is frozen in panic and stares at the woman. She barely makes sense of what she hears. Zippy licks the woman's face and is clearly happy to be in her arms.

"I'm so grateful you found her. She must have been a ragged mess. Her fur gets matted without her daily brushing. I can't offer much, but I'd like to give you the reward for finding her and taking such good care of her. I don't live in the neighborhood, so you probably missed the signs with her picture. My granddaughter was devastated. I can't wait to surprise her!"

Vanessa continues to stare, and the woman asks if she's okay.

"I hope you understand how much she means to me and my family. Zippy pulled me through a dangerous time in my life. I really want to thank you and give you the reward we had written on the 'lost' posters."

Vanessa manages to turn her head left and right in slow motion to indicate "no" to the reward, and the woman in her excitement calls her daughter to tell her she found Zippy.

"My daughter is on her way. I rode public transportation here, and I wouldn't be allowed to take Zippy on the bus. I don't want to lose her again!"

The more the woman talks, the deeper Vanessa sinks into panic. She knows Susie is Zippy, and there's no escaping the right thing to do, but her heart and brain are disconnected. Vanessa is frozen in mind and body and nods "yes" helplessly, as the woman and Zippy get into her daughter's car and drive away.

Vanessa walks with her sandwich and Anton's potato chips, soda and salsa to the studio. Anton opens the door to let her in.

"Where's Susie?"

The question shatters Vanessa, and she breaks down. Anton reaches out and prevents her from falling. He supports her as she sobs in his arms and tells him what happened. He wordlessly comforts Vanessa, and guides her to the siesta couch. He takes the crocheted throw, wraps it around Vanessa and eases her onto the couch. Anton worries Vanessa will slide into darkness so black that she won't be able to come out without Susie.

Margret arrives early and sees Vanessa curled up on the siesta couch. Anton has his finger over his lips as he walks over to Margret to explain. He guides Margret outside, tells her what happened while Margret closes her eyes to stop the tears.

"Margret, Maria and I can take care of the fittings and the final inspections of the kits and accessories. Can you take Vanessa home? As soon as the classes have all they need for the show, I'll take over so you can get back to your mom. I don't think Vanessa should be alone. Her mom,

Catherine, arrives tomorrow at noon. We have our morning two hour rehearsal, and, hopefully, Vanessa can handle it."

"Yes . . . and how are you doing?"

"I'm okay. I'm not sure about Vanessa. It's brutal."

Margret puts the posters on the desk and goes to Vanessa.

"Vanessa we need to go. I'll take you home and stay with you. When the fittings are over Anton will come over, and I'll go home to Mom. We'll be with you all the way."

Vanessa grabs onto to Margret and gets up. She's unable to stand on her own. Margret guides her to the Gorilla and helps her onto the passenger seat. They drive in silence. Margret helps Vanessa find her key. Inside the apartment, Margret makes up the couch into a bed. Vanessa lies down and cries. Margret pulls all the curtains closed, looks around the apartment and thinks to herself,

"Thank God her mother is coming and moving her out of this place!"

Margret picks up the chess book, starts to read and nods off. A knock on the door wakes Margret, and she lets Anton in. Mercifully, Vanessa is asleep. Margret feels Anton's pain.

"She's strong, Anton, stronger than you think, she'll make it through this.

"I'm not sure."

"You'll see."

Margret gives Anton a hug and leaves.

Anton finds an extra blanket in the closet. He lies down with his back to Vanessa and stares into the dark. Susie's gone, Vanessa is destroyed and his mama isn't well. . .

"Luisa!"

Anton sits up, nudges Vanessa and looks to see if she wakes up. Vanessa is groggy but conscious. She suddenly realizes Anton is sitting on her bed.

"Anton! What are you doing here?"

"The news about Susie is so upsetting. Margret and I thought you shouldn't be alone. But I forgot about Luisa. I have to go home to feed her. Are you okay here, or do you want to come with me?"

Vanessa starts to cry.

"Okay, you're coming with me. We'll stay at my house."

"I can't believe it."

"I know. Let's get out of here."

Vanessa is relieved Anton doesn't want to talk. They arrive at the house, and Luisa jumps up on the back porch and howls. Inside the kitchen, Anton feeds Luisa and brews tea.

Vanessa sits on the couch in the living room. Anton comes in, takes her hands, pulls her up and leads her to his bedroom. He gives Vanessa pajamas, towel, slippers and tells her to take a hot bath and go to bed.

"I'll leave a cup of tea on the bed stand. I'm sleeping on the couch. If you need anything, I'm next door."

"Thank you, Anton, but I can sleep on the couch."

"No, Vanessa."

Vanessa wiggles her toes while she soaks in the hot water.

It's been a long time since she had a bathtub to soak in. Her nose is just above the water line. She closes her eyes, and tears squeeze through her eyelids. She holds her breath and sinks down to the bottom of the tub. She feels the water run into her ears, and her hair swirl around her head. She stays submerged until her lungs drive her up to gasp for air. She sees shampoo and washes her hair. Then sinks again to rinse and turns on the faucet. She sticks her head under to do a final rinse. She gets out, dries off and puts on the pajamas. She slips her feet into the floppy slippers and towel dries her mass of curls. She remembers Susie's first bath and feels the heartache of lost love. She goes into Anton's bedroom and slides into bed. She drinks the tea, turns out the light and feels Luisa jump up and curl into a ball at the base of the pillow next to her. Vanessa rolls over and reaches out to stroke Luisa. She listens to her purr, finds comfort and falls asleep.

THIRTY- ONE

Anton is up early. No beach today. He feeds Luisa who marches into the kitchen and demands attention. Anton sits at the table and considers what he can do to help Vanessa move through the loss of Susie. He remembers his mama's sadness with the sudden death of his father. His mama would get up early, before she thought anyone was awake, and Anton would hear her cry. Anton made coffee for his mama and waited in the kitchen like his father did every morning before going to work. She would drink her coffee and pretend she was okay, and Anton helped her pretend so life could go on. Beneath the façade of okay was a potentially fatal cut, but the pretending to be okay helped the family survive the wound and the sadness heal.

Anton hears Vanessa cry. He makes coffee and waits in the kitchen. He hears his bedroom door open, and Vanessa appears in the kitchen. She's surprised Anton is already up. He hands Vanessa a cup of coffee. They sit in silence. The soldier inside Vanessa answers the call to duty.

"We have a big day ahead! I know you're worried, but I'm okay. Susie got me ready for this, and I can manage. Her real owner didn't show up a day too soon, and I'm thankful I had her as long as I did. We gave each other everything we needed. I'm sad, but we saved each other. Besides, she was one hundred percent your dog, and I think if you had been there, the woman would never have been able to drag her off!"

Anton smiles at the thought of Susie refusing to go with her rightful owner. Margret is right. Vanessa will be okay.

"I can see you're going to be alright . . . I'm not sure about me! I've never experienced unconditional love like Susie shared with me. She spoiled me for any future relationships. If they don't love me like Susie did, forget it!"

"Ah, Anton, every girl and woman at Anton Dance Studio adores you! Take your pick."

Anton laughs.

"You mean you'd give me up that easy? You'd just throw me to wolves?"

Vanessa smiles,

"No, just sharing some unconditional love."

Anton smiles while he clears the coffee cups.

"Let's get out of here. Lupe has coffee and pasteles, and we have dance practice. While we drink coffee at Lupe's, we can visualize a robbery at a jewelry store!"

"Anton, be sure to add Lupe to the list of adoring fans."

"As long as you're on the list, that's all I care about."

Anton smiles while Luisa "yowls" and demands breakfast.

Anton confirms,

"There's nothing unconditional about Luisa!"

At Lupe's, Vanessa and Anton sketch out jewelry store ideas and imagine rear screen projections for the *La Vida* set designer. Lupe keeps their coffee hot and their bellies full. Lupe is all about unconditional love.

"Lupe, Vanessa and I will be so full of your delicious pasteles we won't be able to move. I hope you still plan to be part of the pre-show feast!"

Lupe points to Margaret's La Vida poster displayed on the wall behind the cash register.

"Oh yes, Señor Anton, and all the policemen who drink my coffee and eat my pasteles can't wait to see the show!"

"Bravo!!"

Anton, always ready to entertain, gives a preview of the show with a display of intense footwork, arms that twirl and finger snaps to the delight of Lupe's Panaderia customers. He finishes with a flourish, takes Vanessa's hand and leads her out the door to the pricey sports car that saved Lupe from the cruel immigration bullies and transformed them into grateful patrons. Anton opens up the convertible soft top and puts in a flamenco guitar CD. They drive with air blowing music all around them.

Margaret waits on the bench in front of the studio. There's a space in front of the studio, and Anton with Vanessa pulls into the spot and turns up the music. They dance out of the car, pull Margret up from the bench and start a parade on the sidewalk in front of the studio. Mall regulars join in and visitors clap and shout,

'Bravo! It's a pop-up fiesta!'

The song ends, and Anton reaches into the car and turns off the music. Margaret promotes *La Vida*, Anton demonstrates flamenco dance steps, and Vanessa chats with the salon owner about her chipped and broken acrylics. He advises gel polish for the show.

"That's a good idea. I'll tell all the women to come to your salon for the gel polish! Be sure to have lots of bright red in stock!"

"Yes, and tell them they can have special discount for nails this Saturday for *La Vida*!"

"I will!"

Margaret has done her job. It's seems like the whole community is ready to celebrate *La Vida*. Ticket sales are strong and likely to sell out. With Alvaro's reputation, she was able to get some print articles in a few significant publications, and TV coverage of the event. The buzz continues to build, and Anton is astonished at Margret's ability to promote the emergent Anton Dance Company.

The pop up parade disperses, and Anton, Vanessa and Margret disappear into the studio. Once inside Margret touches Vanessa's arm.

"Are you okay?"

"Inside, I'm very sad, but I'm good at letting go. Susie is right where she belongs, and I'm grateful to have had her as long as I did. She saved me!"

"I get it. Before Tilly arrived, I thought your Susie attachment seemed weird."

Now, that I have two goats, I get it. I want to take them with me everywhere! I want to sleep in the barn with them. Flamenco, goats and a Gorilla saved me."

Vanessa and Margret laugh and give each other a high five to celebrate their saviors. Anton is ready to dance.

"Places. Let's review the burglary. Let's see if we can increase our commitment to the story and move the audience to their feet in defense of the defenseless."

Anton puts a flamenco CD on, and each dancer hits their mark. The jewelry store owner (Margaret) is intimidated by the burglar (Anton), and the witness (Vanessa) is convincing. The level of concentration portrayed by each character is a foretaste of what is coming to the Civic Auditorium. The music stops, and all three dancers struggle to breathe. Even Anton is tested by the extreme push to pull out the internal desperation in the armed robbery situation. After today's dance practice each dancer wonders if there is more they can bring to the performance. Anton leads.

"Let's call off rehearsals for today and tomorrow and reset our pace. When Alvaro arrives, he will drive full speed ahead. I want to protect you. Keep rehearsing in your head, but give your bodies a rest."

"I'm relieved you want to take a break. I felt like this the first time I tried my mountain bike and found myself speeding out of control."

"And I revisited the hostage situation at the liquor store. Talk about scary! I don't know if I can sustain that kind of terror in a dance and keep my balance."

"Excellent insights, let's respect the warnings and slow down. Vanessa, I know your mom arrives at noon. We'll close up early, and you can go home and get ready for the big move. Margaret, you and I can have lunch and discuss the pre-show schedule for the audience with the Cuban food truck and Lupe's Panaderia. Maybe at lunch, we have a mental walk through the Civic, so when we pick up the key, we hit the road running – or better yet dancing. We'll show our ideas to Alvaro at the Civic before the band and technicians arrive."

"Sounds good to me, we can ride in the Gorilla, and Vanessa, we can drop you off at the apartment."

Vanessa is subdued.

"Thanks guys. I think I'll walk and get my head screwed on about Susie before my mom arrives."

Vanessa and Anton are silent and concerned.

"No worries. I'm sad, but I can handle it. She taught me a lot."

Vanessa changes out of her dance clothes and pretends to be okay. Anton recognizes the pain and gives Vanessa a quick hug. She bursts into tears.

"Better to cry now and drain the lake of sorrow then dam up the stream and have a flood during the performance!"

Anton agrees.

"Amen to that, Margret."

Vanessa wipes her face with her hands, and Margaret gets a tissue packet for Vanessa.

"Keep these in your pocket, cry as much as you want,

anywhere you want, until the tank is empty."

Vanessa laughs through her tears.

"Anton, let's go get that lunch and give Vanessa time to pull herself together for her mom's arrival. I'll be right back to pick you up. Let the lake drain before your mom arrives. You don't want her drowning with you!"

Anton is tender.

"Vanessa, no worries, you have this handled. You still have your sense of humor. That's what will carry you through now. It's a gift to be able to see sad things as they are and still be able to laugh. I knew a man who lived to be a hundred and two – strong and sharp. He always chuckled at the smallest amusements."

"If my humor can get me through this next week, I'll be grateful! If you hear me burst out laughing during the show, you can blame yourself for your advice!"

Anton and Vanessa high five each other, just as Margret arrives in the Gorilla. Vanessa turns and walks towards her apartment, and Anton watches her go then turns around and climbs into the Gorilla.

"You're caught."

"As in hooked? Yes."

"Stay on the line, she's wonderful, and you deserve wonderful."

"You're next."

"You never know, you never know. . ."

Anton smiles as Margret peals away from the curb in her

untamed Gorilla.

Vanessa walks to her apartment focused on her mom's arrival. When she opens her apartment door, she sees Susie's dish and fights off tears. She puts the dish and extra dog food in the box labeled kitchen.

"I'll give this to mom. When she sees the yard, she'll know it's time to get another dog."

The apartment is filled with boxes and items ready to be packed. Everything is in perfect order detailed with room, closet and cupboard information. Hence, movers can close up the boxes and deliver them to specific locations throughout the new house based on the same schematic Catherine emailed Vanessa after she packed up her house in Texas.

A sharp knock on the door, and Vanessa races to throw open the door to welcome her mom.

"Mom!!!!"

"Sugarcane!!!! I was hoping this was the right door. Now inside, I can't believe you stayed here as long as you have. It's dark and grim as in Grimm Brother's Fairytales. Scary!! I'm glad to see you're ready to move. This place can't be good for anyone's mental health!"

"I know. I wasn't in the greatest frame of mind when I moved in. I can't wait to show you our new digs!"

"I can't wait to rescue you from this hell hole. Thank God you have Susie. Where's the little fox?"

"Mom, it's a sad story but a happy ending. I'll fill you in at lunch."

"Let's skedaddle, Honey. I plan to do everything your

daddy would do, and the first thing would be to get you out of here."

Catherine and Vanessa close the door on the studio apartment. Vanessa sees the Cadillac convertible Catherine rented for her first day in California. It's a warm November afternoon, so Catherine powers down the soft top roof. Vanessa and Catherine pull away in style – exactly how Vanessa's dad would want it. At lunch Vanessa shares the Susie story and her hostage moments. She generally fills Catherine in on her life to date in this Space Force town with its pluses and minuses.

"Honey, I'm ready to meet Jackson and see the house! I can't wait for the movers to roll up with your things and know that chapter of your life is officially over. First thing we'll do is find some English Cream Golden Retriever pups, and you can have the pick of the litter. I know your dad would want you to pick a shabby mutt from the pound, but that's just a bridge too far."

The two women wear big sunglasses and the hats Catherine had in the trunk. They park in front of the real estate office. Jackson sees them through the front window and guesses they must be Catherine and Vanessa. Catherine sees Jackson get up from his desk and walk to the front door.

"Is it possible to have love-at-first-sight twice in one lifetime? He's a prize!"

"And you get to dance with him tomorrow afternoon. Senior-flamenco-dance class starts at three. He signed up before he knew the belle of the ball would be attending!"

"That's quite a chariot you two are riding in, a perfect pairing with your sunglasses and hats!"

"Jackson, let me introduce you to my mom, Catherine."

"Hello, Catherine, you're every bit as charming in person as you are on the phone. Welcome to the California Central Coast, and congratulations on your purchase of the best historic house in Old Town downtown. You and Vanessa are a wonderful addition to the neighborhood."

"Thank you, Jackson, for making it possible. I can't say I'm disappointed to meet you, and I can't wait to see this gem of a house."

"I'll give you the keys, and you can see your house before the movers arrive. You mentioned they are scheduled to start the move-in today at two."

"Yes, and if you can join us, we're going to pick a tasting room and celebrate after we see the house. Wineries are everywhere!"

"I know just the one to go to for a celebration."

Vanessa sees the chemistry between Jackson and Catherine. Jackson is captivated by Catherine's southern charm. The air is electric and watching her mom come alive after the years of suffering with her father's painful decline gives Vanessa a bittersweet lift.

"Let's go! I'll drive, and we can enjoy a California celebration. Jackson, lock this office up and watch a diehard Texas bluebonnet morph into a California poppy."

The trio laughs out loud as the wind ruffles everyone's hair. Jackson sits in the back, and the two southern belles enjoy the front seat. Its Thanksgiving season, and their mood is festive as they pull up in front of the classic Mediterranean house with its backyard enclosed inside a historic rock wall. Catherine is in shock and tears up.

"Vanessa your daddy would have loved this house. We'll find a dog immediately. Jackson, you have made life better than bearable with this California classic and your delightful presence. I can't wait for our flamenco class. The blue in my bluebonnet blossom is now bright orange, and I can feel California orange run through my veins!"

"Wait 'til you see inside, Catherine. California will make a clean sweep over Texas like the San Francisco Forty-niners would trample the Dallas Cowboys!"

"Ha! Not a chance, but I'm happy you like a good football game!"

The tour of the house is equally satisfying, and, at every turn, Catherine expresses enthusiasm with a host of ideas on how to decorate this stately home. Vanessa is thrilled to see a side of her mom come to life that has been buried in sadness for so long.

"Sugarcane, we're going to finish this tour, welcome the movers and be on our way to celebrate. And, Vanessa, I want you to call the local pound, and see if they have a big-scruffy mutt we can adopt today! Your daddy gave us this dream house, and he's going to move in with a big-furry dog to remind us of how he's still looking after us. Male or female, we'll call the dog, Ralph!"

"Mom, California does run in your veins! To get a mutt from the pound is so Central Coast. I can't believe you're saying you want a mutt."

"Sugarcane, I don't want a big-sloppy mutt. You're dad does! And he deserves to have one here or in heaven, so we'll start here on earth!"

Jackson listens to the bittersweet banter between Vanessa

and Catherine.

"Nothing like a loyal mutt to look after two beautiful women in Old Town downtown, and the pound is only minutes away!"

The movers arrive and begin to unload boxes and furniture that is marked with details for each location in the house. Catherine takes charge and tells the crew she will return in an hour and a half, and to expect the second team of movers to arrive with her daughter's boxes and furniture that must go directly to the guest bedroom upstairs. With everything in order Catherine, Vanessa and Jackson ride in the topless Cadillac to the local pound. Vanessa is sure there's a big-friendly mutt waiting for them.

Inside the pound, an attendant encourages the trio to tour the kennels and find their forever dog. Sure enough, as they round a corner, there's a black-shaggy mutt too big for his bench. He lies with his white tipped tail draped down to the floor on one end of the bench, and his long legs with four white paws hang over the side of the bench. His wolfhound head hangs beyond the other end of bench. He likes his perch, but he doesn't fit, and he doesn't care. When he sees the trio, he lifts his head and wags his tail. Catherine and Vanessa speak out together,

"Ralph!!!"

Ralph slides off his perch and comes over to the gate. Catherine is completely taken by Ralph's natural calm and elegance inside his scruffy-fur coat. He's no homeless-downbeat dog. He's a classy hobo down on his luck until today!

Promises made and paperwork filed, the majestic Ralph leads the pack out the pound door. Ralph senses that the Cadillac might be his new ride. Ralph joins Jackson in the back seat, and Vanessa and Catherine look over their shoulders at every stop light and stop sign to observe Ralph. Jackson is comfortable with Ralph as his seat mate, and Ralph appreciates that Jackson lightly scratches his ears. Ralph is satisfied with his new family.

Next stop is Jackson's recommended winery. The foursome parks in the busy lot and waits on the patio for a server to serve them some celebration. This winery doesn't disappoint! A round of wine tasting and sparkling apple cider, tapas and a dog biscuit for Ralph compliment the view of a PGA worthy community golf course. It's an afternoon of toasts to an adopted dog, new friends and a family reunion.

Back at the new-old house, Catherine settles Ralph in the yard while the movers finish up. Jackson thanks Catherine and Vanessa for a fun afternoon, says good bye and confirms he'll be ready to learn flamenco basics tomorrow, at the Anton Dance Studio, at three o'clock.

Vanessa and Catherine seek out their respective rooms and lay down on the beds with a feeling of satisfaction that this day was indeed a perfect day! Both women make their beds, shower and dress in pajamas and slippers to enjoy an evening of complete relaxation. Catherine calls out to Vanessa,

"We forgot to get dog food for Ralph!!"

"Okay. Let's load up. I'll run into Glenn's Market and get dog food and logs for the fireplace while you order take-out from Pepe's."

"Vanessa, we're in pajamas!!"

"No worries, I'll trade my slippers for shoes, put on a coat and no one will know the difference. Ralph can sit in the back seat with the roof up and guard you and the car. We have a security detail now! I can't wait to share our first fire in the fireplace!"

"Sugarcane, I'm telling you, again, how grateful I am you told me to 'consider' a move to California Central Coast! You were way ahead of the curve on this one."

"Mom, I'm so glad you're here, and tomorrow we'll dance Flamenco and celebrate life. Dad would want that for both of us."

THIRTY-TWO

Vanessa wakes to a morning of undressed windows and hears Ralph snoring at the end of her bed. How quickly Ralph has filled the hole Susie left when her rightful owner scooped her up and drove away. Vanessa ponders the way events in life speed by. You either jump on the train or stay stuck at the station.

"I wonder if I'm stuck at the station with Anton. I still feel ill when I think of a relationship, but maybe I just have to board the train and see where it takes me. I understand Margret's fascination with trains!"

"Rise and shine Sugarcane! Let's get this house put together before our dance class."

Vanessa remembers her childhood, and what a drill sergeant her mom was. Remnants of that side of her personality are still in the shadows itching to takeover.

"You can start Mom. I'll take Ralph out for a quick walk and pick up some breakfast at the café I noticed a couple of blocks from here."

Catherine remembers what a feral cat Vanessa was as a child and sees she's still wildly independent.

"Okay, Vanessa, and be sure to go in and out through the kitchen, so Ralph doesn't muddy up the house with his dirty paws."

Vanessa and Catherine laugh. The boundaries are set without discussion. That's Texas charm. They both know that each of them will need their own territory for this household to work.

"Ralph, let's go for a walk. Give me a minute to put on sweats and find something to use as a leash. Mom what do you want from the café?"

"Coffee, Sweetheart, and an omelette with bacon on the side and well-done hash browns! We're still celebrating! Oh and fresh squeezed California orange juice!"

"You got it! My treat this time! You can do the big celebrations like yesterday!"

"Fair enough, and remember milk and sugar in the coffee, Sugarcane."

"That would be like forgetting a lifetime of breakfasts with you and Dad. Let's go Ralph!"

Vanessa and Ralph bound out of the house with Vanessa's robe belt for a leash. They return with breakfast and warm coffee. Ralph has his own sausage paddy. Vanessa starts a fire in the fireplace, and Catherine and Vanessa sit on a couch, face the fire, dig into breakfast and lick their fingers. Ralph licks his paws while lying on his inherited bed that the movers found tucked in the moving van and placed near the fireplace. Three strays are finally home. Vanessa pulls her phone out of her pocket and calls Margret.

"Hey there, my mom, Catherine, arrived and is ready for the senior-flamenco-dance class. Jackson, the real estate agent is eager to join too. I hope Mom and your ranch manager, John, are still up for dancing – three o'clock, at the studio today!"

"Absolutely! Mom picked out a rose-covered skirt and already had me order bright-red-leather-flamenco-dance shoes that were delivered two days ago. I told you she's a gypsy, and I wasn't kidding. She's stepped over the border. I hope I can convince her to leave Tilly and Gypsy at the farm!!"

"This is wild! See you at the studio at ten for the usual Cuban pretzel workout!"

"No, Vanessa, remember he's giving us a break before the fireworks."

"That's right! Thanks for the reminder. I could feel my body start to ache before we even started. Okay, well, remember Alvaro's arrival tomorrow."

"Oh, yeah, I have a small film crew coming to document the drama. I'm milking his reputation for all its worth."

Vanessa and Margret laugh at Mom's obsession with gypsies, plan Alvaro's grand entrance then hang up.

Catherine starts to open the living room boxes and places a few framed photos of Vanessa's father on an end table by the couch. Ralph sniffs the pictures, wags his tail, as if to say "thank you" and romps to the backdoor barking to be let out.

Vanessa checks her phone clock.

"Mom, we need to leave in fifteen minutes to get to the studio on time. You can change into dance clothes and shoes at the studio. You won't believe this loan closet! I'll run upstairs and change. Ralph can come too!"

Catherine, Vanessa and Ralph arrive as Margret, Mom and John pull into a space in front of the studio. Anton finishes up calls to the *La Vida* stage manager and lighting director. He opens the door to the crowd and is bowled over by Ralph. Anton laughs as he regains his balance.

"And who is this handsome gentleman?"

Vanessa beams with happiness and introduces the shaggy-gentle giant and her mom to Anton, Margret, Mom and John. Jackson slips into the studio and stands next to Catherine.

"Anton, Margret, Mom and John, I'd like you to meet my mom, Catherine and finally, Ralph, a local mutt from the pound who is now part of our family. Jackson, standing next to Catherine, is the real estate agent who sold us our dream home. Margret, do you want to introduce John?"

"Sure. Everyone this is John. He manages "Tilly's Farm" and is master of the rose garden."

"Goodbye Texas, hello California! So many handsome men in one room and my dance card is empty!"

A round of laughter and Mom shouts,

"Every one of them is a catch! I can't decide who to take home!"

There's another round of laughter.

Anton speaks,

"It's great to have you all here at the studio. Vanessa wants to get started with the class, so I say 'hasta la vista.' We'll meetup and get to know each other well during this week of rehearsals and the final *La Vida* performance. Ralph, I'll put a spare blanket down, and you're welcome to stretch out on the siesta couch or the floor – whichever you prefer. Tomorrow, we welcome international-flamenco sensation, Alvaro, from Cuba. All of you are welcome to join us to celebrate his arrival at the local airport. See Margret for details. Have fun dancing flamenco everyone!"

A chorus of "thank you" follows Anton out the door.

Vanessa puts on the teacher mantle and asks the dancers to line up in front of the mirrors. She stands with her back to the row and demonstrates a basic flamenco dance step. Vanessa is thorough and slow in her instructions. Everyone catches on in a hurry, so much so that she turns on flamenco guitar music and has the group dance the basic step. Next, she adds arms and turns. By the end of the forty-five minutes, the group actually dances through a simple routine. Each dancer is ecstatic with their beginning flamenco experience. Jackson and Catherine stamp their feet in rhythmic patterns together, and Mom shows John her variation on the routine. Ralph sleeps on a blanket on the couch. The senior class is an unqualified success.

The senior dancers want to go to the airport and greet Alvaro the next day. Margret offers rides in the Gorilla, and Catherine offers room in the Cadillac. The flamenco fiesta is just getting started! Catherine and John decide to go for an early dinner together and invite Ralph to come along, while Margret, Mom and John head back to "Tilly's Farm" for evening chores.

Dancers enrolled in the adult class begin to arrive, and

Vanessa turns her attention to a review of *La Vida* dances and organizing rehearsals at the Civic. Margret, with Mom, returns to announce she has a van available for anyone from the adult class that wants to go to the airport. She is determined to have crowd optics for the film crew to prove that Alvaro is a star, and works to bring the "seeds" to grow a spontaneous audience.

Margret and Mom head home in the Gorilla. Mom is deeply impacted by her time at the studio. It's been a long time since she spent any time in society, and her mind tries to make sense of it all.

"Margret, thank you for the Flamenco class. John is a nimble dancer. It was difficult to keep up, but it's the first time, in a long time, that I wanted to do something besides prune roses. It tickled my brain! I can't wait to dance again!"

"Mom, it was great to have you there! We'll practice in the morning, and, before you know it, you'll be center stage."

"Yes, and John said he would be right there with me! He was surprised at how much he enjoyed the class, and he loved the music! He might even learn to play guitar and accompany me."

Mom is overwhelmed with joyful emotion.

"Margret, you and John are very dear. I can't wait to tell Tilly and Gypsy. We can listen to flamenco guitar while I work on my pastels!"

It's been a curious road with Mom, but in the end the rewards are mighty. Margret hopes the dance class can help clear the fog in her mom's thinking. Now it's time to get back to the farm and feed Mom some dinner. Tonight, Margret will dedicate some hours to showtime follow-up and get ready for tomorrow.

Vanessa is still at the studio. She rehearses the adult class and fields questions about the Civic auditorium rehearsals. The childrens class is excited, and, to get them to focus, Vanessa decides to follow Anton's approach and take the pressure off. Once they get to the Civic everything will become serious, so today she laughs. She praises the kids and reminds them to bring the beach rehearsal to the stage. The children love the reference to the beach rehearsal and joyfully dance around the room making up footwork and songs. Finally, all the parent's questions are answered, and Vanessa calls her mom for a ride home.

Anton returns from dinner to find Vanessa waiting for her mom outside the studio on the bench she graced months ago as an unrecognizable and desperate victim of PTSD. Anton sits next to Vanessa.

"How did the senior flamenco class go?"

"I'm amazed! I haven't had that much fun teaching ever."

"What made it so wonderful?"

"The innocence. No ego, no competition just fresh enthusiasm for learning something new. Mom, Margret's mom, was completely engaged. I think it might be the greatest thing we can do to serve the community. The class offers a place where seniors can be childlike without being childish. I was blown away."

Anton sees the Cadillac pull in and walks to the driver's side of the car. Catherine rolls down her window while Vanessa gets in the car on the passenger side. Ralph sits on the backseat and watches.

"Vanessa told me how wonderful the senior dance class was. I'm happy you were able to join us and experience flamenco first hand."

"Anton, I can't thank you enough for what you have done for Vanessa, and now what you are doing for the seniors here. John and I spoke about the class at dinner and are thoroughly on board. You are obviously kind, and that is a rare quality in today's hard-edged world. I'm happy to meet you, and thrilled I listened to Vanessa and made the move to California! And I can't wait to see *La Vida*!"

"Your daughter is an extraordinary dancer. You will be in awe of her performance! Now I say, 'buenas noches.' Hopefully, you will join us to greet Alvaro tomorrow. He is a stunning ambassador of Cuban flamenco."

Anton nods in a small bow, goes to Vanessa and kisses her on both cheeks then goes to open the door of the PR sports car. Catherine is not immune.

"My stars, is that little motorized gem, yours?"

Anton laughs.

"I hold the pink slip. Vanessa can tell you the story."

Anton slides behind the wheel, rolls down the window and calls out,

"See you tomorrow at the airport. That's when the show begins!"

Catherine and Vanessa wave "Adios."

"Vanessa, you never told me that your dance instructor is a saint and a flamenco champion! Mom is spot on! He's a catch!! It's evident he's crazy about you! I want to hear the whole story!"

"Anton is the apple of every eye, including mine."

"I'm certainly glad to hear that! Your daddy would be beyond pleased."

"Mom, let's go home, steep some tea, stoke the fire and share stories."

"Vanessa, that's the best idea you've had all day!"

Meanwhile, Margret says good night to Tilly and Gypsy and walks Mom back to the house.

"What did you think of your first flamenco dance class?"

"Oh Margret, I love the gypsy life with gorgeous men and blood-pumping music. I feel alive. I know I forget a few things, but I remember what it is to celebrate! Flamenco celebrates everything! Olé!"

"That's wonderful Mom! I feel the same way!"

"Thank you Margret, you are such a good friend. I just love you!"

"Love you too, Mom."

The full moon rises early, and Tilly's Farm is lit bright as daylight. The rose blossoms that still cling to their beauty remind Margret of her past moment-by-moment hell in the mall parking lot. Things can change moment-by-moment, in an instant, in the "twinkling of an eye." All those archaic-trite adages are true.

Anton watches Vanessa and Catherine pull away and remembers to lock the door to the studio. He glances over and sits on the bench where he first pulled Vanessa from her passed-out flop onto the sidewalk, after mimicking the flamenco dance she observed through the studio window. He remembers how she accused him of stealing her purse. He remembers her transformation into a beautiful young woman who wanted flamenco dance lessons, and Susie that created an unbreakable bond between the three of them. He remembers Vanessa come to his rescue as he descended into hypothermia when he nearly drowned in the riptide. He tears up and begins to silently cry at the terrors of war, and how they damaged Vanessa to the point of unmanageable reactions to everyday life. He wonders if she will ever regain her innocence so that she might be able to love. The bench and it's waterfall of memories becomes unbearable. He gets up and goes to his sports car to break the sadness.

Anton is not one to wallow. He sits in his car and touches his Rosary to circle through prayers for a round of concerns regarding the upcoming performance at the Civic. Alvaro's arrival tomorrow will raise the event to a new level. He's reassured to know that his friend and colleague will be on the stage with him, and will give everything he has to elevate the dance. He feels blessed to have a star of Alvaro's stature appear in a small town, at a common civic auditorium, solely to help his friend make a splash in the world of flamenco. Anton closes his eyes and imagines the final moment of their flamenco "duet." He feels the audience rise up to whistle, and shout "Bravo!" and "Olé!" while they stamp their feet.

Energized, Anton starts the car and drives to the beach to watch the full moon light the ocean waves. The park closes at dusk, so he hikes past the wetland to the train trellis and walks through the dunes to his dance floor now bathed in moonlight. Unafraid, he releases his body to his inner muse, springs across the hard sand and dodges small rocks and seaweed while the ocean roars through its own instrument of rhythm and sound. He transcends the earth with joy and completely immerses himself in his memories of his studio and dance company in Cuba. As he moves down the beach, he leaves Cuba behind, embraces a lonely strip of sand for his partner and exhausts himself dancing on the packed-sand floor. He achieves oneness with nature that surpasses anything he has known before. He lies on his back and looks up at the moon. He loves this wild beach and dedicates himself to a deeper commitment to know the wild within himself.

Anton returns to his car, and a coyote watches him. Distracted from tracking the wetland birds, that float on the water in the moonlight, the coyote follows him. Anton admonishes the coyote and suggests he become a vegetarian. Anton laughs at himself and remembers, "And the lion shall lay down with the lamb." Anton fully comprehends this is possible. Surely, Saint Francis knew the secret, and Anton commits to listen better to the inner voice. The moonlight enlightens him. He's been washed in ocean spray, and he feels he is one with all creatures great and small. He gets into his car and drives away, but tonight's experience stays with him, and he recognizes that he has, once again, been forever changed.

THIRTY-THREE

The parking lot at the local airport is almost full. The caravan from the studio files through the automated gate, drives to the end of the lot and parks. The Cadillac with Catherine, Vanessa and Jackson, the Gorilla with Margret, Mom and John, the Dodge van with Maria and the adult class and four additional cars with parent drivers and kids fill the last few spaces. Margret's ad campaign must be working. It's rare to see a full parking lot at this airport.

    Anton jumps into the lead and takes a fast pace to be sure to be in place to greet Alvaro. The caravan's occupants walk together into the arrival area for passengers who disembark, ride the escalator down to the lobby and head to baggage claim. Margret sees her film crew in place at the escalator and breathes a sigh of relief. Mom, John, Catherine and Jackson hang out together to observe the feeding frenzy. At Margret's request, John is particularly tuned in to protect Mom from any confusion. When Catherine sees Alvaro step onto the escalator she gasps. Mom does a double take and says aloud, "another catch!" Jackson and John laugh. Mom knows a star when she sees one.

Excitement and expectations are contagious, and curious on lookers want to know what's going on. The crowd grows, and Margret is satisfied with the optics. Now it's up to Alvaro to wow the crowd, and he does. He steps onto the escalator and recognizes Anton standing in the front of the crowd. Alvaro slings his bag over his shoulder and waves to Anton while his heels rattle flamenco steps on the escalator stairs. Anton answers back with his heels, and a wave of his hand that whips through the air. The two dancers relish the opportunity for a spontaneous performance.

Travelers going up the escalator are intrigued with the dance dynamic between Alvaro and Anton, and the people behind Alvaro coming down the escalator enjoy the exchange. It's all happening so fast, Margret hopes her filmmaker is able to capture the event. People start to clap and shout "Bravo!" which emboldens Alvaro, and he rips into a complete performance while he accompanies himself with claps and finger snaps so intense they ricochet against the far lobby wall. Anton follows his lead, and the two dancers break into wild displays of footwork and spins. The improvisation ends with Alvaro's hug for Anton and hearty laughter from both dancers.

Margret, always well prepared, hands out flyers about *La Vida* and the dance studio to the expanded crowd that wants to know more about the man that descended the escalator with so much style. Some people in the crowd recognize Alvaro from articles in the newspaper and ads and ask for autographs. The event is more than Margret hoped for and is a harbinger for a successful performance at the Civic.

When Anton introduces Margret to Alvaro, Margret is

consumed with how to get the right shots and make sure the film crew is where they need to be. Alvaro watches Margret and is taken by her stunning appearance. Her indifference to his presence is a new, and Alvaro is intrigued.

"It is good to meet you, Margret. Anton tells me you are responsible for this overwhelming airport welcome. Thank you!"

Margret laughs and curtsies.

"You're welcome! And thank you for putting on a show and warming up the crowd for the Anton Dance Company and Dance Studio and the *La Vida* event at the Civic auditorium. We don't have many celebrities come to our town. It is such an honor to have you here!

"My pleasure, Anton and I have history. I am curious how he puts on such a show. Now I know. You are, how you say, force of nature. He is lucky man."

Margret blushes, but keeps up the banter.

"Wait until you see my car!"

The group around Margret and Alvaro surges in for autographs, and Margret takes the opportunity to disconnect and concentrate on her film crew. The crew continues to film Alvaro and Anton on their walk to baggage claim, and they along with the crowd begin to disperse.

"Hey guys, I have one more shot I want to capture. Can you film as I pull up curbside to pick up Alvaro, Anton and Vanessa? After that we can all go to lunch, on our tab, at The Pizza House near the studio. After lunch, it's off to the Civic to meet the various technicians and prep for tonight's rehearsal. You guys are super stars! I think we have some great material, and you will come up with an excellent documentary!"

Margret goes back to the dwindling crowd to make sure, along with Vanessa, that all the Anton Dance Studio people are accounted for and invited to lunch at The Pizza House. Catherine, Mom and Jackson tag along in awe of Margret, and the photo op that unfolded in front of them. They make their exit and tell Margret they'll see everyone at The Pizza House. Alvaro and Anton have Alvaro's baggage and are ready for lunch. Margret teases the flamenco stars about their twin outfits.

"Did you two call each other to be sure you matched? All black everything is stunning!"

Alvaro speaks up,

"Actually, Anton had us wearing hot pink everything, but I settle him down."

Good humor and laughter follow Anton, Alvaro, Margret and Vanessa to the Gorilla at the curb. Alvaro drops his jaw.

"Ay, Carumba! You don't make joke! This is monster car!"

Margret, Anton and Vanessa laugh. Margret continues,

"This is just the tip of the iceberg!"

Alvaro and Margret have met their match. Anton and Vanessa look on with amusement. One camera person documents the drive to the Pizza House. The rest of the crew meets up at The Pizza House. After lunch everyone ends up at the Civic. It's a busy day, but Alvaro seems to enjoy the schedule and is obviously interested in Margret.

At the Pizza House another spontaneous performance

erupts. Free beer, sodas and pizza flood and feed the crowd. Catherine, Jackson, John and Mom say goodbye to the fiesta and head back to Tilly's Farm to drop off Mom and John. Mom is tired and misses her goats. Catherine drives John to his real estate office to pick up his car.

"Thanks, Catherine, for a spectacular day of celebration! Your daughter Vanessa is quite a woman. You raised a good one!"

"Thank you, John. It's a delight to share all this with you. I hope we see each other often. It's not every day I meet someone who is such good company!"

"We will, we will. I feel the same way. And we have *La Vida* Saturday night!"

John leans over and gives Catherine a kiss on the cheek.

"Catherine, I think we're in for a lot of fun together."

Catherine agrees.

"Yes!"

Back at The Pizza House the fiesta ends, and the patrons are eager to watch soccer. Anton, Alvaro, Vanessa and Margret make their way through the appreciative crowd and leave in the Gorilla to meet the technicians. The rest of the Anton Dance Studio dancers leave to prepare for an informal rehearsal and walk through at the Civic. Margret has the schedules for the week printed, and she passes them out with her phone number on the sheet to answer any questions. Maria is the go-to person for details regarding outfits and green room protocol. Alvaro is stunned by Margret's attention to detail.

"Anton, where did you find Saint Margret? She is, how

you say, phenomenal!! Does she dance too?"

"Oh yes! Wait till you see Vanessa and Margret dance in *La Vida*!"

"I put you on notice. I steal Margret for my dance company in Cuba."

"I'm sure you would have no trouble stealing her. How about we share her? She can easily run two dance companies. But no stealing Vanessa, she's mine."

"No worries, I could see it from moment I met her."

Anton laughs.

"No worries until you see her dance!"

Anton and Alvaro shake hands.

Margret parks the Gorilla near the side entrance of the Civic Auditorium. The four dancers enter the building, and three of them wonder how this sold out show is going to shine in this dated performance hall. Margret, on the other hand, thinks about the company she hired that transforms interiors to the client's specifications. Margret spares no expense and knows from experience that the interior of this building will be unrecognizable on the night of the performance. She decides to surprise the three other dancers the day of the final dress rehearsal.

Alvaro is impressed with the hall despite its outmoded appearance. He races to center stage and tests the floor with part of his solo dance.

"The floor is excellent!"

The footwork leaves observers gasping while they shout "Bravo!" and "Olé!" Vanessa and Margret are stunned.

Breathless is a good word. He arrived from Cuba a few hours ago, and now he is attacks his dance like a wild beast.

"I told you he would take us to a new level."

Margret comments,

"I'm glad you warned us and gave us those two days off to rest before the hurricane made landfall!"

Alvaro laughs and leads Margret to the stage. Alvaro begins to dance and instructs Margret.

"Follow me."

Margret follows Alvaro without looking at her feet. Like any great professional, he makes Margret look like a native-Cuban-flamenco dancer with invisible cues that lead her seamlessly to wherever he wants her in the dance. Anton starts to clap and Vanessa sings. The quartet transports to Cuba and a curbside café where a flamenco band plays. The dance grows in intensity, and Margret is suddenly Cuban in every fiber of her flamenco loving soul.

Anton smiles while he continues to clap. Vanessa sings higher and higher while the song expands and bounces around the hall.

"Alvaro, I think you have a dance partner worthy of your talent. Bravo!"

Alvaro spins Margret around and hugs her.

"Bravo Margret! You come to Cuba with me to dance in my company. This was your audition."

Alvaro winks at Anton.

"Vanessa, I would steal you too, but Anton would never

forgive me!"

Margret is mesmerized. She is halfway between Cuba and the California Central Coast while she catches her breath and looks for familiar landmarks. Vanessa comes to her rescue.

"I say we all go to Cuba after this show to relax and visit with Anton's family to diminish his mama's disappointment to miss *La Vida*."

"Yes! Yes! And my family meet Margret. We can put on show for las familias!"

Margret pinches herself and remembers how much she still must to do to keep the momentum up for the La Vida production. She gracefully disengages from Alvaro's embrace and regains traction. She excuses herself to draw a layout for the Cuban food truck and Lupe's Panaderia at the Civic Auditorium entrance. Alvaro puts his arm around Anton and thanks him for asking him to perform in his premiere event.

"We share Margret, my friend, and we bring Cuba to the California Central Coast and the California Central Coast to Cuba. Bye bye Miami!"

Anton and Vanessa laugh. Anton continues,

"I'm glad you're sold on the Central Coast."

"I'm sold on Margret! And Vanessa, you have extraordinary voice. You must have experienced great sufferings to pour out those words and notes."

"Thank you, Alvaro. I made friends with the dark night of the soul."

Alvaro studies Vanessa a long moment.

"Not friends, lovers!"

Vanessa pulls back and moves halfway behind Anton.

"Vanessa is an Afghanistan War veteran."

"Anton tells me you are amazing dancer. No wonder. You have much pain. Flamenco is good for you."

"Flamenco saved me."

Margret interrupts the conversation, and tells Anton the flamenco band has arrived. Anton and Alvaro turn their attention to music, choreography and dance and leave Margret to continue her work with the stage manager, set designer, lighting designer and lighting technician. Vanessa leaves to introduce the green room to the dancers.

Margret understands eye candy. The visual experience is the strongest take away in any show, and Margret intends to make this event memorable.

The band is working out placement and sound check with Alvaro, Anton and the recording engineer. Margret and the lighting designer come in on the tail end of the sound check and discuss colors, moods, spotlights and the set up with Alvaro and Anton. Margret carries production details on a clip board and wastes no time in conversation. The hall holds 1,500 people, and she's determined each ticket holder will experience the ultimate show.

Vanessa vanishes into the back of the building where the greenrooms are filling up with dancers and the children's parents. Vanessa checks in with Maria, and they coordinate dressing rooms. They reserve three small rooms for Alvaro, Anton and the professional male dancers hired for special scenes in *La Vida*. The women hang up dresses and shelve shoes, mantons, fans and their makeup kits. The atmosphere is electric, but the children are subdued by the magnitude of the event. Everywhere are Vanessa's posted instructions for greenroom protocol, and who to contact if there's a problem. The production machine is well oiled with Vanessa's military training, and her passion for order.

"Maria, what do you say we give the dancers a tour of the building to build familiarity and confidence. We have the house for three days leading up to the performance. This is a luxury we can use to make everyone feel at home."

"Good idea, Vanessa!"

"I'll find the house manager to lead us on the building tour while you corral all the dancers and parents."

Maria has a triangle and strikes it to get everyone's attention. They line up in twos and follow Maria to the front of the stage. The house manager leads the centipede of dancers and parents through the building and shows them each area of the hall. She doubles as a docent and shares brief historical notes regarding the interior and the historical performances that have graced the hall.

Wall sconces and a large-crystal chandelier, donated by a wealthy patron back in the day, light the interior of the building. In the auditorium, light reflects off the chandelier and speckles the walls with small points of light. The stage, on the other hand, is fully lighted and hums with various theatrical professionals that work out details for an exceptional and then some event.

In the red-carpeted lobby are large posters that show the former glory days of the auditorium. Two isles split the audience into thirds, and the slant of the room provides excellent line of sight for everyone. Three large double doors at the entrance provide easy access and exit, and additional exits are well marked in the front and back of the auditorium. Audience restrooms are on both sides of the lobby so congestion is eased.

Elegant tables on each side of the entrance to the isles are covered with programs and postcards advertising the Anton Dance Studio and Anton Dance Company. Posters are for sale of Alvaro in his signature black-slim-fit pants, boots, pirate shirt and head band to hold back sweat and hair. The posters capture his intensity and a perfect item for a fan collection. Volunteer ushers are prepped to help the audience find their seats, and other volunteers are assigned to the tables to sell posters, various flamenco souvenir accessories like *La Vida* fans and embroidered shawls. Margret wants the audience to go crazy for flamenco!

The house manager leads the group to the front entrance to show them where they can purchase food from the soon-to-arrive Cuban Food truck and cappuccinos plus pasteles from Lupe's Panaderia. The flamenco band does a short sound check at the entrance for pre-performance entertainment, and dancers stamp their feet and clap in anticipation of what is to come. No one knows, but Margret and the company she hired, what it is that will up the ante for the atmosphere in the hall on the morning of the final dress rehearsal when Cuba comes to California.

THIRTY-FOUR

The rehearsal schedule works, and each day the production moves closer to its peak. Today the final dress rehearsal begins at 5:00 p.m., and Margret lies in bed with her hands over her face unable to get up. The sheer enormity of the event she has underwritten is a tsunami of responsibility, and she nervously questions if she has tied every loose string into a knot to prevent unraveling. Add to the pressure of the event, Alvaro's magnetic pull that presents serious danger to her legendary focus. Each day, Margret falls prey to Alvaro's presence that overwhelms, and his sincere affection for her quirky ways confuses. Each day, Margret battles to come back from her emotional precipice and hold to her purpose.

    Margret peeks through her fingers at the clock on her bedside table. It is 4:30 a.m. and counting. She closes her eyes and deep breathes for three minutes. She feels a small release of tension and decides to get up, light a fire in the bedroom fireplace and read writings of her favorite poet, Pablo Neruda. The irony of reading Neruda poetry to calm her anxiety is not lost on her. She knows the nature of Neruda's passion for women and his soulful connection to Cuba.

At 6:00 a.m. Margret gets up and dresses for a ride on her mountain bike to mentally prepare for a day fraught with requests, questions and problems from every side. Today is the day Anton runs the entire show from start to finish without a break. Margret takes comfort in the superstition "disastrous dress rehearsal – great opening." Not that she thinks the dress rehearsal will be a bust, but the saying gives her the feel of a safety net.

The ride up the dirt road, where she initially met Tilly, is still her favorite. She works the pedals like the locomotives she watched as a child worked the rails. She stands on the pedals and forces her way up the road to a new lookout. She dismounts, leans her bike against a wiry-scrub oak and sits on a boulder to survey the expansive valley. She sees the river that runs through it and thinks of her father. She knows how proud he would be to see her blossom in her passion for the outdoors, and her triumphant effort to learn to dance flamenco. Yes, Vanessa is right. Flamenco saves them all with its call to rise up and share a story with feet, legs, arms, hands and voice. John, Jackson, Catherine and Mom are the latest beneficiaries, and it doesn't end there. Anton's Dance Company is going to rock the world. Margret stands up and embraces the landscape with outspread arms.

"Thanks Daddy. You knew it all along. I can see you smile and hear you say, 'I told you so!'"

Margret jumps on her bike and races down the mountain devil-may-care, because that's what her dad taught her to do. Back at Tilly's Farm, she gets ready to meet the moving van that brings the construction materials and design elements to transform the California Coast Civic Auditorium into Cuba.

Farm manager, John, and Mom's assistant both know it's a long day ahead and prepare Mom for time on her own with Tilly, Gypsy, art supplies and roses.

Vanessa wakes up to Ralph shoving his damp nose under her arm and wagging his white-tipped tail. He wants out and chooses Vanessa for the job. Sleepy, but happy to accommodate, Vanessa puts on her robe and calls Ralph to follow her down the stairs and out the back door. Ralph bounds around the yard like a freestyle gymnast. Vanessa thinks he would make a sensational flamenco dancer. When she laughs, Ralph responds with higher and more daring jumps and flips.

Catherine hears the commotion and meets Vanessa at the back door. She offers to make breakfast. Ralph sees another admiring human and gallops over to Catherine to say "good morning!" Ralph, unknowingly, has struck the perfect chord to celebrate this day. Catherine puts her arm around Vanessa's waist and reassures her brave daughter.

"Sugarcane, your daddy would be so proud to see you dance. The dress rehearsal is the warm up exercise! I can't wait to see the show tomorrow night! John plans to take me to dinner beforehand, and we'll arrive in time for dessert at Lupe's pop-up panaderia. Honey, you did it! You took those bitter lemons, and you squeezed them dry to make the sweetest lemonade in all of Texas and California combined!!"

Susie was my guardian angel. I miss her terribly, but Ralph makes me smile. He's a character for sure."

"Sugarcane, Anton is your guardian angel, and he will be there for you. I can see that from a hundred miles away."

"It means a lot to me that you see Anton that way. He's everyone's hero, and I'm grateful to have him as a friend.

Too, it is fun watching Anton and Alvaro interact. They have a bond."

"Yes, Sugarcane, and Alvaro is quite taken with Margret. The four of you can look forward to some adventures with flamenco! I felt it in the air when we welcomed Alvaro at the airport."

"I'll take you up on that breakfast, Mom, and… how about a game of chess? I've practiced for days just so I could, at least, hold my own against you!"

"You want to play a game of chess today??"

"Yeah, I need something to take my mind off everything that's coming up. I need a brain clear, and chess is the perfect game to shut out the world."

"Sugarcane, bring it on! I've missed clearing the board and holding a king hostage!"

Ralph comes in the back door and lies down near the table as they set up the battlefield. The morning is relaxed and exactly what Vanessa needs to prepare for tonight's dress rehearsal.

Anton and Alvaro are both early risers, and Anton takes Alvaro to his favorite dance floor at Ocean Park Beach where the two of them cavort along the edge of the sea and drink in the damp air. After forty-five minutes of playful-gymnastic dance moves, the two friends walk back to Anton's car and head to Lupe's Panaderia.

"So, Margret gave you this car??"

"Yes. My little sedan was wrecked by a lifted truck. My whole life was in collapse when Margret and Vanessa saved everything. I was broke, and they put me back together."

"You, my friend, are lucky hombre!"

"And so are you. Margret is your fan."

"You think so? I can't tell. She is completely focused on *La Vida*. I like it if she is my fan. I find her beautiful and interesting."

"You love all your fans!"

"True, but Margret is different. Her intensity matches mine. This is good."

"It is good, and since you are stealing her, we must be sure to keep her in the family. Two dance companies would be exceptional, and when you witness Vanessa dance you will join forces without a backward glance!"

"Vanessa is fragile, no?"

"Vanessa suffers from PTSD. She has made great progress, but demons still chase her."

"You, my friend, are in love!"

"Yes, I admit it."

"Well…Cuba and California are good places to share. Margret and Vanessa would be good partners. Let's see where this *La Vida* takes us!"

Anton and Alvaro enter the panaderia. Lupe sees Anton and orders two cappuccinos and two pasteles for Anton and his friend.

"Hola Anton! Sit over there. I bring you breakfast!"

The panaderia is busy. Alvaro notices the poster above the cash register and smiles. Margret knows how to promote a show. The panaderia patrons shout,

"Bravo! Anton. We'll see you tomorrow night!"

Anton introduces Alvaro and the crowd cheers. Alvaro comments,

"Anton, you are famous!"

"Not like you, but as I said, Vanessa and Margret saved me. I owe all I have to them."

Alvaro is subdued.

"Perhaps, they will save us both."

***

Margret directs the delivery of the instant transformative design for the Civic Auditorium. In the front lobby, an interior design is constructed to represent a fishing community on the edge of Havana Port with cafes and shops. The lobby is transformed into a Cuban gathering place, and the spirit of flamenco is well represented with clothing, fans and castanets. The atmosphere is fiesta, and, after the flamenco band practices, it will play for the patrons before it takes the stage for the show.

The step railings that lead up to the entrance of the Civic Auditorium are draped in fishing nets with large hand blown glass balls that float the nets when cast into the ocean. Volunteers will dress as local fisherman and act as servers. Every detail is authentically Cuban. Even San Cristobal La Punta Cigars, which are under embargo, will be legally offered as gifts to the patrons while they sit outside and savor a starry evening or visit the Cuban Food truck and Lupe's Panaderia. With Cuban street lamps, cafe and the flamenco band, the setting is perfect for *La Vida*.

Margret inspects each area to insure a consistent atmosphere and guarantee a suspension of disbelief so that all patrons experience flamenco – Cuban style. By 1:00 p.m. the "setting" is established, and patrons will enjoy dinner in Cuba, and dessert in Mexico before the Anton Dance Company's *La Vida* transports them beyond time and space to Havana.

The stage itself is transformed into a section of downtown Havana with a jewelry store and the neighborhood café. Rear screen projections show large images of jewels and bracelets that sparkle. Actual jewelry cases are placed in the center of the shop. The lighting emphasizes the precious value of the stones and the upscale neighborhood in contrast to the fishing village in the lobby. The effect is the separation of rich and poor which Margret hopes will be bridged by *La Vida*.

Margret leaves the auditorium for lunch and rest. She heads to Glenn's Market for a deli sandwich and soda. As she leaves Glenn's, preoccupied with details of the production, she literally bumps into Alvaro on a mission to get lunch for Anton and himself, before they rehearse their dance at the studio.

"Excuse me, I'm so sorry…Alvaro! It's you! I'm so focused on the show, I didn't see you! Forgive me!"

"No problema, Margret. I see you have sandwich and soda. Join us at studio for lunch."

"I'd love to, but I have so many loose ends to tie up before tonight, I'm eating on the run. My Mom has some memory issues. I have to check in before I come back for tonight's dress rehearsal. Can we do a raincheck? Oh God, you probably have no idea what raincheck means. . ."

"Of course, we have time tomorrow or after show! We celebrate together!"

"Exactly, yes, let's celebrate after the show!"

Margret excuses herself and goes to her Gorilla to get home and chill out with Mom. She realizes how rude she must seem to rush off and pulls up to the curb to wait for Alvaro to come out of Glenn's Market.

"Alvaro, over here . . . forgive me for being rude! I would love to stop for a moment to eat lunch with you and Anton!"

"I thought maybe you don't like me. Now I know we are friendly!"

Margret laughs and parks the Gorilla in front of the studio. Alvaro helps her out of the Gorilla.

"Aren't you afraid Gorilla will hurt you? Gorillas can be dangerous!"

"Oh no, this Gorilla is tame, except when I'm driving on the freeway. Then she is fierce!"

"Good to know, Señorita."

Anton sees the Gorilla and comes out to greet Margret. He sees Alvaro with lunch and invites Margret into the studio to join them.

"Alvaro is way ahead of you. I literally ran into him at Glenn's! He was polite and invited me to have lunch at the studio. I was rude and said I had to get home, but I corrected my manners and will take a lunch break with you!"

Anton laughs, Alvaro smiles and Margret grabs her soda and sandwich and joins them for lunch.

"How is the Civic shaping up?"

"Oh you won't believe it. You and Alvaro will think you're back in Cuba!"

Anton continues to question while Alvaro continues to smile.

"What?"

"It's a surprise! I thought in honor of Alvaro, we would make him feel more at home! I even have a permit for contraband Cuban cigars! Hopefully, you won't recognize the auditorium when you arrive this evening for rehearsal!"

"Margret you have outdone yourself with this event! Alvaro wants to steal you and take you to Cuba to dance and run his company. You already passed the dance audition, but I told him he must share. You can run two dance companies and dance in both!"

Margret sparkles with the idea of dancing in two companies.

"Let's see how this show comes off, and then let's talk about Cuba and dance companies! If this show is all I hope for, we'll dance all over the globe!!"

Anton and Alvaro laugh, and the trio chats about future events. After Margret literally ran into Alvaro, and realized she was rude, she discovers she is completely relaxed around the star.

"Guys, I need to get back to the farm. I'll see you at the dress rehearsal. I can't wait to watch your reaction when you see the transformation."

Margret is amused and surprised at Alvaro's obvious interest in her. Somehow, today, he seems so normal and kind. He's not at all what she imagined.

"Strange what celebrity status does to alter one's perception of a human."

The final dress rehearsal sneaks up on everyone, and the air is charged with anticipation. Anton pulls all the disparate parts into a cohesive whole, and the dancers gain confidence from Anton's natural grace and self-assurance. Even Alvaro is stunned at his good friend's ability to calm the nervous dancers.

Anton gathers all participants in the production – from backstage personnel to lead dancers and everyone in between – onto the main stage. He assures everyone that the show is ready to shine and thanks each one for their contribution. He passes out programs and insists each participant study the contents and memorize the order of the show to put everyone on the same page. He is convinced that if everyone feels a sense of importance in the part they play, the show will reflect a spirit of cooperation, allow each individual to shine in their role and benefit the event as a whole.

The curtain closes, lights go dim, participants find their marks and the program begins. There is no intermission. The dress rehearsal rolls out, mistakes are noted but nothing slows this train. From beginning to end, the flamenco band sets the tempo and mood. The singers in the band are the soul of the show.

When Alvaro and Anton take the stage for their dance together, the show jumps to a whole new level. They pace themselves just below one hundred percent – like thoroughbreds on a race track ridden by expert jockeys – they allow room to peak. The dress rehearsal so far is seamless, and the dancers gain confidence with each successful dance. The final performance in the rehearsal, *La Vida,* is up.

All is well until the jewelry thief (Alvaro), continues to stumble after he trips in his attempt to escape with a stolen necklace. Vanessa, as an observer of the robbery and tasked with sounding the alarm, sings higher and higher with agonized phrases that pull her inside out. She suddenly snaps and runs around the stage desperate to find a safe hiding place for her descent into a delusional flashback that has her running through a backstreet in Kabul to escape a car bomb that has rocked the square. She crouches underneath one of the jewelry tables and hopes she'll go undiscovered in the rubble.

Anton sees Vanessa is delusional and quickly improvises to incorporate the irrational panic into the story. He rushes to Vanessa and assures her, in Spanish, that the explosions are over and her wailing soprano voice is the way to tell everyone that the square is secured and people are safe. He gently pulls Vanessa out from under the jewelry case and begins a slow tango to engage Vanessa's attention. He whispers in Spanish,

"I'm your Susie, and you are safe in this dance."

A hush falls over the auditorium. The band intuits the situation and corresponds with soulful music that weds the two dancers into one and gives Vanessa time to find her way back to *La Vida*. Everyone watches in awe, as Anton gracefully weaves Vanessa's horrific panic attack into choreography that brings everyone to tears. Anton whispers again,

"Vanessa, you are safe inside this story. Come back and carry on. You are no longer a soldier. You are a flamenco dancer. Dance like your life depends on it. Sing like a liberated canary. . ."

Vanessa hears the soft tones of Anton's Spanish and follows his instruction like a lost child seeking comfort. She curls around him, clings to his body as the tango grows bolder, and she regains her voice. Suddenly a glorious high C issues forth from her relaxed torso and throat. She disengages from Anton and shoves herself into a flamenco solo that brings the surrounding dancers into gentle whistles and mumbled bravos that grow in intensity to match Vanessa, as she gathers momentum and dances with fierce determination to chase every vestige of the flashback into nothingness. Her liberation is tangible and everyone in the hall begins to shout,

"Bravo! Olé!"

Anton skillfully keeps the show on track, and *La Vida* continues on to the end without further incident. The dress rehearsal officially concludes with the joyful *La Vida* fiesta on stage where police and cafe patrons dance flamenco on stage, down the aisles and out to the lobby where panaderia pasteles and cappuccinos greet the celebrating cast.

Alvaro approaches Anton with deep reference and pulls him aside.

"Mi amigo, you are wonder. Never have I seen such generosity and kindness expressed so beautifully that it transforms disaster to glory. You are master and our two dance companies will shine like stars in same sky. And no, I have never seen dancer like Vanessa. She is lava that spills down mountain after volcano erupts. She is beautiful and terrifies all at once."

Alvaro backs away, as others press forward to thank Anton for *La Vida*.

Margret sees Vanessa surrounded by parents and excited children. She gently pulls Vanessa over and whispers,

"Vanessa, that was incredible. I am in awe."

"Anton saved me. It was me that drowned this time, and he rescued me. What can I say? I too am in awe."

Alvaro sees Vanessa and Margret together and approaches.

"Never do I see such dancers like you two! *La Vida* captures fragility of jewelry store owner and horror of observer. Cuba goes crazy for you! Pablo Neruda is on knees."

Alvaro gives Vanessa a gentle hug. He turns to Margret and gives her a full bodied embrace which Margret returns in kind. Vanessa returns to the adoration of the children and their parents while Margret, in a romantic fog, connects with the technicians, flamenco band and volunteers. She assures them their checks will be ready for them tomorrow night. Alvaro watches her handle questions with patience and waits for her to be free.

"Can I help close up?"

"Alvaro, how thoughtful, please, and yes, we will celebrate tomorrow night after the show! Your solo and your duet with Anton are extraordinary! I feel so privileged to be on the same stage with you!"

"It is spectacular production. Much praise to you. You are incredible dancer, and you know how to make show. When I saw the fishing village in front, and Havana downtown on stage, I am amazed."

Margret laughs.

"None of it would be anything without a dancer like you to raise the bar. We are so fortunate to have you here. I hope you are happy."

"I am very happy! And I will be happier tomorrow night, when we celebrate together!"

"Yes, tomorrow night we celebrate. Now let's get this place closed up, go home and get some rest!"

Anton goes from station to station to thank various personnel and make sure each person is accounted for and appreciated. The auditorium clears, and it is Anton and Vanessa, Margret and Alvaro left to thank the auditorium staff and leave before the doors lock.

Anton and Vanessa wave goodbye to Alvaro and Margret on their way to the sleek-little sports car. Alvaro and Margret do a bold improvisation and dance to the Gorilla.

"Hasta la manana, Anton y Vanessa!"

"Buenas noches mis amigos, Alvaro and Margret!"

THIRTY-FIVE

"Hola mamá! ¿Como estas?"

"Hi, mama, how are you?"

"¿Anton?"

"Anton?"

"Si mamá, estoy aqui. ¡Esta noche abrimos nuestra primer espectáculo flamenco! ¡Te extraño a ti y a toda mi familia! ¿Te sientes major ahora?"

"Yes, Mama. I'm here. Tonight we open our first flamenco show! I miss you and my whole family. Do you feel better?"

"Si mi hijo. ¡Yo estoy muy bien! ¿Cómo estas?"

"Yes son. I am much better! How are you?"

"¡Estoy muy feliz! ¡Mi amigo Alavro está aquí para actuar con nosotros!"

"*I am very happy! My friend Alvaro is here to perform with us!*"

"¡Oh hijo, eres muy afortunado! Es un gran artista flamenco!"

"*Oh son, you are very lucky! He is a great flamenco artist!*"

"¡¡Si mamá!! Y planeamos venir a Cuba, despues de show y hacer un show para ti y la familia de Alvaro. Quiero que conozcas a mi amiga Vanessa y a mi amiga Margret."

"*Yes mom!! And we plan to come to Cuba, after the show, and do a show for you and Alvaro's family. I want you to meet my friend, Vanessa and my friend, Margret.*"

"¿Te gusta esta mujer Vanessa, hijo?"

"*Do you like this woman Vanessa, son?*"

"Si mamá. Me gusto mucho Vanessa. Y Alvaro quiere mucho a Margret."

"*Yes, mom. I really like Vanessa. And Alvaro likes Margret very much.*"

"¡Esta noticia me hace muy feliz!"

"*This news makes me very happy!*"

"¡Necesito decirte que te amo y que te vere pronto! Tengo que colgar ahora, pero pensare en ti esta noche. ¡Hasta pronto Mamsita!"

"*I need to tell you that I love you, and that I will see you soon! I have to hang up now, but I'll think of you tonight.*"

"¡Hasta pronto hijo!"

"See you soon, son."

The connection is lost, and Anton settles back into the leather seat of his racy-sports car, smiles at the thought of a visit to Cuba and the opportunity to introduce his mama to Vanessa. He fingers the Rosary that he still keeps in his car, whispers prayers for all aspects of the show and all the people that work hard to bring it to life.

The sunrise is cloudless, and the warm air that clings to the middle of November is an omen. November is when leaves bid goodbye to their branches and float to the ground in anticipation of colder air that freezes the branches and seals the buds for spring. It is a perfect time to dance flamenco and show the Central Coast the flamenco side of Cuba. Anton foregoes his beach time for quiet meditation in his casita and a day of solitary confinement. He learned long ago that he must protect himself from all distractions the day of an opening performance. It is easy to lose concentration, and the power of the moment, in superficial conversation. He has advised everyone to do the same – to stay within themselves and maintain the focus necessary for success. Not every artist works this way, but for Anton it is sacrosanct like his workouts at the studio. His craft and art demand all he has to invest, and he is prepared to keep himself safe from crowd babble on the day of the opening.

Alvaro, on the other hand, thrives on the energy of others, and finds himself at Lupe's to share stories with the police patrons and flirt with women young and old while he dances a little and laughs a lot. He is so alive he wiggles with energy that waits to explode whether the stage is a table at the panaderia or front and center in a grand hall. He is the consummate performer. His joie de vie is irresistible, and his charisma hypnotizes with every encounter. When he leaves the panaderia and takes a walk through Old Town, he begins to understand Anton's affection for this neighborhood. He thinks about Margret – her mysterious ways and her captivating intensity. He has never encountered anyone like Margret, and it confuses him. He loves women, but this woman is unlike any he has ever known. He is sometimes afraid that he is on the same hook others have experienced, but for him this is new. He looks forward to when he introduces Margret to his family and shows her his homeland. Cuba is everything to Alvaro, and he is eager to bring Margret to Havana. He is both terrified and happy to bring Margret into his Cuban world and wonders what will come of it.

Margret sleeps in and welcomes a day of freedom. She has delegated every duty, so that she is free to dance with total concentration and fierce commitment. She gets up, enjoys a simple breakfast and homemade cappuccino. This day is a day of celebration, and she intends to celebrate every moment. She leaves the house in the same outfit she wore the day she bought her mountain bike, the Gorilla and drove up the coast to that little hill for her first mountain bike downhill-adrenaline rush. She heads to her preferred dirt road up the canyon to "Goat Lookout" and stops to survey her favorite view. Today is dedicated to her daddy, and she dedicates it all to honor him. He has afforded this entire event. She is struck by the profound impact it is having on this community, and the potential of what is to come. She has no doubt the Anton Dance Company will make history. Alvaro slips into her thought while she sits on her favorite boulder and surveys the valley. She smiles and shakes her head.

"Who knew . . . who knew. . ?"

At the same time, Vanessa is still in awe of how Anton saved her from the dark visions of war and carried her through the smoke to a place of safety. She savors the morning with reading in bed. She allows Ralph to lay his big head on her stomach while she turns the pages of Hemmingway's novel *The Old Man and the Sea* written when Hemmingway lived in Cuba. Since the idea to visit Cuba took hold, she started to read about the island neighbor and the birthplace of her favorite human, Anton. Today, she enjoys the luxury her mom brought with her when she moved to California. The dark studio apartment is already a distant memory – now that Anton has established himself as her official guardian. Susie has passed her baton to Anton, and Ralph is the goofy-furry friend that takes away the sting. This level of peace is new. Vanessa intends to keep this secret deep inside and let it infuse everything she does. She hopes Anton will have great success with *La Vida,* and that she, Anton, Margret and Alvaro will be able to relax and enjoy Cuba together.

Fortunately, the weather is unseasonably warm at 5:00 pm. Early-bird guests who arrive and wait on the terrace for the Cuban food truck and Lupe's Panaderia to open the event are comfortable. Cuban cigar smoke floats over the terrace and into the parking lot. Servers, dressed in Cuban regalia, are in place. The authenticity that Margret insisted on convinces the audience that it's a night in Havana Port. String lights strung between poles add an intimate-festive air to the auditorium entrance. The flamenco band comprised of three guitarists, flute player, stand-up bass player, a singer, two drummers accompanied by an array of Cuban flamenco drums and the three professional male flamenco dancers enliven the café atmosphere. The dancers challenge each other with difficult routines and wild footwork. The patrons settle down to enjoy Cuban food truck specialties: sandwiches, empanadas, croquettes and sweet plaintains and Lupe's Panaderia. The crowd favorite is Castilo de Wajay wine or Bucanero and Mi Cristal beer with Cuban steak sandwich and Lupe's Panaderia pasteles for dessert.

It's obvious that the event is sold out, and the patrons wait in an atmosphere of a laid back fiesta to enter the auditorium. The doors open and the crowd moves through the lobby that is now an authentic Cuban fishing village with large poster murals that show off Havana Port.

Chimes ring, lights dim and patrons are encouraged to settle into their seats for the show. The camera and film crew work their way through the crowd to document the event, before they make their way to Alvaro and Anton for a brief backstage interview that is live streamed into the lobby and auditorium. The crowd goes wild when they see the Cuban principal dancers talk to each other and to the audience via big screens. Every instant is designed to make the audience feel they are in time travel to Havana. Even the volunteer ushers, that hand out programs and speak Spanish, are dressed in their Cuban-style-fishermen outfits to blur the borders between Central Coast California and Havana, Cuba.

The Mayor of this seaside town catches everyone's attention. Her bright colored outfit, and her short history of the flamenco tradition in Cuba is the perfect touch.

"Tonight we welcome you to Cuba! We thank the Anton Dance Studio and Anton Dance Company for the World Premiere of *La Vida*. We give a special welcome to Cuban-international-flamenco sensation, Alvaro Ramirez."

The audience erupts with whistles, shouts, Bravos and Olés.

"This show is dedicated to the late Mr. Walter Finch. Mr. Finch was committed to help people in every country his business touched, and, through his international bio-chemical company DECCA, he funded hundreds of events that brought attention to different cultures worldwide. His daughter Margret dances in the Anton Dance Company and follows in his footsteps. Tonight's performance is made possible by a gift from The Margret and Walter Finch Charitable Foundation. It is a privilege for this community to have such an event presented in our historic auditorium. Your programs have a brief history of our town, biographies and details of the show. Now it's time to sit up, fasten your seatbelts and get ready for your trip to Cuba!!"

The crowd whistles and cheers. The lights dim, and the curtains draw back. The flamenco band is on an elevated balcony above the stage, and each player is placed under an arch but still united with the other musicians. A dramatic-rainbow light shifts from player to player as they perform their opening solos. Below the band, Alvaro sits alone at the café surrounded by rear screen projections of upscale Old Town downtown stores and the jewelry store next to the café. This is Alvaro's time to shine. He lights up the entire auditorium with his presence.

The setting is sunset, and the colors of the sky are pastels against the dark. Supported by the flamenco band, Alvaro stands, follows the lead of the soloist and moves the audience through dance from life to death in a painful story of a brutal street fight that leaves his best friend mortally wounded. Alvaro's body expresses every emotion associated with loss. The audience is silent until the end, when Alvaro finds peace in his surrender and acknowledgement of what he has lost and walks off stage in the dark. The audience goes wild, whistles, shouts "Olé" and "Bravo" as Alvaro returns to the stage to take another and another bow under a single spotlight.

The children's class assembles in the wings, and Vanessa encourages them in a whisper,

"Remember the beach rehearsal, and dance with confidence!"

She remains in the wings while the children enter to the music they have been rehearsing with for weeks. The band is so good it seems like the music and dance come together as a spontaneous event, but in fact Vanessa has drilled the choreography with prerecorded music so that the dance flows seamlessly. The matching polka-a-dot dresses with ruffles on the bottom of the skirts whirl, swirl and twirl like a flock of starlings. The children lift their skirts and end their dance with an acapella footwork routine that lifts the audience out of their seats to cheer. The children give a classic-dismissive wave and leave the stage. The crowd continues to shout "Bravo" while they anticipate the second children's dance to come.

Gone are the ruffles and skirts. The children wear black pants with suspenders over white peasant shirts and red sashes tied around their waists. Their small-stiff-black hats stay firmly in place to the end while the children show off footwork that mimics a flock of snowy plovers that race back and forth in the sand and scratch for bits of seafood. In the end, the line of children stretches across the front of the stage and displays synchronized footwork that, once again, lifts the audience out of their seats. The children do a final spin, dismiss the audience with a wave and leave the stage. The roar in the hall deafens with whistles, foot stomps, hand claps and more shouts of "Olé" and "Bravo."

The adult class enters and waves mandons in circles as they dance. Each dancer then drops her mandon and unleashes a fan held in the neckline of their tight red satin dresses that cover the hips and spread out in layers of colored ruffles to the floor. The dancers fold their fans, lift their skirts and reveal their heels as the source of the sound of hammers against the hardwood stage. The spotlights on each dancer bring another appreciative roar from the audience. The band soloist presents a romantic story in song while the adult class pairs off and flirts with the classic flamenco fans. Finally, they tuck the fans back into their well fitted necklines, pick up the mandons and continue to dance while the classic scarves circle around them to the end. The audience jumps up to whistle and shout.

Moments later the adult class re-enters now in full floral print skirts with polka-a-dot fitted tops that look like confetti on a dress. The crowd is on their feet to clap while the dancers take their marks and wait for the band to start the dance. The dancers wear big smiles, and the party continues. The hired male dancers keep the rhythm with claps, and the dancers show off their fiesta dresses as their arms move from side to side. The ring of castanets compliments the rattle of their footwork. The playful celebration of fabric and dance continues to build. Each dancer offers a solo, and the crowd is stunned at the variety of expression while the castanets continue a steady rhythm in contrast to the feet that tap. The audience continues to stand and dances in place or spills into the aisles inspired to bring their own solos to the auditorium. The last adult dancer completes her final solo, and the class forms a line across the stage to take a coordinated bow. The audience cheers, stomps, claps and the proud-adult-dancers parade off the stage and disappear into the wings.

Dressed in black, Alvaro silences the crowd with finger snaps and cat-like steps that bring him center stage into a spotlight in a dark auditorium. He stands in place and snaps his fingers until the silent hall is filled only with the sound of Alvaro's finger snaps. Little-by-little, Alvaro adds claps, slaps and footwork that hammer the hardwood floor. The only sound in the auditorium is the sound from this one-man-percussion kit under a single spotlight. The circle of light around Alvaro is how a circus show would present a lion. Alvaro continues while sweat pours down his face. His legs pound faster and faster to support the rocket-fast-heel-toe patterns that shift minute by minute. The audience is mesmerized.

Unlike Alvaro's opening dance, this dance is full of positive vibes like a drum solo from a great rock an' roll band. Alvaro is his own drummer and drum. He whips in circles until he must stop to keep his body from shredding. At the end, he collapses to his knees and looks up through the funnel of light that shines down on his still body. The crowd leaps up and cheers. The claps and shouts of "Bravo!" begin to diminish only after Alvaro disengages from the spotlight and leaves a blacked out stage.

The audience waits in darkness. No one moves. The lighting and sound technicians create sunrise on stage and release sounds of cranes that unload containers from ships, in Havana Port. Alvaro returns to the stage, sits in the café and drinks a cappuccino. Seagull squawks mix with cargo-ship-horn blasts. The three professional male flamenco dancers sit at a table next to Alvaro and play cards.

When the rear screen projection changes to a blue-sky morning, the three card players challenge each other to a dance-off on the dock. Alvaro watches while he drinks his cappuccino. The three, dressed as Cuban dock workers, wear classic white Panama Jazz Caps and bait each other to up the ante and take it to the limit. Alvaro, who has no limit, jumps onto the café table, and the flamenco band cuts loose, as three flamenco guitars lead the way. The audience cheers, and Alvaro shows these young dock workers how to dance flamenco.

An admiring group of tourists (performed by the adult and children's classes) watch the contest on stage, and the audience watches the scene with amusement. Alvaro refuses to leash himself to the confines of the café and uses the entire stage – front to back and side to side. Again, he takes no prisoners. The three dock workers are soon spent, and Alvaro breaks the heel of one of his boots, as he finishes with a ferocious drumroll of legs and boot-sleeved feet. He helps himself to the boots of one of the dock workers and continues to savage the stage with continuous footwork that leaves the King of Havana Port on the flamenco throne. The audience confirms his status with a standing ovation and shouts for more. Alvaro collects his broken boot, sits down at the café table ready to order breakfast while the morning blues dissolve into evening pinks on the dock.

Anton joins Alvaro at the café. They listen to the flamenco band, before they hold a dance-off of their own. However, when Vanessa and Margret make a surprise entrance the audience completely loses it. These two beautiful women that visit Havana Port have decided to have dinner at the downtown café. They watch with interest the two roosters showing off to each other. The singer in the band serenades with a story of chance encounters. The two women rise to the occasion. They pull out fans and mantons from leather bags and begin to dance flamenco at the café. In the end, it is the women who win the dance-off, and the tourists on the dock crowd around them and ask for autographs. The men stare in disbelief that they have been pushed aside. The audience is beside itself, but finally sits down and respectfully waits for the last performance of the night. The Anton Dance Company's *La Vida*.

While the curtain is drawn shut, and the stage is set for *La Vida*, the Mayor returns to give a few notes.

"Thank you for coming out tonight in support of the Anton Dance Studio and newly formed Anton Dance Company. When the curtain closes tonight, you will have witnessed an event when three cultures come together to celebrate a fusion of classical flamenco, tango, rock and opera to give us an expanded artistic experience! As you leave, be sure to enjoy Lupe's Panaderia after the performance. Everything is on the house! And now, what we've all been waiting for, *La Vida*!"

The house lights dim, the curtain opens to rear screen projections of precious gems and one exquisite necklace of opals and diamonds in an arch above the jewelry store. Inside the store are jewelry cases filled with necklaces. Next door, the café is serving dinner to patrons (Anton Dance Studio students) who are there to enjoy early-evening life in Cuba. The band is assembled between the jewelry store and the café.

A man (Alvaro), sits alone at the café table nearest the jewelry store and watches the jeweler (Margret) as she finishes crafting her precious necklace. A second man and woman (Anton and Vanessa) sit and hold hands at a nearby table while they watch the jeweler put on the necklace. The music from the flamenco band with the soloist's song tells the story and draws the jeweler to center stage where the jeweler's necklace reflects in a spotlight. The man leans towards his date, points to the jeweler and mimes putting the neckless on his girlfriend's neck.

The jeweler begins a dance to celebrate her store, her freedom from oppression and her superb creation – the opal and diamond necklace. Her dance is timid at first. She takes small steps and keeps her head down then lifts herself up and begins to dance with bold footwork, as she carries her valuable necklace around the stage. The band soloist sings the story of a journey from poverty to riches, and the jeweler identifies. Her dance becomes one of joy, and she abandons all reserve. She is an artisan of great skill, and, as the owner of the store, she answers to no one as regards design and gems. The necklace symbolizes all she has achieved, and she dances with authority. Suddenly, the man who sits alone in the café comes into her store. Shy, she is embarrassed and hurries to put the necklace back in the case and forgets to close it. This man who entered the store sees that the case is open. He pulls out a gun, threatens the jeweler and grabs the necklace from the case.

The only couple in the café to witness the robbery is in shock, and the man jumps up and races toward the thief. The drums intensify and guitars scrape and squeal to sound a warning. One of the guitarists picks up his electric bass guitar and wails with a rock solo that elicits shouts and whistles from the audience. The girlfriend sings a shattering high C that terrifies the thief. He drops the necklace and runs away from the store. He dances in panic across the stage, down the stairs, up the first aisle and into the darkness. The push and pull of the dancers signifies chaos and danger – no one is safe. The audience is in shock and stays glued to their seats.

The band soloist continues to sing the story. The three dock workers race from the café through the auditorium to look for the thief. Two downtown police hear the high C siren and rush to the scene, find the necklace and return it to the jeweler. The officer in charge then begins to focus on the jeweler's immigration status and downplays the robbery. His dance is aggressive and shatters the confidence of the jeweler.

The man who wants to buy the neckless comes to the defense of the jeweler who is more terrified of the police than a would-be robber. Her dance folds in on itself, and all her confidence is cast aside. The police ask for papers, proof of residency and business license. The policeman's bigoted dance threatens the jeweler. The would-be buyer of the necklace moves in to stop the intimidation and offers to buy the priceless necklace for thousands of dollars. The suspicious policeman is stunned and stops his cruel immigration priority. He asks the potential purchaser of the jewelry how he is able to offer so much for the necklace. The buyer tells the policeman he owns the café, the jewelry store and the entire downtown block. The policeman is shocked and humiliated.

The man buys the necklace and gives it to his girlfriend. She puts it on, and they dance a tango that relaxes the scene and gently moves the focus to their romantic relationship. The band then marches across the stage under buckets that spill confetti while all the dancers follow and show off flamenco moves and footwork. The stagehands and technicians join the parade, and the larger group begins to dance down the steps to the auditorium floor and streams up the aisles where audience members join the throng. An energized flow of humanity celebrates justice while the flamenco fiesta moves up the aisles and surrounds Lupe's Panaderia for free coffee and pasteles.

The crowd is animated, the night is warm and the stars twinkle as the quarter moon rises over the ocean. The Anton Dance Company is launched. Anton, Vanessa, Alvaro and Margret thank everyone they meet for their support and invite them to join the Anton Dance Studio. Catherine and Jackson are in awe and can barely speak. Catherine hugs Vanessa, and Jackson shakes Anton's hand. Catherine exclaims,

"I had no idea! I had no idea!!!"

Mom and John are equally overwhelmed. Mom is charmed by the three male flamenco dancers, and John can't wait for his next senior-flamenco dance lesson! Mom says it all,

"So many catches, where do I start?"

The well-wishers keep coming, and Catherine, Jackson, Mom and John move away. They are aware it's going to be a late night for the flamenco stars.

"We'll catch up tomorrow! Congratulations!!!"

***

The audience gone, the terrace cleared and the auditorium closed, Anton, Vanessa, Alvaro and Margret stand together on the terrace of the, once again, shabby auditorium. It feels like a dream, as if none of it happened, but Alvaro breaks the spell. He starts to dance with finger snaps and claps. Anton does a baseball steal a la flamenco and Vanessa starts to sing. Margret heel-toes her way across the terrace, and Alvaro scoops her up into a tango. Margret exclaims,

"Let's celebrate! I know just the spot! The Gorilla is ready!"

Anton takes Vanessa's hand and twirls her around.

"Yes. Where are we headed, Margret?"

"The wetlands Anton!! The ocean! We'll sit in the Gorilla, look out from the cliff and toast to success! I already packed champagne, sparkling apple cider and dessert!"

Alvaro picks up Margret and carries her to the Gorilla.

"When do you come to Cuba? Do you have passport? I leave tomorrow!"

Margret hugs Alvaro,

"We're right behind you!"

Anton jokes,

"Do we bring the mamas too?"

"Yes, yes! Everyone, bring them. We have little flamenco fiesta in Cuba! And Margret stays to run Cuban dance company."

"This train runs too fast, but I'm packed and ready!"

The quartet climbs into the Gorilla, and Margret drives the beast like a mountain bike in free fall.

"Hold on!"

Vanessa is thrown into Anton's arms with a tight turn onto the highway and stays there. She volunteers show dates,

"Let's do Christmas in Cuba and New Year's here!"

Anton agrees,

"It's Christmas at Sergio's Café, where papa smoked his last cigar!"

Margret pulls onto the scenic viewpoint off the highway. The quarter moon adds a silver edge to the marine layer on the horizon. The ocean rumbles in the semi-darkness. Alvaro opens the champagne and sparkling cider, and Margret cuts the cake.

Anton proposes a toast.

"Alvaro . . . thank you for coming to California. So many nights I came home to my cat, Luisa, opened my laptop, watched you on the news and celebrated your success.

Now we are a two-in-one dance company in Cuba and on the Central Coast. Margret and Vanessa are stars aligned in flamenco. Our destiny is set. Viva *La Vida*."

Four glasses touch and shouts of "Olé!" fill the Gorilla.

Alvaro proposes a toast.

"Margret and Vanessa, thank you for family for crazy flamenco men. It is women that inspire flamenco!"

Alvaro leans over and gives Margret a kiss on the cheek.

Anton does the same to Vanessa. He remembers his first encounter.

Vanessa laughs and kisses Anton on the lips.

"I want to kiss you all day and night forever!"

Anton gives Vanessa a hug and affirms,

"Yes."

Margret exclaims,

"Look, look the train is on the bridge!"

A train horn blasts across the wetlands, and an engine light leads the train through the dark. Margret puts her hand on Alvaro's cheek.

"There's our inspiration. Our gypsy camp is on the move. Hello Cuba!"

¡OLÉ!

Priceless support and essential editorial contributions:

R. J. Smith

Theresa Duer

Chris Ward

Ryan S. Bruemmer

Author Biography

Born and raised, in Santa Monica, California, Catalina spent weekends and summers on the family ranch, in the east end of Ojai, California.

A University of California at Los Angeles honors graduate and Otis Art Institute MFA recipient, Catalina practiced painting, photography, printmaking and creative writing. She worked as a printmaker and professional photographer, and won the New York Art Director's Award for *The American Cowboy* poster.

In 2009 - 2019 Catalina founded and directed The Art of Peace aka Art. Peace. Imagine 501 (c) 3. She created Artist Peace Chairs with at risk young men residing at Los Prietos Boys Camp and distributed the chairs throughout Santa Barbara County schools, public libraries and beyond. The final project was making Artist Peace Benches in India, working with the Piyali Learning Center for disadvantaged girls from Piyali Junction, two hours outside of Kolkata, India.

Three years with the Santa Barbara Actors Forum and writing the book and lyrics for the full stage musical *Toad Hall*, shopped by Cornerstone Entertainment International, along with the selection of her short play *Rose*, for Edward Albee's New Frontier Theatre Conference, in Valdez, Alaska, and her plays *Lizards* and *Clarion Call*, screenplay *Sweet Grass*, and novel *The Long Ride Home* all prepared the way for her second novel *La Vida*.

Catalina McIsaac currently lives in Santa Barbara, California and spends the majority of her time in her studio where she writes and paints.

Visit
www.catalinamcisaac.com
to sign up for the next novel release

HOBOVILLE
October 2023

Made in the USA
Las Vegas, NV
02 June 2023

72851099R00225